A Dozen Black Roses

Nancy Collins

White Wolf Publishing
780 Park North Boulevard, Suite 100
Clarkston, GA 30021

World Wide Web Page: www.white-wolf.com

DEDICATION

For my husband, Joe Christ
Always and Forever

AUTHOR'S NOTE

As this is a crossover between the world of Sonja
Blue and the World of Darkness, there are matters of
continuity that do not match up exactly with the
respective universes; I have attempted to graft them
together as well as possible. This story can be
considered to be taking place sometime following the
events detailed in *Paint It Black*. I would also like to
give a tip of the hat to the following: *Yojimbo, A
Fistful of Dollars, Dawn of the Dead,* and *Warriors*.

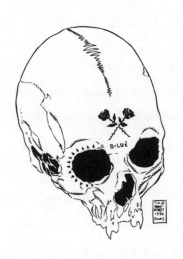

DEADTOWN

A considerable percentage of the people we
meet on the street are people who are empty
inside, that is, they are actually *already
dead.* It is fortunate for us that we do not
see and do not know it. If we knew what a
number of people are actually dead and
what a number of these dead people govern
our lives, we should go mad with horror.
— *George Gurdjieff*

I believe in children
I believe in life
But I'd have to be deaf, dumb and blind
Not to see the strife.
Faces of death, faces of death
Faces of death all around me.
— Love Theme from *Faces of Death 4*

Chapter

1

The city was founded over two hundred and sixty years ago by those who fled the intolerance of their various homelands. It sits at the head of an estuary, a stone's throw from the huge bay that first welcomed the settlers who came to this strange new world. Its proximity to water shaped its future, much as a growing child is shaped by its environment.

From its earliest days the city's destiny was linked with that of sailing ships and those who ply the waves. By the time of the American Revolution it was a bustling seaport and shipyard, its wharves busy with trade, legal and otherwise. The shipping companies that crowded the waterfront exported tobacco, flour, indigo, and fish to Europe, while accepting darker human cargo from the Gold Coast and beyond.

In the years that followed, the city's livelihood became even more tightly linked with the sea and the adjoining rivers that occasionally threatened to swallow it whole. Time passed. Ships were no longer made entirely of wood, so steelworks and oil refineries arose to build the battleships and freighters of the steam era.

Like all seaports, in the beginning it was a brash and roughshod town—but as the decades turned into centuries, it came to see itself in a more cosmopolitan light. As the city matured, it became more sophisticated in its pleasures, giving birth to opera houses, museums, and coliseums. The seminary birthed first colleges, then universities. There were ups and downs—fires and floods, recessions and inflation—but the city always recovered, just as a human body recovers from fevers and ills.

The symbiotic parasites who thought the city their own thrived, producing sports figures, surgeons, newspapermen, philosophers, statesmen and poets. The wheels of progress, industry, and business moved in sync without grinding against one another's gears. It was a city with a past and a future.

And then came the present.

Forty years ago the denizens of the inner city began to abandon the brownstones and row houses of their ancestors for the roomier, greener environs of the outlying suburbs. Soon the only people left were those too poor or disenfranchised to move. The neighborhoods began to decline as the working class gave way to working poor.

Thirty years ago the wheels of progress and industry began to shift as advances in technology made brute strength less and less necessary. The shipyards began to mechanize, as did the refineries and steel plants. Fewer and fewer jobs were open to the unskilled and uneducated.

Twenty years ago the oil embargo drove the price of oil from two dollars a barrel to thirty-two. Americans, no longer able to afford to drive the lumbering gas-guzzlers Detroit manufactured, turned to foreign imports. The demand for domestic steel dropped drastically. The wheels of progress were no longer lubricated and the gears began to grind loudly, sending sparks in every direction. Dockworkers, shipbuilders, foundry and refinery employees were laid off in droves. It became increasingly difficult for even the educated to earn decent wages once inflation turned a college degree into the equivalent of a high school diploma. Entire city blocks were abandoned and left to rot.

Fifteen years ago the federal government began cutting back on aid to the poor and disadvantaged stranded in the inner cities. The city was left to face its declining years bereft of services, neglected and abused. What had once been an industrial economy gave way to one based on services. College graduates found themselves underemployed, flipping hamburgers and changing sheets, while the poverty-stricken watched stockbrokers, investment bankers, and realtors drive their Beamers and Volvos into the slums to score cocaine. Crime rates soared. Political corruption was everywhere. Gangs began to proliferate, and with their growth, wars over turf escalated as well. At some point during the heated battles between Uzi-toting gangbangers, the city was delivered a mortal wound.

Cities are living things. They are born and grow, mature and age. Sometimes they even die. But cities, unlike organic things made of flesh and blood, bone and sinew, do not know that they are dead. The symbiotes that labor so busily within the carcass are often determined to continue the pretense of life long after its vitality has bled away.

Deadtown was the largest of the maggots thriving within the corpse.

Most of the humans dwelling within the city are unaware that there is a sector that the elected officials pretend does not exist. It is not located on any street map. Neither patrol cars, ambulances, nor firetrucks venture into this lost neighborhood near the river. Cries for help are often heard echoing from its dark alleys and twisting streets, but seldom answered—and for good reason. For this is the rotting heart of a once-vital city. And what better place for the children of the night to gather than in a city that is already one of the living dead?

The stranger stepped out of the shadows and onto The Street With No Name. She studied the ancient brick buildings, rough cobblestones and nineteenth-century lampposts, nodding silently to herself. This was the place.

Although the "quaint" street fixtures might fool the unwary tourist into thinking they'd wandered into some attempt at a yuppie urban commercial center, the illusion was only momentary; piles of rotting garbage lumped in the alleyways and gaunt, ashen-faced derelicts lurching down the street were proof that the neighborhood did not boast a Crabtree & Evelyn.

Still, for a portion of the city that did not technically exist, The Street With No Name seemed surprisingly busy. Though most of the storefronts were boarded up, a handful of *bodegas* serviced a steady stream of solitary men and women.

She paused in front of one of the windows, peering in at the wall of faded Froot Loops boxes and expired baby-food jars that had been erected as a barricade against prying eyes. Whatever they sold inside, it certainly wasn't groceries. Her attention was attracted by the stutter and flash of neon from farther down the street. She moved toward it, keeping a cautious eye on the darkened mouth of the alley, where something mewled to itself and rustled like dry leaves.

In the middle of the block were a couple of bars and a liquor store that looked to be the only thriving businesses in the neighborhood. One was a titty bar called Dance Macabre; its logo was a woman cradling a serpent with a flickering neon tongue. Directly across the street was a pool hall called Stick's. Both establishments had knots of young men dressed in gang colors hanging outside on the curb, glaring at one another across the cobblestone road.

The stranger paused to watch the young men as they talked among themselves, drank malt liquor from forty-ounce containers and smoked reeking blunts, gun-butts jutting from their waistbands. Both groups seemed of equal size, their members a mix of white, black and brown—surprising, given the city's tendency toward unofficial segregation.

The gang loitering in front of the Dance Macabre wore black leather jackets festooned with chrome studs outlining inverted five-pointed stars across their backs. The gangbangers milling outside Stick's wore identical leather jackets—except that the backs were decorated with Jolly Rogers. Instead of legbones, however, the grinning skulls hovered above crossed spoons. Despite the intense, glowering stares flashing between the groups, neither side offered to move from its respective post.

A late-fifties Cadillac, its tail fins raised high like the dorsal of a shark, turned the corner. The suitcase-sized speakers blasted out hip-hop so bass-heavy it made the stranger's ribs vibrate in time with the beat.

"Here comes the Batmobile," announced a Hispanic youth with a blossom of acne across his thin face. The gangbangers outside the Dance Macabre tossed away their blunts and bombers and pulled out their guns, moving to form a human corridor.

The vintage Cadillac pulled up to the curb. The windows were so heavily tinted they looked like mirrors. One of the gangbangers sprang forward and opened the rear door. The first person out of the car was a tall, striking woman dressed in low-cut black leather pants and steel-tipped boots. As she turned to face the others, her black leather jacket swung open, revealing naked breasts with stainless-steel rings piercing the nipples. The right side of her head was shaved to the skull, while the hair on the left hung to her waist like a drape of black silk. Her features were strong and clean and would have been considered classically beautiful if not for the plethora of metal hoops and studs dangling from her nose, lips, and brow ridge. In her right hand she held a loaded crossbow. She quickly checked the perimeter, then gestured to her fellow passenger that the coast was clear.

An extremely pale young woman, her hair the color of smoke, climbed out of the back seat. She was dressed all in white, from her satin pumps and plunging silk evening gown to the mink coat she clutched like a life preserver. Her face was so perfect it looked more like a china doll's than a living woman's. Yet, for all her loveliness, there was something wrong. Her movements were jerky and deliberate, like those of a marionette, as the other woman hustled her toward the entrance of the club. Her lavender-colored eyes were as glazed and slightly out-of-focus as a tranquilized gazelle's.

"Mama! Mama!"

The woman in white froze in midstep, a flicker of emotion crossing her otherwise placid face.

"Ryan?"

"Mama!"

A young boy, no older than five, darted between the legs of the gangbangers. He was thin and ragged, but there was no mistaking where he'd gotten his coloration and hair. He made a grab for the woman's dress, narrowly dodging the archer's steel-tipped boot. The woman in white's eyelids began to twitch, like those of a sleepwalker emerging from a dream. The archer cursed and made a grab for the boy, only to have him scoot between her legs and into the open street.

The archer pointed her crossbow at the pimply-faced gangbanger who'd opened the car door for her. "Cavalera! I thought I told you dumb fucks to deal with that little cocksucker!"

The gangbanger she'd addressed jumped to something resembling attention.

"You heard what Esher said about lettin' that brat get near her! Don't just stand there with your fuckin' thumbs up your ass! Get him! And take Cro-Mag with you!" the archer snarled over her shoulder as she propelled her charge toward the open door, revealing strong white fangs and eyes the color of wine.

Cavalera and Cro-Mag promptly sprinted down the street in pursuit of the boy. The kid had a half-block headstart, but their legs were twice as long, and within seconds they closed in on him.

The one called Cro-Mag, a hulking Anglo youth with a lantern jaw, made a flying tackle, knocking the terrified child to the ground.

"Way t'go, Mag!" Cavalera, the thin Hispanic with the skin problem, chimed. "Mebbe you shoulda kept playin' football."

"Nah. Can't read. If I wanted t'stay on th' team, I had t'take retard classes. Fuck that shit, man!" Cro-Mag grinned as he got to his feet. He held the boy by his shirt collar, dangling him above the ground like he would a baby rabbit. "What we gonna do with this little shit?"

Cavalera shrugged as he pulled the .38 from his waistband. "You heard Decima, homeboy."

"Let him go, assholes!"

Cro-Mag and Cavalera turned in the direction of the voice. Cro-Mag swore under his breath and let the boy drop. The child instantly regained his footing and scampered off into the shadows.

An older white man with a gray-flecked beard and long flowing silver hair that fell almost to his belt stepped out of the alleyway and onto the street, closing the distance between them. Except for his tie-dyed T-shirt, faded jeans, and beat-up high-tops, he could have passed for Gandalf the Grey. The sawed-off shotgun in his hands did not waver.

"That's good. You did the right thing that time, pal. You—with the gun—you gonna do the right thing, too?"

"Fuck you, old man!" Cavalera spat, trying his best to keep his voice from cracking.

"I may be old, punk, but I still know shit when I smell it! Now throw down the gun or I'll cut you off at the knees!"

Cavalera bit his lower lip to keep it from quivering. For all his bravado, he looked as if he were about to cry. "We gonna fuck you up, motherfucker!" he warned as he tossed the .38 onto the sidewalk. Without being told, the boy scuttled forward and snagged the gun. In his hands it looked like a vicious oversized toy. "You fuckin' with the Pointers, asshole—you fuckin' with *Esher!*"

"I'm quakin' in my boots, punk! Now you, big boy—kick the gun over to me!"

Grumbling, Cro-Mag did as he was told.

"If you boys had half the brains God gave you, you'd get the hell outta this stinkin' place and forget you ever heard of Esher," the bearded man sighed. "But something tells me thinking's not your strong suit. Get outta here—and if I see either of you near that kid again, I'll let you have it with both barrels! And next time I won't bother to announce myself!"

Cro-Mag and Cavalera turned as if to leave. Just as the old hippie let out his breath and lowered his weapon, they rushed him. Cro-Mag grabbed for the shotgun while Cavalera dove after the boy.

"Give it up, old man!" Cro-Mag grinned, displaying crooked teeth. "Cav's right—you're fuckin' with the wrong gang!"

A shrill, high-pitched shriek of pain cut the night, but it was not the boy's. Cro-Mag looked to his friend in time to see Cavalera collapse in the gutter, the hilt of a switchblade buried in his chest.

"Cav!"

The old hippie slammed the butt of the shotgun into the bigger man's jaw. Cro-Mag staggered backward, looking stunned. He touched his dripping mouth, stared at the blood for a moment, then looked at his attacker.

"That hurt."

"I meant it to," the old hippie retorted, driving the butt of the shotgun directly between Cro-Mag's eyes with all his might. This time the banger went down and stayed there.

The bearded man stood on the curb, gun in hand, and stared down at the Goliath he'd toppled. His hands trembled and his breath came in ragged gasps.

"What you did was very brave. Foolish, but brave."

The bearded man pivoted on his heel, bringing the shotgun to bear on the stranger standing behind him. He saw a woman in her early twenties, dressed in tattered jeans, scuffed Doc Martens, a black leather jacket, and mirrored sunglasses. She held the boy against her so that he clung to her side, riding her left hip.

"Jesus, lady!" he rasped as he lowered his weapon. "Don't go sneakin' up on me like that!"

"It's what I do best," she replied as she lowered the child to the sidewalk. The boy shot forward like an arrow, wrapping his thin arms around the older man's waist.

The hippie ruffled the child's hair, then held him at arm's length, frowning down at him in reproof. "I told you to be careful when you left the house tonight and this is what happens! What'd you do, Ryan? Did you try and see your mom again?"

"I saw her, Cloudy! I even touched her this time! She said my name!"

The bearded man rolled his eyes. "Christ-on-a-crutch, kid! You're gonna get us both killed doin' shit like that!"

The stranger stepped over Cro-Mag's sprawling form and bent to pluck the switchblade from Cavalera's lifeless heart. As she wiped the blood from the knife onto her pantsleg, she nudged Cro-Mag with her steel-tipped boot, frowning slightly. "This one's still alive. If I were you, I'd put a round through his heart."

The bearded man shook his head. "I don't do shit like that unless I can't avoid it."

The woman shrugged. "It's your call."

"Look, lady—I appreciate you steppin' in like you did—"

"You can thank me later. Now, are you going to keep us standing on the sidewalk the rest of the night or are we going to find someplace to hide? I suspect these goons' friends are already headed this way."

The older man nodded and scooped up the boy. "You're right. We better hurry. My place isn't that far."

The stranger followed the white-haired man down the narrow, foul-smelling passageway, emerging onto the next avenue. If anything, it was even more blighted than The Street With No Name. The hippie hurried down the steps that led to the basement entrance of a crumbling brownstone tenement. Swinging the boy onto his back, he pulled a keyring from his pants pocket and unlocked the heavy metal door. Once inside, he shrugged the boy off and quickly slammed the door, securing it with a crossbolt made from an old railroad tie.

The stranger turned to scan the interior of the basement apartment. The front room was quite large, and books surrounded them on every side, spilling from narrowly spaced bookshelves that reached to the ceiling. The place smelled of the genteel decay of old paper and moldering leather.

The older man let out a deep breath and allowed his shoulders to slump, but he did not unload the sawed-off he held cradled in his arms. He gave the stranger a curious glance. "I make it a point not to let people around here know where I live. You're the first person besides the boy I've allowed in my place in years. You try anything funny, lady, and I'll spray your brains all over the walls. I'd really hate to have that happen, seeing as how you saved the boy and that I'm such a lousy housekeeper."

"I'll keep that in mind."

"You do that."

"Cloudy?" the boy whispered, tugging on the aging hippie's shirt. "Cloudy?"

"What is it, kid?"

"Can I have some cookies?"

He ruffled the boy's prematurely gray hair. "I don't know—can you?"

The boy gave an exaggerated sigh and rolled his eyes. "*May* I have some cookies?"

"I guess so. But leave me some Oreos this time!" He smiled indulgently as the boy sprinted along the narrow trail that wound through the towering mounds of books to the rear of the apartment.

"Is he your son?"

He shook his head and laughed. "Hell no! I don't know who his daddy is—neither does he. But I couldn't let the poor kid starve to death on the street—or worse."

"His mother was the woman I saw in the escort of the vampiress?"

"Was she wearing white?"

"Yes."

"That's Nikola, all right. And the vampire—was she a kinky-lookin' mama with fishin' lures stuck all over her face and tits?"

"Yes."

"That'd be Decima. Esher's lieutenant."

"Who's this Esher everyone keeps talking about?"

He gave her an odd look. "You really don't know?"

"I'm new in town. Why don't you fill me in?"

"Sure—let's go in the back. We can sit down there. I'll tell you what I know over coffee."

The back of the apartment was considerably neater than the front half, although books challenged the major appliances for territory in the small kitchen. The boy was sitting on an upended plastic milk crate in the corner, a dog-eared comic book draped across his knees and cookie crumbs smeared over his chin.

"Excuse the mess," he grunted as he moved a pile of old paperbacks from the only other chair in the room. "But I don't get much in the way of visitors nowadays. Normally I don't let anyone past the threshold—but I've learned to listen my instincts."

"And what do your instincts have to say about me?"

He looked at her for a long moment, as if trying to read a message only he could see. "I think you can be trusted. God knows why. I hope it's not just an acid flashback."

"I will take your vote of confidence as a compliment." The stranger picked up a copy of *Fate Magazine*, blowing a cloud of dust from its faded cover. "How long have you lived here, if you don't mind me asking? By the way, I don't believe I caught your name—?"

"Eddie McLeod. Friends call me Cloudy. The kid's name is Ryan. I don't know his last name. Neither does he. And, no, I don't mind you asking: I've lived in Deadtown since the late sixties."

"Has it always been like this?"

Cloudy shook his head as he lit the gas range. "It hasn't always been this rough, but it's always been a weird scene. I mean, this is six square blocks of Nowhere in a major city! And I *do* mean Nowhere! I remember hearing some story that back in the Colonial days this part of town was a safe haven for rebel smugglers, and ever since then it's been an unofficial "neutral zone" for those outside the law.

"Back during the Civil War, Confederate sympathizers and other tough characters used to hang out here. Toward the end of the last century, it was full of immigrants and lowlifes. Me, I found out about it in '68. I moved here to dodge the draft. I can't stand cold winters, so Canada was never an option."

The stranger raised an eyebrow in surprise. "You've been hiding out in Deadtown for thirty years?"

Cloudy shrugged as he ladled instant coffee into a pair of chipped mugs. "I'm not really hiding out anymore—leastwise, not from the draft. I took advantage of the amnesty a few years back and made myself legit with the government on that score. But I got used to living here, and I'd be hard put to get by this cheaply anywhere else in the country—or the world! I don't pay rent. No one does here! It's a squatter community."

"Where do the water and power come from?"

"Rumor has it the city has some kind of deal with Deadtown. Maybe it's to keep the worst of Deadtown from spreading out into the surrounding area."

"From what you tell me, I'm surprised there aren't more people living here."

"Oh, they're here—you just don't see 'em, that's all!" Cloudy chuckled dryly. "Those who call this neighborhood home have learned it pays to be invisible. But there's not as many people as there used to be, that's for certain. Deadtown always did have its price for living here—but now it's higher than ever."

"You mean the gangs?"

"Gangs, schmangs! I mean the bastards behind them."

"The vampires."

Cloudy grimaced. "You don't hear that word used much around here. They call themselves Kindred. They've been here since the beginning, too. That's one of the reasons this place ain't full to overflowing with the homeless! It's haunted! I didn't believe the stories when I first moved here. But one night, back in '70, I saw one of them take down a friend of mine. I was plenty scared by what I saw—but I was even more frightened of going to Viet Nam! I just made it a point to get indoors by sundown after that. Besides, it used to not be as bad as this."

The battered teakettle began its shrill shriek and Cloudy quickly removed it from the heat. He continued to speak as he poured the hot water into the waiting mugs. "For the longest time, there was only one bloodsucker running things here. Sinjon. Then, about five years ago, this new vamp moves in—calls himself Esher. Next thing I know, they're going at it hammer-and-tongs, bringing in these teenaged psychos as muscle!

"Sinjon's boys are the Black Spoons—they're his front men when it comes to drugs. Rumor has it Sinjon controls most of the hardcore smack-and-crack trade on the Eastern Seaboard. Esher's boys are the Five Points Gang—they call themselves Pointers. They're gun runners, mostly. Esher's big into illegal weaponry. Everything from Saturday Night Specials to heatseeking missiles, if the scuttlebutt's true. I wouldn't put it past him fencing a thermonuclear device! Once the sun goes down, all traces of "normalcy" around here disappear and you only set foot outside at your own risk. Not that it's much safer during the day. But at least while the sun is out the Kindred stay off the streets."

The stranger nodded her head in the direction of Ryan, who had abandoned his comic book and was curled up on a pile of old blankets under the sink. "What about the boy's mother?"

Cloudy took a sip of his coffee and grimaced. "Her name's Nikola. She used to be an exotic dancer, over at the Pink Pony Club, a few blocks outside Deadtown. She was real good at it, I guess, because word got around to Esher. One night Esher comes into the club to watch her dance and the next thing she knows he's deciding to make her his new "star." You see, one of the first things Esher did when he moved into Deadtown was take over the old titty bar across the street from the Black Spoons' hangout and change the name to Dance Macabre. Of course, she had no idea what she was getting herself into. But I guess she found out soon enough. The next day some Pointers showed up at her apartment—she was packing in a hurry—and took her away to Esher's stronghold."

"And the boy?"

"He only wanted the woman, not her child. He was left behind, without any money or family or friends to help him. I'll give the kid credit—he's strong! Lot stronger than most kids twice his age. When he realized his mom wasn't coming back, he went out looking for her—which is how I stumbled across him. He was eating out of a garbage can outside my building. I knew if I didn't do something, he'd either starve to death or end up killed by Esher's goons. Poor kid! He spends most of his time watching the house where his mother's being kept, hoping for a chance to see her." He shivered, as if trying to shake himself free of an unpleasant memory, and held out the second cup of coffee to his guest. "I'm sorry! Where are my manners? Here's your coffee—how do you like it? Black or white?"

The stranger smiled without showing her teeth and waved aside the proffered mug. "Don't bother with me. I don't drink—coffee."

She got up and knelt beside the sink, looking down at the boy's thin, pale features. She reached out and brushed the fringe of hair on his forehead. He murmured something in his sleep and pulled his blanket tighter.

"The undead do not like children—except as prey. Children are unpleasant reminders that they are frozen in time, changeless and unchanging, locked outside the chain of Nature. Although vampires feign disgust as to how humans reproduce, they are secretly jealous. The boy was lucky Esher did not order him killed immediately."

"Yeah," sighed Cloudy, as he poured the extra coffee into the sink. "Real lucky." He glanced at her suspiciously. "You sure know a lot about vampires, lady. And I don't think I've caught your name—?"

The stranger straightened up, wiping her palms against her jacket. "No, you didn't."

Cloudy felt the pit of his stomach tighten. The hair on the back of his hands and the ridge of his spine began to tingle. "You're one of them, aren't you?" he whispered, taking a step away from the sink. He started backing toward the front room, where he'd left his shotgun propped next to the door. The stranger turned toward him, but did not move to follow.

"Shit! I should have known it! Who's your master? Who you working for—Esher or Sinjon?"

"I serve no one but myself."

"I don't believe you, sucker! Either answer me straight or get the fuck out of here! I don't have to be Van Helsing to figure out you'll stay dead if I blow your fuckin' head off!"

The stranger smiled again, this time revealing sharp fangs. "You *are* brave. You and I both know I could bring you down long before you could reach your weapon, Cloudy. Very well. If I prove to you that I am not like the others—will you hear me out?"

Cloudy glanced down at where Ryan was still sleeping under the sink, then back at her. "Okay."

The stranger reached into her jacket pocket and produced the switchblade she'd used earlier on Cavalera, the handle of which was decorated with a sinuous golden dragon. Her thumb brushed the dragon's ruby eye and the blade leapt from the hilt. In the dim light, the knife resembled a frozen flame.

Cloudy's eyebrows lifted in surprise. "I didn't get a good look at that before—but that's real silver! And something else is weird about it too. Gives me a really creepy feeling."

"It's enchanted. Specifically to slay Kindred. For someone who may not be Van Helsing, you know much."

"You learn fast if you want to survive in Deadtown," he replied tersely.

"Then I don't have to explain what this means." She drew the blade across her left palm. The cut was deep; dark, almost black blood welled from the wound and dripped between her fingers. Then, as Cloudy watched, open-mouthed, the lips of the wound began to seal themselves, leaving a scar that pulsed bright red for a second or two, then rapidly paled.

Cloudy frowned. "What the hell are you, lady?"

The stranger shrugged as she folded the blade back into its hilt. "It's a long story. Let us say for now that there is more than one kind of vampire, my friend. And more than one kind of vampire slayer."

Chapter

2

Nikola sat in front of the dressing-room vanity and stared at the black paint covering the mirror as she applied her mascara. Over the last few months, she had grown adept at putting on her makeup without the aid of reflective surfaces. Lord Esher did not approve of looking glasses. Still, she had managed to glimpse enough of herself in shop and car windows to know that she no longer looked like herself.

Whoever that might be.

She knew that her name was Nikola, that she was a dancer, and that she was betrothed to Lord Esher. Beyond that there was only mist and the occasional murky recollection. She had the nagging suspicion that her life had once held more than these few reference points, but every time she tried to focus on remembering, her head began to hurt and the mist surrounding her thoughts grew thicker.

Sometimes—but not that often—the fog would lift for a moment, and she would become painfully aware of what was happening to her. During those brief moments of clarity, horror and helplessness so overwhelmed her that she would deliberately wrap herself in the mist. It was less scary that way.

Like what had happened outside the club earlier. When the street urchin darted forward and touched her—it was as if she'd been startled from a waking dream. She had looked down into the child's unwashed face and recognized it. Even now, the boy's features were trying to swim out of the mist, as if he were drowning and desperate to reach her. The face had a name. And on some deep, instinctual level, she realized she should know it.

Nikola put aside her mascara, fearful that her trembling hands would ruin her makeup. Lord Esher was most particular when it came to how she looked while dancing. It would not do to displease him. Nikola blinked her eyes and, to her surprise, found that she was crying.

How strange.

Why should she weep? She was Lord Esher's newest bride-to-be. Shouldn't that make her the happiest woman on the face of the earth?

She wished she knew.

The door opened and Lord Esher, accompanied by his lieutenant, Decima, entered the dressing room. The vampire lord wore tight-fitting black leather jeans, a black muscle shirt, dyed-black lizardskin cowboy boots, and a floor-length black leather duster. His dark, square-cut hair fell well below his wide, heavily muscled shoulders. Although quite striking physically, the vampire lord did not look much different from the mortals who inhabited the city's rowdier districts. The only things that marked him as one of the Kindred were the black-and-gold enamel clan totem, a squared circle and captive triangle, pinned to his left lapel, and the chromium-plated skull of a human infant he wore as a belt-buckle.

"Good evening, my dear," he smiled, standing behind Nikola so that his sinewy hands rested on her bare shoulders, the thumbs pressed lightly against her carotid artery. "Are you ready for tonight's performance?"

"Almost." Her voice was as dry and brittle as papyrus.

"You look ravishing, my pretty. Doesn't she, Decima?"

The vampiress shrugged. She folded her arms over her bare breasts, making the nipple rings jingle. "If you say so, milord."

Nikola felt her flesh grow chill under Decima's gaze. The vampiress made no attempt to disguise her contempt for her sire's new bride. After twenty-five years as his consort, Decima had been cast aside in favor of the mortal dancer. She was too heavily enthralled to Esher to rebel against him openly, but Decima took great delight in making Nikola's life as unpleasant as possible.

"You look troubled, Nikola," Esher commented as he stroked her hair. "Is there something bothering my sweet?"

Nikola hesitated for a moment, then spoke in a voice as soft and uncertain as a child's. "There—there was a little boy on the street outside the club. He looked familiar. Who is he, milord? I feel that I should know him."

Esher turned Nikola around in her chair so that she faced him. His eyes gleamed red and wet, like fresh wounds. When he spoke, it was as if thunder echoed in his voice.

"You do not know the boy! You have never seen him before! He is a stranger to you! In fact, you did not see a child tonight at all! Do you understand me, Nikola?"

"There was no child," she murmured, her pupils out of focus.

"Very good! That's much better, isn't it? Don't you feel much nicer not thinking about things?"

"Yes, milord. Very nice."

"Now hurry up and get ready! You don't want to be late for your performance!" Esher smiled. "We'll leave you to finish your preparations. Come, Decima!"

The vampire lord stepped into the hall outside, but the moment the door closed the indulgent smile twisted into a scowl of anger. "Why didn't you tell me the boy had been here?!?"

Decima shifted uncomfortably and glanced at her boots, unwilling to meet his gaze. "I—I didn't think it was important, milord. I sent a couple of the Pointers to handle it."

"Which ones?"

"Cavalera and Cro-Mag."

"And did they succeed?"

"N-no. Cro-Mag was found unconscious in the gutter with most of his teeth knocked out. Cavalera is dead. Stabbed through the heart."

"Seeing as how they're a congenital idiot and an illiterate, I'm not surprised they failed so miserably!" Esher snorted in disgust. "Do you have any clue as to who did this to them?"

"Cro-Mag said something about an old man, but I don't know how reliable his account might be. He's suffering from a serious concussion. There's some brain damage—"

"As if anyone would notice! See that he's made tonight's Example."

"Yes, milord."

"And have that child destroyed, once and for all! How can I hope to finish conditioning my new bride if her wretched brat keeps getting in the way? I've nearly got her turned, except where the boy's concerned! As long as he continues to live, he endangers the entire process! I have not spent all this time and energy on Nikola to have it ruined by something as insignificant as a human brat! Have I made myself clear, Decima?"

"Perfectly, milord."

In earlier, if not better days, the Dance Macabre was a bar frequented by motorcycle gangs and other social misfits. Now it was an exotic dance club that catered to tastes far darker than anything dreamed up by even the most depraved of its former clientele.

The interior of the club was divided into three areas: the vast dance-floor area, where pale-faced Kindred and humans mingled at tables; the combination runway/stage, where the dancers paraded for the audience; and the upper balcony, which was reserved for Esher and his minions. There was a standard bar that served alcohol, and a far more elaborate system for those whose tastes ran to things warmer than wine.

A dozen humans, male and female, were shackled to the far wall by bondage harnesses attached to spools of stainless-steel chain, similar to those used to restrain large dogs. Phlebotomy shunts jutted from their right elbows, while bags of anticoagulant pumped into intravenous feeds attached to their left arms. Some looked terrified to the point of madness; others seemed oblivious to their surroundings; a few appeared to be lost in ecstasy. All were exceptionally pallid.

Esher paused at the balcony's railing to scan the floor below. The evening looked as though it was getting off to a good start. He spotted a couple of new faces clustered near the feeders. The Dance Macabre attracted Kindred from as far away as New York and Atlanta and had proved handy in recruiting unaffiliated vampires. Soon his enclave would be as large as Sinjon's brood—if not larger.

Satisfied with the turnout, Esher returned to his seat, a rosewood throne outfitted with crimson velvet cushions, which had been presented to him by the human mage, Crowley. The little charlatan had thought he could learn the ways of Thaumaturgy from Esher, but had quickly lost interest upon discovering the price of such knowledge. Not that Esher would have Embraced the power-hungry dilettante in the first place.

He snapped his figures and his private stock stepped forward and knelt at his feet. This evening's private stock was a woman whose wan complexion and drawn features made her look far older than her nineteen years. Without his having to gesture or speak, she automatically lifted her right arm. Esher quickly uncapped the shunt and plugged a hypodermic needle attached to a length of IV tubing into the access port. He then brought the end of the IV to his lips and began to suck. The private stock rolled her eyes back in her head and voiced a deep sigh as her head nodded back and forth.

Once the private stock's blood darkened the tube, Esher pinched it shut and motioned for Decima to hand him a shot glass. The private stock gasped as if on the edge of orgasm and swooned, laying her head atop Esher's boots. The vampire lord grunted and kicked her away as he would a bothersome pet. The private stock barely flinched. Judging by the thinness of the blood he'd drawn, she was close to empty. He made a mental note to remind Decima to see that another vessel was chosen from his cellar.

As he sipped fresh blood from the shot glass, Esher settled back into the wizard's throne and allowed himself a moment's relaxation. His eyes flickered to the series of closed-circuit television monitors mounted near the ceiling.

One presented him with a closer view of the club floor, another was trained on the stage, and two more showed views of the street just outside the front door. Esher liked to keep an eye on things. It was a trait that had helped him become one of the more powerful lords on the Eastern Seaboard.

At one hundred and ninety-one years, Esher was little more than an adolescent, as the Kindred measure age. Most were well into their third century before they accrued a power base as sizable as his. But then, he'd always been exceptional, even as a mortal. All anyone had to do was look at the impression he'd made on his unofficial "biographer."

He'd been born into Tidewater aristocracy thirty years after the signing of the Declaration of Independence. Indeed, his maternal grandfather had signed that very document. Raised by doting mammies, he had wanted for nothing as a boy. Nor had any limits been placed on him. By turns inquisitive and cruel, he'd shown signs of interest in becoming a physician, so he was sent to the University of Virginia to continue his schooling. Once there, he began a life of carousing and abandon that would eventually end in his being expunged from the school's records.

It was there that he met the poet.

They became acquainted over the gaming tables. Esher found the younger student intriguing, as they both shared a morbid turn of mind. Although Esher found his friend's inability to hold his liquor alternately amusing and disgusting, they remained on familiar terms after the poet's gambling debts forced him to quit his studies.

Of the two, Esher was clearly the stronger personality from the very beginning. The sensitive young poet seemed both fascinated and appalled by his comrade's *sang froid*. Esher believed that the world and the wonders in it belonged to whoever was strong enough to take them. There was no room for the incompetent, the weak, and all those unwilling, or unable, to make the most of their situation.

Although the poet argued heatedly with Esher over these points time and again, he could never quite bring himself to break their friendship. It was as if the strength of Esher's charisma compelled the poet to seek his company. But there were other, more prosaic reasons behind their relationship: it was clear that the poet envied Esher his money, position, and charm; and as they grew older, the interests they shared in death and dying continued to bind them. But where the poet's obsession took the form of fanciful stories and poems, Esher trod the path of the occultist. As the years passed, they saw less and less of one another. The poet drifted in and out of various editorial jobs up and down the Eastern Seaboard, publishing the occasional slim volume of gothic poetry. Esher, on the other hand, was expelled from the University of Virginia, and then from Harvard's medical schools. In each case he was accused of harvesting organs from cadavers for occult purposes.

After his expulsion from Harvard, Esher decided to take the Grand Tour and "broaden his horizons." It was in an isolated portion of Romania known as Transylvania that he first learned of the blood-cult called the Tremere. Rumor had it they were a group of immortal wizards who practiced a very obscure, but exceptionally powerful brand of magic known as Thaumaturgy. This occult discipline was said to involve the drinking and manipulation of blood during its rituals.

Intrigued, Esher was compelled to find out more about these secretive "vampire wizards." At first his inquiries as to the Tremere's whereabouts were met with evasion, if not outright hostility. The peasants who tended the fields and the thick-witted boyars that ruled over them were clearly unwilling to help anyone asking questions about the Tremere. In some villages the mere mention of their name was enough to cause every door to be slammed in his face. Still, Esher was not the type to be dissuaded by superstitious villagers.

When he heard stories of an elderly Eastern Orthodox priest named Father Magnus who claimed to be an expert on Romania's darker secrets, he decided to search him out. Father Magnus was old and blind in one eye and given to drinking at a local inn, but Esher found the ancient cleric to be extremely knowledgeable about the dark arts. Despite his physical infirmities, he possessed a mind that was a virtual encyclopedia of the occult.

At first the old priest hedged concerning his knowledge of the Tremere, but after a few sherries he became increasingly voluble. Father Magnus claimed that the Tremere were not mere wizards, but true creatures of the night—*vryoloda*. Vampires. According to the legend, a thousand years ago a group of ambitious magi had sought immortality by any means possible. One experiment after another had failed them until, in desperation, the coven captured an ancient vampire from a clan that had long dominated the region. Concocting a potion from its blood, the magi had attained an undead state similar to that of their victim. They then returned to their monastery and transformed their fellow warlocks, growing in size and strength until they were powerful enough to assert their control as a clan in their own right.

It was Magnus who told him that the Tremere no longer made their home in Transylvania, but had migrated to Vienna prior to the Renaissance. He also told Esher how to recognize them by their totem—a squared circle wed to a captive triangle.

Esher lost little time in booking passage to Austria. While on his way to the city of the Hapsburgs, he wrote to his friend back in the States of his adventures and plans to infiltrate the blood cult. It was a foolish thing to do, he later realized—but at the time he wanted someone to know what had happened to him should he never be heard from again.

He was in Vienna less than a week before he was contacted by the blood-wizard known as Caul; apparently his inquiries in Transylvania, while unanswered, went far from unnoticed. The Council of Seven, said to be the self-same adepts who founded the cult, had appointed Caul to investigate the inquisitive stranger and discover his intentions. Apparently he was impressed by Esher's strength of personality and ambition, for it was he who proposed to the Council of Seven that the American be apprenticed to the clan under his tutelage.

And so Caul—he of the beautiful blond hair and milk-pale skin—became his mentor. The Tremere, unlike many other vampire clans, spent a great deal of time and care grooming their "recruits" before actually transforming them. It was important that any human chosen to become one of their number be first indoctrinated as a wizard, then subjected to the ritual that would make them one of the Kindred.

Esher studied under Caul for several years, until such time as it was decided that he was ready to receive the Embrace. The Council of Seven called Esher before their august presence in 1838 and told him that he must return to his homeland one final time, to set his affairs in order and arrange for his estate to be inherited by a "distant relative"—actually himself, under an assumed name. Esher did as he was told and returned to America. His ship put to port in New York, and it was there he saw the poet for the second-to-last time.

They met in a dark and dire pub in the city's notorious Bowery. Esher wasn't terribly sure why he'd arranged the meeting, except that part of him wanted to say goodbye. Over absinthe, Esher found himself rattling on about his drive to bend death to his will and his pursuit of "forbidden knowledge." After a few minutes he realized that his companion was regarding him with open ill-ease, if not outright fear. Only then did he recognize his mistake in confiding in his one-time companion. He quickly found a reason to leave, hoping that the poet would dismiss his story as the raving of an absinthe addict and nothing more.

Having put his mortal affairs in order, Esher quickly returned to the chantry in Vienna. Once there, Caul greeted him. He was dressed in the blood-red robes of an initiate and brought before the Council of Seven. Clan Tremere prided itself on its closely knit ties, so unlike the rest of the vampire community. Where the others were haphazard in the selection and conversion of their neonates, producing creatures ignorant of their dark heritage, the Tremere controlled the process assiduously.

Since Caul had served as his tutor during his apprentice stage, he was given the honor of draining Esher's lifeblood. As he lay dying on the altar, one by one the Seven came forward. Each pricked their thumb with a sacred knife reserved for such rituals, and squeezed a single drop of their own tainted blood onto his parted lips. When he awoke three nights later, he was shown his death certificate and his obituary in the paper. And so did his mortal life end and his unlife begin.

It wasn't until some years later that he discovered his final conversation with the poet had born fruit, in its own way. Deeply disturbed and agitated by what he'd been told, the poet had written two stories whose title characters bore more than a passing resemblance to Esher. The Council of Seven was displeased by what it saw as an indiscretion on Esher's part that might someday endanger the clan, but Esher convinced them that their worries would come to nothing. After all, the humans who read the poet's stories dismissed them as mere fantasy, nothing more. And the poet's own problems with drink prevented those who might glimpse the truth hinted at in the stories from taking them seriously. Besides, in a decade or more, who would remember the jottings of a delirious drunkard?

A decade passed, during which time Esher honed the occult skills he'd learned while still alive, becoming adept in the practice of Thaumaturgy. He curried favor with the Seven and was chosen to supplement the clan's strength in America.

In 1848 he returned to his native land once more, but this time greatly changed. He claimed his "inheritance" and drifted from city to city along the eastern coast, spying on the competing clans and gathering information for later use. It was during one of these forays that he came across the poet one last time.

He spotted the poet lurching out of a grog shop on the low end of town. He was exceptionally drunk and looked to be in very bad health. Esher decided to follow his former companion as he continued on his bender. He stayed in the shadows, never betraying his existence to his prey or casual passersby. Most of the people on the street gave the poet plenty of room, as he was babbling to himself, calling out the name of his wife and quoting fragmented lines of his own poetry in a heavily slurred voice.

He followed his prey into an alley and watched from his hiding place as the poet leaned against a wall and vomited noisily. It was then that he finally stepped forward and tapped his old school chum on the shoulder.

"I say, old fellow, are you all right?"

The poet wiped at his mustache and turned unsteadily, doing his best to keep from collapsing. He peered at Esher for a long moment. "I know that voice—or at least I used to."

"I'm insulted, old man! Don't you recognize me?"

The poet's brows knotted even tighter, then suddenly went slack, his eyes widening. "My God! They said you died of typhus while in Vienna!"

"You shouldn't believe all you read—or what you write, old friend!" Esher chuckled, clapping him on the back. "Come—let's have an absinthe! My treat! We have so much to catch up on!"

It wasn't hard for him to cloud the minds of the patrons of the absinthe house, since their minds were befogged to begin with. Still, Esher did not want anyone to notice that the poet's last hours were spent in the company of anyone but the green fairy. As the poet drank, he told Esher of his life— or what was left of it. Although he had experienced some success with his writings, there had been a scandal involving a poetess and a libel suit, which robbed him of what little money he'd accumulated. Not long after this, his wife had died of tuberculosis. He'd come back to where he'd grown up in hopes of overcoming the temptation of drink, and had been largely successful at it. But then a friend invited him to a birthday party in the city. He made the mistake of toasting the hostess with a sherry—he did not remember much after that.

As Esher watched the poet weep and babble over his drink, he contemplated, for the briefest second, Embracing him, but quickly rejected the notion. In order for the poet to be made one of the Tremere he would have to be taken to Vienna, and he was certain to die before their ship could arrive. Secondly, he had not undergone the rigorous preparation necessary to join the ranks of the blood-wizards. And, most importantly, the poet was simply too romantic and weak-willed for such a transformation. Besides, bestowing the gift of immortality on artists was more in keeping with clans such as those degenerates, the Toreador.

So when the poet suffered a seizure and collapsed in the gutter, Esher simply left him there to die of exposure. He had more important things to attend to.

That was one hundred and fifty years ago.

In the years since his return to America he'd established himself as a Pontifex among the Tremere in North America. His power had grown with each passing generation, making him one of America's most feared and respected Kindred. But it wasn't until five years ago, upon his return to his old stomping grounds, that he'd dared to make his boldest moves.

Deadtown had been the domain of the vampire Sinjon for close to two centuries. Sinjon was a prince of the Ventrue—a clan that prided itself on its aristocratic background. It was Esher's intention to move in and shatter the old fool's power base and set himself up as prince. Since Tremere law forbade the indiscriminate creation of whelps, his plan for deposing his foe involved recruiting as many unaffiliated Kindred as possible and binding them to him through the taking of blood oaths. Luckily, he had no shortage of raw material.

In the years since the First World War the number of carelessly spawned neonates had quintupled. There were more untutored fledglings wandering the world now than ever before, thanks to the rise of modern technology and the downfall of superstition. Most were by-blows of thoughtless seductions, brought into a new existence wherein they knew nothing of their heritage. They wandered the earth, eternal and alone, searching for some meaning to their existence. And Esher was more than happy to give it to them.

Deadtown was different from other American cities in that it had been damned for a very long time. Here he could operate openly, without fear of discovery from the human authorities. Throwing caution to the wind, he set out on a blatant campaign against the resident prince. He opened the Dance Macabre, which drew both unaffiliated Caitiff and rebel anarchs alike; those who were new to unlife were the easiest to snare. They were so pathetically desperate for someone to tell them what to do and explain the intricacies of Kindred society to them that they gladly agreed to the blood oath. By drinking of his blood three times, they became bound to him, trapped in a kinship far stronger than that between themselves and their original sires. From then on they were his—mind, heart and soul—if they possessed one.

Esher considered himself dedicated to his clan. All he had done since the night of his Becoming was to the betterment and advancement of the Tremere. Yet, even the most dedicated of sons may sin against his father. And so it was that Esher had broken one of the most important laws of his clan; he had created whelps outside the rituals of the Tremere.

Like all Kindred, he had created them out of a combination of love and loneliness. He'd been forced to destroy the first one. He'd forbidden her to create her own brood, just as the Seven had forbidden him, but then had caught her in the act of Embracing a human. Although it grieved him to do so, he'd had no choice but to consume her, taking back the gift of immortality he had bestowed upon her. He never spoke her name after that and his servants had been instructed never to mention her again on pain of death.

Decima was his second attempt, and he had made a point of Blood Bonding her to him immediately following her creation, ensuring no troublesome display of free will on her behalf. And now he was preparing his precious Nikola to accept the Embrace. For the first time two of his by-blows would exist at the same time.

Esher was drawn from his reveries by the flashing lights and the sound of the disco music being switched off. He straightened himself and leaned forward in his seat. The floor show was about to begin.

The club's emcee, a stocky vampire dressed in a black cassock and floppy beret, raised his hands for silence. He held a cordless microphone and his voice boomed out over the club's speakers.

"Welcome and good *eveeee-ning*, children of the night, and fellow-travelers, to Dance Macabre: Deadtown's premiere nightspot! We've got a fine floor show lined up for you, if I do say so myself! Something for everybody! We've got blood sports, beautiful women, gorgeous men, and the one-of-a-kind dance stylings of our very own Nikola to look forward to before cockcrow! I don't want to hold up the festivities any longer, so let's get started with tonight's Example!"

The curtains behind the emcee opened to reveal two figures standing center stage: one white, the other black. Both were completely nude except for leather fighting harnesses and heavy manacles around their wrists and ankles that secured them to an eyebolt set in the floor.

"Ladieees and Gentlemen! On your left is none other than the six-foot-four, two-hundred-and-thirty-three-pound tower of terror known as Skald! Type AB Negative! Three wins!

"And on your right, weighing in at six foot three, two hundred and twenty pounds, is the challenger and tonight's Example, Cro-Mag! Blood type O Positive!"

The Pointers in the crowd shifted uneasily as they recognized their friend, but said nothing. Their eyes went from Cro-Mag to Skald, whose mouth was twisted into a permanent sneer by a scar that ran from his left cheek to where his ear had once been. His head was shaven clean, along with his eyebrows. On closer inspection, there wasn't a single hair to be seen on the massively built African-American's body.

Cro-Mag, while impressive in his own right, did not look quite as intimidating. A large purple bruise discolored his forehead, and his right pupil was fixed. He looked dazed and seemed unsteady on his feet. His penis dangled like an albino python between the pillars of his thighs. Both men were outfitted with special razor-studded gloves.

Skald lifted his razored fists over his head, his sneer tightening even further. The gleam in his eyes was that of a man nearly beyond the boundaries of sanity. The vampires in the audience clapped and cheered. The Pointers glowered at the scarred fighter but said nothing.

The emcee gestured to someone offstage, and the sound of a diesel engine added to the already considerable noise. A large metal cage was lowered from the rafters. The bars looked rusty, but they weren't. The emcee removed a keyring from his voluminous sleeves, quickly unlocked the fighters' manacles and opened the cage door. As the two men entered, the diesel motor changed gear and began to lift the cage high into the air, swinging it out over the dance floor.

Skald stared coldly at Cro-Mag as they gripped the gore-flecked bars for balance. Cro-Mag kept shaking his head, as if trying desperately to clear his vision.

The emcee smiled, exposing his pearl-white fangs. "Let the dance—begin!"

The taped electronic music kicked back in, louder than before. Skald surged from his corner of the cage, razored fists slicing Cro-Mag's naked flesh. The odor of adrenaline-heavy blood filled the air. Below them, the club patrons lifted their voices in an ululating howl of raw pleasure.

Cro-Mag landed a punch on Skald's jaw, neatly slicing off most of his lower lip. The black man staggered backward, his sneer transformed into a crimson grin. Before Cro-Mag could savor his coup, Skald grabbed his opponent's scrotum and yanked.

Cro-Mag shrieked and instinctively grabbed his wounded groin, allowing Skald the chance to smash a razor-studded fist into his unprotected face, nearly severing Cro-Mag's nose. Cro-Mag's eyes bugged as he strove to keep from strangling on the wash of blood filling his sinuses. The spectators below laughed and jeered as they jostled one another for prime positions beneath the cage, their heads thrown back and mouths open wide. Even some of the Pointers, caught up in the blood-frenzy, were laughing and clapping. Besides, Cro-Mag had never been well liked.

Cro-Mag was losing and he knew it. He grabbed at Skald's hairless crotch. The fighter tried to sidestep him, but there wasn't enough room to maneuver. Skald bellowed like a bull in a gelding stall. The crowd screamed its delight as the black man's sex landed on the dance floor. There was a minor scuffle as some of the vampires fought to retrieve the tidbit.

Maddened by pain, Skald pounded Cro-Mag's face unmercifully, slicing open his eyes and gouging huge ruts along his forehead and cheekbones. Blood fell from the dangling cage in a crimson shower, splashing the wildly dancing vampires underneath.

Blinded and mortally wounded, Cro-Mag offered Skald his throat in ritual defeat. The killing blow was swift and—compared to what had gone before—relatively painless. Cro-Mag dropped to the wire-mesh floor of the cage, his life pumping from his severed jugular onto the dancers below. His last thought before he died was maybe, just maybe, he wouldn't have come to such an end if he'd only learned to read.

The cage was lowered to the stage, where a man wearing a white coat and carrying a doctor's bag stood beside the emcee. Now that the killing lust had fled, Skald began to feel the effects of his emasculation. He collapsed across Cro-Mag's body, his eyes glazing as he gripped his opponent's cooling flesh. The shivers caused by oncoming shock made it look as if he were grieving for his fallen foe.

The vet hurried into the cage and squatted next to the crippled fighter. He glanced at the emcee and shook his head. Either way, this would be Skald's last fight.

The emcee stepped forward, waving the chattering crowd into silence. "Well, ladies and gentlemen—what shall it be for our brave contestant? Is it 'yea' or 'nay'?"

There was quiet for a second, then the audience answered as one, their voices joined in a primitive singsong:

"One of us! One of us! One of us!"

The emcee nodded his understanding and turned to look in the direction of Esher's balcony. Sighing, the vampire lord stood and leaned against the balcony railing. The revelers gathered on the floor below, human and Kindred alike, tilted their faces upward, and began chanting, *"Esher! Esher! Esher!"*

"So, milord? What will it be?" asked the emcee.

Esher glanced at the dying champion, then nodded. A ragged cheer burst from the spectators. The veterinarian pocketed his stethoscope and returned the premixed lethal injection to his little black bag.

"Do it," ordered Esher.

The veterinarian sank his fangs into Skald's neck, rewarding him with the prize that every champion who enters the cage strives for—immortality.

Esher looked away, already bored.

"I don't think Skald's going to appreciate an eternity without a dick," Decima smirked.

"What does he need a dick for?" Esher replied with a casual shrug. "He'll be one of the Kindred."

"Old habits die hard. You know that better than anyone, milord."

Esher stiffened and turned to glower at his lieutenant. "Mind your tongue, whelp—if you want to keep it in your head!"

Decima lowered her eyes in deference, but offered nothing else in the way of an apology. Esher made a mental note to see that she was properly chastised, then returned his attention to the stage.

While Dance Macabre attracted unaffiliated vampires to his banner, it served a twofold purpose. In the past the Kindred had utilized bands of social pariahs, such as gypsies. But ever since the end of the Second World War, gypsies had become scarce and far too conspicuous. Luckily, the late twentieth century had seen fit to provide the Kindred with disaffected urban youths that wandered the streets of America's and Europe's cities. There were always those willing to betray their own kind in hopes of sharing the power of the Kindred. Indeed, they often proved so dedicated they would recruit their friends and family. Right now the club was full of such Judas goats, eager to taste forbidden delights.

Esher had discovered over the years that the best way to bind human servitors to him was by indulging their vices. Drugs, alcohol, sex, violence—these were the tools most often used to bend humans to his will. Not even the sight of one of their own being beaten to death was enough to make them doubt the wisdom of their pact.

The curtains parted again, this time to reveal a padded couch outfitted with leather restraining straps and stirrups similar to those found on an examination table. A large raffle drum filled with plastic chits stood to one side of the stage.

"And now, on to the audience-participation part of tonight's entertainment!" the emcee announced as he waved in the direction of the wings.

Two Pointers dragged a struggling woman onto the stage. The woman wore an expensive, if unexceptional business dress, and a pillowcase smothered her head. The emcee stepped forward and yanked the pillowcase away, revealing tousled blond hair and the terrified face of an executive secretary in her early thirties. The woman was trying to scream but her cries were being blocked by the ball-gag in her mouth.

The secretary was dragged to the couch. As her captors tried to force her to sit down, she experienced a burst of panic-born strength and kicked one of them hard enough to make him let go of her. Catching the other off guard, she wrenched herself free of his grip and made for the stage door.

Suddenly the emcee was there in front of her. Grabbing her by the sleeve of her jacket, he backhanded her hard enough to send her reeling. The secretary dropped to the floor, stunned. Her guards unceremoniously grabbed her elbows and dragged her to the couch, then began roughly removing her clothes and gag. The Pointers in the audience began to hoot and stomp their feet in unison.

"Bang-bang! Bang-bang!"

Having finished stripping and restraining their captive, the two Pointers moved to the raffle drum. One of the youths turned the crank on the drum to the accompaniment of a prerecorded drum-roll, halting at the crash of the cymbals; his companion opened the hatch on the drum and reached in, removing one of the plastic chits and handing it to the emcee.

"Tonight's lucky winner is—467!"

There was a brief moment of silence as the humans in the audience consulted their ticket stubs, then a hoarse bellow of triumph. A Pointer with a spiderweb tattooed across the back of his shaved head began pushing his way toward the stage, pumping his fist in the air as his buddies clapped him on the shoulders.

"M'man, Webb!" one of them hooted, punching him in the arm.

Esher had already lost interest by the time Webb clambered onto the stage to claim his door-prize. Something was bothering him—but he couldn't put his finger on it. As the secretary woke to find Webb on top of her and began screaming, he motioned for Decima to draw near.

"You said Cavalera was stabbed. Who is responsible?"

"Cro-Mag insisted that the old man did it, although from his description of what occurred, that would have been impossible. The child may have stabbed Cavalera, but I seriously doubt it."

"How so?"

"I saw Cavalera's body. His chest was heavily bruised and there were several broken ribs—as if whoever stabbed him drove the knife in with a mallet. He could have died by human hand—but I think otherwise."

"You believe he was slain by one of Sinjon's brood? But why? Why would one of them bother to come to the aid of a human child and an old man?"

Decima shrugged, her gaze fixed on the ritual rape being enacted below. "Sinjon is your enemy. Whoever slew Cavalera did it because he was a Pointer, not because they were helping the child—doubtless a fledgling thinking he was honoring his sire by killing one of your servitors."

Esher nodded. It made sense. He leaned back, stroking his chin thoughtfully. "Cavalera was a pathetic idiot, but his death is an affront to my honor. It cannot go unavenged. Besides, the Pointers will not expect me to let such a transgression go unpunished. Kill a Black Spoon in retaliation tomorrow night."

Esher glanced back down at the stage. Webb had finished and was pulling his pants back up. The secretary's face was bruised and her mouth bleeding, her eyes swollen with tears. Webb winked, leered at his comrades clustered around the stage, and made a thumb's-up sign. The crowd roared like a hungry animal and the synchronized clapping and foot-stomping began again.

"Bonk-bonk on the head! Bonk-bonk on the head!"

The emcee sidled up, holding a tray on which were arrayed various different blunt instruments—everything from a monkeywrench to a sawed-off bat. Webb studied the selection for a long moment before deciding on the traditional lead pipe.

"Bonk-bonk on the head! Bonk-bonk on the head!"

The secretary saw what was coming, but did not struggle or plead for mercy. She was surrounded by monsters—human and otherwise—and recognized the futility of her situation. Instead of screaming, she simply turned her head and closed her eyes. After five blows there wasn't much left of her skull. Satisfied that he was finished, Webb held up the bloody length of pipe for his gang's approval. A ragged cheer went up from the audience.

Webb jumped off the stage and was greeted by his homeys, who congratulated him on his performance. The clean-up team quickly removed the secretary's body and hurried it backstage. It was up to them to see that anything that might possibly identify the corpse was removed before it was weighted and dumped in the river. Esher was not so careful with every door-prize—just the ones who would be missed.

The lights dimmed and the canned throb of the house music abruptly disengaged. Esher leaned forward in his seat, clutching the armrests with his powerful hands. His full attention was now riveted on the darkened stage below. The vampires and humans milling on the dance floor fell silent, their conversations forgotten, as the speakers crackled back to life, this time straining out the opening notes of Philip Glass' soundtrack for *Misihima*. A powder-blue spot blossomed on the stage, spilling its light onto a solitary figure curled in upon itself on the boards.

The figure was that of a woman dressed in a classical-length tutu fashioned of white gauze. Underneath it she wore a white satin leotard and tights, which showcased her dancer's build. Her feet were laced into blood-red ballet shoes, the ribbons elaborately knotted just below her knees. Her hair was pulled into a soft bun that hung against the nape of her neck like a silken cloud. Her already pale skin was made even more so by a layer of clown-white greasepaint and a generous dusting of talc.

As the music swelled, the dancer languidly raised her head, looking out into the audience. Her eyes were heavily outlined in mascara, like those of an ancient Egyptian princess, and her lips were painted a brilliant scarlet.

Nikola's gaze swept across the upturned faces—some pallid, some human, all of them hungry—and the doubt and confusion filling her head disappeared. She had an audience. It was time to dance.

Esher's eyes narrowed, his features set in extreme concentration, as he watched his bride-to-be rise and go *en pointe* as if pulled upright by invisible strings. Her grace was what had drawn him to her in the first place, and it never ceased to awe him.

Moving with the tranquil ease of a jungle cat, Nikola displayed to her audience the shunts embedded in her arms. As she swayed to the music, she slowly opened the valves. Several of the vampires gasped in excitement as the smell of her blood filled the air. As the rhythms intensified, so did her movements, as her glissades gave way to pirouettes, arabesques, and grand *jetes* that carried her across the stage like a young gazelle, her blood flying in crimson arcs into the crowd.

The Pointers usually found Nikola's dancing boring, if not disgusting, but watched for fear that Esher would take offense. In contrast, the Kindred gathered at the edge of the stage, their wine-dark eyes gleaming in anticipation. For creatures decades, if not centuries removed from human sexuality, this was the ultimate in erotic dance. Those lucky enough to be spattered with her blood moaned and swooned in ecstasy as they licked the precious fluid from their fingers.

Nikola spun across the stage like a dervish as the music neared its climax. As she came out of her final pirouette, she stumbled and nearly lost her footing. Her pristine tutu and tights were stained so bright a red it was impossible to see where the blood ended and her shoes began. She collapsed onto the stage, her bosom heaving as she gasped for air. The smell of fresh blood was overpowering, and Esher felt himself grow excited.

So did a few members of the audience, judging from the noise below. One of the vampires, an anarch dressed in a plaid shirt and backward baseball cap, jumped onto the runway, baring his fangs in anticipation of slaking his lust.

A collective gasp rose from the audience as Esher leapt from his place in the balcony onto the runway. He lifted the anarch by the scruff of the neck, holding him at arm's length as he would a miscreant pup.

"I will not destroy you, whelp, for you are new to Deadtown and its rules! But know this now and forever: The woman Nikola is mine! Have I made myself understood?"

"Y-yes, milord!"

Satisfied, Esher hurled the young vampire back into the crowd. Turning his back to the audience, he bent to pick up Nikola. He shut the valves on her shunts as he gently cradled her in his arms. Her face was pressed against his chest, her features as still and perfect as a porcelain doll's.

Chapter

3

Father Eamon looked up from his prayers when the screaming started. He narrowed his eyes as he tried to gauge its distance and direction. Light cast from the flickering votive candles made the shadows surrounding the plaster saints pulse and shudder. Sound had a tendency to echo inside St. Everhild, and even after all these years he had yet to develop the ability to pinpoint the exact location of the noises that filtered in from the street. Not that it mattered. He never set foot outside the church doors after sundown.

His knees groaned as he rose from the prayer rail, his rosary swinging from his fingers like a carpenter's plumb. Hardly a midnight went by without Mass being disrupted by screams or gunfire from outside. Then again, since he kept the doors to the sanctuary barricaded, what difference did it make? Certainly none to the archdiocese, which had desanctified St. Everhild years ago. Actually, expunged was closer to the truth. The parish had been erased from all records, yet it continued to exist as a rumor—an ecclesiastical urban legend, if you will.

He had first heard of "the parish of the damned" while attending the seminary, where it had been whispered of in the tone of voice reserved for campfire ghost stories. Little did he know then that one day he would seek it out and make it his own.

He grimaced as the rheumatism sent a sharp jolt of pain into his right knee. Sleeping on a pile of rags in an unheated room with a leaky roof was hardly the best thing for his condition, but he had little choice—or desire— to live elsewhere. As he hobbled down the aisle, he glanced at the line of heavy wooden pews knocked over like dominoes and made a mental note to right them and see that the hymnals scattered across the floor were properly dusted and put back in place. Just because St. Everhild had been forsaken by the Church did not mean it had been forgotten by God.

As Father Eamon reached the stairs leading to the bell tower, the screaming heightened in intensity. It sounded as if it was coming from the direction of the Black Lodge. Father Eamon hesitated for a moment, then began to mount the rickety wooden steps. As he wound his way up the narrow, dusty confines of the tower staircase, he knew he was helpless to change the outcome of whatever was transpiring below. Perhaps this was his punishment—to witness horror upon horror and stand idle. Once, long ago, he had been tricked by Satan into thinking he was acting as an instrument of the Lord. Because of his sinful pride he was fit only to tend St. Everhild's altar.

With a mighty grunt, he pushed open the belfry trapdoor. His occasional trips to the tower were the closest he'd come to venturing out-of-doors after dusk over the last decade. The bells that had once hung in the belfry were long gone when he'd first arrived, but judging from the thickness of the rotten coils of rope and the size of a solitary clapper left behind, they must have been impressive. The tower had four large, narrow windows that faced the compass points, allowing him unobstructed views of Deadtown. From this vantage point he followed the comings and goings of his "parish."

To the east was the river, gleaming dark as sacramental wine in the light reflected from the city. To the north was Pointer territory. To the south was The Street With No Name, the neighborhood's unofficial neutral zone, where the few remaining shops were clustered. And to the west, almost directly across the avenue from St. Everhild, was the Black Lodge.

Father Eamon was uncertain which had come first, the church or the Masonic lodge. Both were quite old. Perhaps the Holy See had elected to build St. Everhild in defiance of the antipapal bigotry of the Freemasons. Or perhaps the Masons had erected their lodge as an affront to the Pope. There was only one person in Deadtown who knew for sure, and that was Sinjon, and Father Eamon had no intention of ever asking him.

The priest glanced down the street and saw the source of the screams. He glimpsed the silvery grin of a Black Spoon death's-head in the moonlight as the jacket's owner held a gun to a quaking woman's head. The girl was either a prostitute or a hapless tourist who had wandered into the area by mistake, since no citizens of Deadtown would be so foolish as to leave the relative safety of their squats once the sun set.

Father Eamon's attention was drawn from the attempted rape by a flicker of movement in the opposite alleyway. There was a sound like that of a book being snapped shut and the Black Spoon stiffened and stretched, as if trying to get a crick out of his back. He dropped his gun, his victim forgotten, as he tried to reach behind him and pull the crossbow bolt out of his spine, then collapsed with a choked gurgle. The woman stared down at her attacker, then looked in the direction the arrow had come from. Before she could thank her rescuer, there was another snap and a second bolt sank into her throat, pinning her to the wall like a butterfly.

Although Father Eamon could not see who had fired the shots, the killer's mocking laughter rose on the night air, making him shiver like a wet dog. He crossed himself and quickly recited the prayer for the dead. He hurried down the tower stairs to the comparative warmth of the sanctuary. He did not want to think about what he'd just seen, but he could not help but feel that it was the start of something bad, even by Deadtown standards. That one of Esher's minions had dared to kill one of Sinjon's men on his doorstep was Not Good.

The pain in his leg was now so intense it made his vision blur. He reached behind the pulpit, retrieving a quart bottle of yellow-label bourbon. He cursed his weakness as he knocked back a stiff slug. The liquor burned his gut almost as badly as his shame.

The first swig of the night was always the guiltiest. After that, they began to blur and soften, as did his memories and pain. He eased himself into the one pew he'd managed to upright in the ten years since he'd first arrived at St. Everhild, angling his bum leg so it was supported by the hard wooden bench. As the cheap bourbon dulled his senses, he decided that he was going to get around to righting the rest of the pews.

Tomorrow.

Ryan was trying very hard to be quiet. Cloudy had told him not to disturb the strange lady while she slept. Not that there was much chance of that happening, since she was dead.

Well, maybe not really dead, like the rat he'd found in the alley the other day. The strange lady—the one who had helped him and Cloudy—was one of the Kindred. Sort of. Cloudy had told him, when he woke up that afternoon, that the strange lady wasn't like the other vampires in Deadtown. Ryan didn't know exactly what to make of this, but if Cloudy said it, then it must be true. As far as Ryan was concerned, Cloudy knew everything. He wondered sometimes if his real dad was as smart and good as Cloudy, but somehow he didn't think so, or else his mom would have let him stay around.

Ryan thought about his mom all the time. Sometimes he would dream of how it had been before the monsters came and took her away. They'd moved around a lot—usually from one dingy studio apartment to another. His mother slept all day and worked all night, so Ryan spent a lot of time with babysitters. If his mom couldn't get someone to watch him, she'd lock him inside the apartment by himself. He'd learned how to take care of himself early. By the time he was three he already knew how to call 911 and microwave a burrito. Most of the time he sat up watching TV until his mother came home. After she fixed herself something to eat, she'd read him a story, like *Curious George Rides A Bike* or *Mike Mulligan and his Steam*

Shovel, and they'd go to bed. Until recently, Ryan had never slept anywhere but beside his mother. Their life was spent one day ahead of the eviction notices, but Ryan had no way of knowing that. As far as he was concerned, theirs was a normal and happy existence.

And then the monsters came.

Ryan still had nightmares about that. It was just before dawn and he and his mother had just gone to bed for the day—because of her hours they usually slept until two or three in the afternoon—when there was a horrible crash and the front door of the apartment flew open and a bunch of strange guys and a scary-looking woman came in. Ryan's mom screamed for him to run away, but he was too scared and didn't want to leave her, so he grabbed her hand and held on tight.

The scary-looking woman pointed at Ryan's mom, and the guys started dragging her off the bed. Ryan was still holding onto his mother's hand, so he was dragged along, too. The scary-looking woman grabbed him and yanked him free and held him up by his hair, looking at him like he was a bug or something. Ryan screamed, more out of fear than pain, and his mom broke away from the guys holding her and punched the scary-looking woman, calling her a bad word and telling her to put him down.

The scary-looking woman just laughed and backhanded his mom, sending her flying onto the bed, though the slap had been a light one.

Ryan was too scared to fight or cry or do anything except hide under the sofa, which is what he always did when the shows on TV got too scary for him. No one seemed to notice. The guys grabbed his mother and dragged her out of the apartment, the scary-lady following behind them. Just as she was about to close the door to the apartment, she turned and looked right at where Ryan was hiding under the sofa, and grinned. That was when he saw her sharp, pointy teeth and red eyes. That was when Ryan knew his mom had been captured by monsters.

The policemen never showed up, like they always do on TV, and after a day or so it was obvious that his mom wasn't coming back. So Ryan packed what few things he owned—mostly a few articles of clothing and action figures—and went in search of his mother on the streets of Deadtown.

He spent most of his time avoiding the gang kids, scrounging food out of dumpsters and garbage cans, and looking for a safe place to hole up. Being a little kid, he was able to crawl into spaces most people would never think to look in. Unlike most of Deadtown's residents, Ryan actually ventured out at night. It was the only way he could catch a glimpse of his mother. He'd actually gotten pretty good at sneaking behind Pointer lines—he even experienced a weird thrill, knowing he was getting away with something he wasn't supposed to. But it wasn't a game. It was survival.

Ryan had been on the street for several weeks when he met Cloudy. There were a handful of people living in Deadtown who left scraps and old clothes on the doorsteps for him. Even though these offerings were clearly intended for him, he'd become so cautious he would wait until no one was around before darting from his cover and collecting them. Then one day, as he was hungrily wolfing down the half-eaten chicken salad sandwich left for him, the door opened and a pair of masculine hands grabbed him and dragged him inside.

Ryan's first instinct was to try to escape, and he began to kick and scream, biting the hands until they let him go. Ryan scampered across the room and tried to make himself as small as possible, wedging himself under a table. He glowered at the white-bearded man in the tie-dyed shirt who was standing between him and the door. Ryan had seen enough TV to realize that the old man was supposed to be a hippie.

"Damn it, kid! I'm just trying to help you, that's all! There's no call for you biting me like that!" he snapped, sucking the blood from his wound.

The bearded man didn't look very threatening, but then Ryan had learned through painful experience that things in Deadtown were often deceiving. The anger in the hippie's face drained away after he got a good look at Ryan.

"Jesus, kid! I've seen fatter alley cats than you! Look, I'm sorry if I scared you—it's just that I didn't want you to run off, dig? I've been seeing you from a distance for some time now, and it's been botherin' me that a li'l dude like yourself is on his ownsome. Where's your mama, kiddo?"

"The monsters took her."

"Monsters—? Which monsters?"

"The Pointy ones."

The bearded man made a face. "Your old lady's Esher's squeeze?"

"My mommy's not old!"

"I know she's not, kid. It's just a turn of phrase—never mind."

There was something about the bearded man that Ryan liked. Maybe it was because he looked like Tim the Bouncer, who worked at one of the clubs where his mom danced. Tim the Bouncer had a beard, but it wasn't white, and he wore tie-dye, too. He also wore a leather jacket and rode a motorcycle. His mom had told Ryan that Tim the Bouncer was an angel, although Ryan had never seen any wings or a halo on him. Maybe this man was an angel, too.

No longer afraid of being attacked, Ryan looked around his surroundings for the first time and saw that the whole room was full of books. He slowly crept out from under the table, his head swiveling in every direction.

"Are these all your books, mister?"

"Sure are. Do you like books, kid?"

Ryan nodded vigorously. His eyes widened as he spotted a familiar dustjacket. He picked up a copy of *Make Way For Ducklings*, holding it as if it were an ancient treasure. The gleam in his eyes was that of someone who has seen an old friend.

"I used to have this book! My mommy would read it to me before I went to bed!"

"Would you like to read that book, son?"

"I—I can't read yet."

The bearded man smiled and motioned for Ryan to bring him the book. "That's okay. I'll read it to you, if you like."

Ryan looked at the hippie, then down at the book, then back again. "My name's Ryan."

"Hi, Ryan. My friends call me Cloudy."

Ryan giggled. It was the first time he'd done that in a long while. It felt good. "That's a funny name."

Cloudy laughed. It sounded like he hadn't done it in a long time, too. "Isn't it, though?"

From that moment on, Cloudy was Ryan's friend. He loved and trusted the old hippie more than anyone in the world—except his mom. And if Cloudy said the strange lady was okay—then she was okay.

Even if she *was* a monster.

Ryan put aside the picture book he'd been pretending to look at and walked over to stare down at the strange lady. She was lying on the floor, on top of an old Army blanket. Cloudy had pushed aside some of his books to make room for her. She was still wearing her street clothes—she hadn't even bothered to remove her boots or jacket. Her arms were folded across her chest, hands resting atop her jacket. She didn't seem to be breathing. Ryan couldn't tell if her eyes were open or shut because they were covered by sunglasses. Ryan leaned closer and stared at his twinned reflection in the mirrored lenses. He'd gained some weight since hooking up with Cloudy, but he still looked thin. It made him look a lot older than five. He crossed his eyes and stuck out his tongue, giggling as his mirror image did the same.

"Good morning to you, too."

Ryan yelped and scuttled backward as the stranger unfolded her arms and sat up. She swiveled her head to follow his movements, her gaze still shielded by the sunglasses.

"I wasn't making fun of you! Honest!"

"I believe you, Ryan. You needn't be afraid of me." She stood up and stretched, her leather jacket creaking. "Where's Cloudy?"

"Out doin' stuff. He'll be back soon. It'll be dark in an hour." He paused for a moment, eyeing her speculatively. "Are you really a monster?"

The stranger nodded as she patted down her pockets. She didn't seem to take offense at the question. "You could say that."

"What kind of monster?"

The stranger grinned at the boy, revealing pearly white fangs. "I guess you could say I'm the monsters' monster."

"Cool!"

"Point out the ones that are normally posted as guards," the stranger whispered.

Ryan squinted for a moment, then pointed at a youth whose shaved head was covered with a web-shaped tattoo. "He's one." He paused for a long moment, then motioned toward a thick-set black man with tangled dreadlocks and a wicked-looking machete hanging from his belt. "He's usually there, too. I think they're friends."

They were watching the safe house in which Esher kept Nikola imprisoned when she wasn't dancing at the club or keeping him company. Although they were less than thirty feet away, the handful of Pointers hanging outside the entrance did not notice them because they were standing in the storm drain across the street. Ryan was perched atop a plastic milk crate so he could see over the drain's concrete lip.

"Do you watch from here every night?"

"Mostly. Unless it's rainin'—then I can't. That's how come I can get away from the Pointers so easy—I slip down the old drains and hide from them."

"Aren't you scared of the rats?"

Ryan shrugged. "At first I was scared—they'd hiss at me and stuff, but I learned that if I carried a stick or threw stuff at them, they left me alone. Cloudy says they're more scared of me than I am of them, anyway. Besides, they're just animals."

"You're a brave kid, Ryan. Braver than most men." The stranger smiled and patted the child's head. Ryan went completely rigid. At first she thought it was because she'd touched him; then she glanced up and saw the door to the safe house opening. The vampiress from the night before—the one armed with the crossbow—stepped out and motioned to the black man with the machete, who briskly clapped his hands. The Pointers gathered on the stoop snapped to attention. One of them produced a cellular phone, and a second later the black '57 Cadillac pulled up to the curb.

"That's Decima," Ryan whispered, pointing to the vampiress. "I hate her. She's mean." There was a vehemence to the boy's voice that was far older than his years.

Decima turned to the door of the safe house and gestured with an impatient wave of her crossbow. Nikola stepped through the door and stood under the entrance light, blinking as if confused. She was dressed in a white velvet sheath that clung to her like a second skin and exposed plenty of thigh and cleavage. One of the Pointers at the foot of the stoop broke into an unabashed leer. The machete-wielder saw the banger was looking at Nikola and came barreling down the steps toward him.

The Pointer's leer disappeared, to be replaced by a look of genuine fear. He took a couple of steps backward, raising his hands as if to shield himself from a blow. "I didn't mean nothing by it, Obeah! I swear t'God I didn't—!"

"There's no point in swearin' to your god to me, *fool!*" Obeah thundered. "This is Deadtown—only devils hear your prayers here!" With that he brought down his machete with one powerful stroke. The Pointer screamed as blood geysered from the stump where, moments earlier, his right hand had been. His companions swore and jumped back, but did not offer to come to his aid as he collapsed onto the sidewalk, clutching his wrist.

"You dissed Lord Esher with your thoughts, if not your words!" Obeah intoned. "Such insolence is not tolerated!"

Obeah struck quick as lightning. The Pointer cried out as the machete sliced down toward his face, severing his nose as cleanly as a surgeon's scalpel.

The stranger was more impressed than shocked. "So Esher has a Tonton Macoute guarding his intended. Interesting." She suddenly remembered Ryan and glanced down at the boy. He was watching the Haitian take apart the Pointer with an eerie calm. When she looked up again, the errant Pointer was lying on the sidewalk in a widening pool of blood and Obeah was carefully cleaning his machete blade.

Decima grabbed Nikola by her upper arm, hurried her down the stairs, and pushed her into the back of the waiting car. Obeah climbed in after her, while the tattooed skinhead got into the front passenger seat.

The moment the car doors slammed, Ryan hopped down off the milk crate and gathered it in his arms. "C'mon—we've got to follow her!" He wiggled down the concrete throat of the drain, pushing the milk crate ahead of him until he came to the open mouth that fed into the main sewer. He then carefully lowered the crate onto the narrow walk that flanked either side of the sluiceway.

"We're underground. How can you follow them when you can't see where the car's going?"

"It's Thursday!" Ryan explained as he hurried along the walkway. "She always goes to his place on Thursdays—just like she always goes to the club on Wednesdays and Saturdays!"

"Whose place?"

"Esher's, of course!" Ryan replied, rolling his eyes.

Chapter

4

The House of Esher was exceptionally large, dating from a time when people built in a grand manner. What distinguished it from the other buildings on the block was the fact that there *were* no others on the block— only piles of rubble and yawning, symmetrical holes that had once been basements. This was not the handiwork of urban renewal—Esher had ordered the demolition himself. He liked to see company coming long before it arrived. It had taken the Pointers the better part of two years to raze the neighborhood. There were sentry posts at either end of the block, manned by older, more experienced gang members armed with Uzis and repeating shotguns.

Still, the block was not without its residents. Candlelight flickered and reefer smoke rose like ground mist from the outlying basements the Pointers used as combination crash pads and barracks. The holes closer to the House, however, were completely dark, their contents far more sinister. These served as entrances and exits to the House, connected by subterranean tunnels, and were used exclusively by the Kindred. Many unaffiliated fledglings and those who had yet to bind themselves fully to Esher waited out the daylight in their shadowy depths.

The street outside the House was alive with Pointers sporting colors, milling about aimlessly. Some lounged on the wide stairs leading to the building, while others perched on makeshift stools fashioned from cast-off crates. The oldest of their number looked to be no more than twenty-five, while the youngest couldn't have been more than thirteen. There were no women to be seen among their number, but the lack of female company was compensated for by a plethora of firearms, as each gangbanger sported some kind of weapon in his waistband.

"Interesting," the stranger muttered from her perch atop a six-story tenement two blocks away. "This Esher has built himself quite a little army of sociopaths."

"How can you see that far with those glasses on?" Ryan asked, squinting in the direction she was staring. "I can't see anything from here!"

"My eyes aren't like yours. I can see things better at night than most people can at high noon."

"Neat! Like a kitty, right?"

"Kind of."

"I used to have a kitty named Koko, but the landlord found out and made us get rid of him. He said Koko had fleas. He was really mean and I hated him. The landlord, not Koko."

The stranger knelt and placed her hands on Ryan's shoulders. The boy's collarbone felt like the strut of a kite under her fingers. "Ryan—I need you to do as I say, understand? I'm going to try and get inside Esher's stronghold and find out what I can about your mom. But there's no way I'm going to be able to sneak in."

"So how are you gonna get in?"

"I'm going to ask him for a job."

"Huhn?"

"It's clear he's looking for hired muscle—both human and Kindred. If he thinks I'm his friend, then maybe I can catch him while he's not looking. But I can't let him know that you and I know each other. I want you to get back to Cloudy's as fast as you can without being noticed and stay there, okay? And if you see me on the street again, pretend you don't know me, understand? Your mother's life depends on it."

Ryan nodded, his features taking on a solemnity made even more poignant by his extreme youth. "I understand. You're going undercover, like the cops on TV."

"You've got it. Now get on back to Cloudy's. It's not safe out here."

Ryan headed for the rooftop door, then turned to look at her. "Do you have kids, lady?"

The stranger nodded, smiling sadly. "Once. A long time ago. A little girl."

"What happened to her?"

The stranger paused for a long second, looking across the rooftops to the stars dimly twinkling through a pall of pollution and light reflected from the city. "She grew up and didn't need me anymore."

Ryan fidgeted for a second, playing with the doorknob. "I need you, lady. My mom does too."

The stranger took a deep breath and let it out slowly while massaging her forehead. "Kid, this isn't a TV show. I didn't come to Deadtown to save your mother."

"Why did you, then?"

"I have my own reasons. I don't expect you to understand them. Sometimes I wonder if I understand them myself." She stared at the ragged preschooler for a long moment, then a small smile pulled at the corners of her mouth. "I can't promise anything, okay? Remember that. Now get going, before someone sees you!"

Ryan grinned, his eyes lighting up with real delight. It was the first time since she'd met him that he'd looked like a real-live boy.

Satisfied that Ryan was safely gone, the stranger straightened the shoulders of her leather jacket and stepped from the shadows of the tenement doorway.

She didn't want the boy to see her in full action. He had every reason to hate and fear creatures such as herself, and she didn't want his trust shaken by seeing her play up her Kindred nature. More to the point, she did not want him to realize just how difficult it was for her to control her vampiric tendencies. God forbid the child should come face-to-face with the Other.

She strode down the deserted street in the direction of Esher's block. Occasionally she glimpsed the faint glow of electric lights or a wan, frightened face peering out from a second-story window, but to all outward appearances Deadtown seemed as moribund as its name implied.

Appearances, in this case, were indeed deceiving. Three figures suddenly moved to block her way. Their movements were fast and fluid, like those of stalking panthers. The stranger halted in midstride, but did not try to flee.

"I told you we'd find her if we bided our time," said one of the vampires, his voice as dry as corn husks.

"I was the one who suggested staking out the neighborhood!" growled the second.

"Shut up! There will be time enough for arguing over who gets the credit after we give her head to Sinjon!" snapped the third.

"My-my," the stranger smirked. "What have we here? The Three Billy Goats Gruff!"

The first vampire made a disgusted noise and drew himself up to his full height. "Your days of insulting the Ventrue are over, Tremere witch!"

The stranger smiled and shook her head. "Look, fellas—I think you've got me mixed up with someone else."

"Do not seek to confuse us, witch!" growled the second vampire. "We know you were responsible for the execution of one of our prince's human servants! You left your calling card jutting from his back! You sought to insult our master by slaying one of his own on the very steps of the Black Lodge! Such effrontery must be punished!"

"Will you idiots get this through your thick heads? I'm *not* the person you're looking for! Now, I'm only going to ask you nicely once more to clear out of my way—"

"Enough!" thundered the third vampire, and they were on her.

The first circled behind her, while the second came in high and the third came in low. The stranger caught the third vampire squarely in the jaw with her steel-tipped boots, kicking so hard it hung like a busted garden gate, the tongue flapping like a pink worm. The second vampire's momentum sent him headlong onto her switchblade, skewering his right lung like a toy balloon. Normally such wounds are meaningless to the Kindred—but not when dealt by a weapon specifically enchanted to slay them.

The second vampire shrieked like a stallion in a gelding stall, pulling himself off the knife with a convulsive jerk. He tore open his shirt to expose his pallid, hairless chest. The flesh surrounding the puncture was already turning black and swelling with infection, becoming instantly gangrenous.

"What manner of Tremere wizardry is this?" rasped the first vampire.

The second vampire coughed, spewing forth the remains of his recent feeding, and collapsed onto the cobblestone street—well and truly dead. The stranger wasted no time rounding on the first vampire, plunging her silver switchblade into his right eye. The vampire shrieked, and within seconds his left eye ballooned outward, like some absurd Tex Avery cartoon character, then burst.

The third vampire turned to flee, but found his way blocked by his erstwhile prey. He lifted his hands in supplication and sputtered something that might have been a plea for mercy as the stranger drove the switchblade into his abdomen. The vampire dropped to the ground and lay writhing at her feet like a worm stranded on a hot sidewalk after a rainstorm. It took a lot longer to die from a gut wound than from a shot to the heart or neural system.

Bored, she stepped over her third and final victim, resuming the direction in which she'd been headed before she was sidetracked. She took three steps, then froze at the sound of automatic weapons being chambered.

A woman's voice barked out: "Halt!"

Several Pointers armed with AK47s emerged from the shadows. At their head was the vampiress the stranger had seen previously—the one called

Decima. She was dressed in a black leather jacket and leather jeans and carried a loaded crossbow. Decima scanned the carnage and frowned, looking back at the stranger.

"What's going on here?"

"Nothing. Now."

"Don't get cute with me, childe!"

She nodded to one of the Pointers, who rolled over the dead vampires with the toe of his boot. All three were already well on the way to putrefying.

"They're Sinjon's brood, Dec—er, milady!"

Decima's frown deepened and she turned her gaze back to the stranger. "You killed Sinjon's get—why?"

"I had no quarrel with them. They attacked me."

"Why?"

The stranger smiled crookedly, nodding to Decima's crossbow. "Apparently it was a case of mistaken identity. They thought I was you."

Decima's spine straightened as if it had been transformed into solid steel. *"Ridiculous!"*

"Yeah—imagine how *I* must feel!"

"Impudent bitch!" snapped Decima, lashing out with a vicious open-hand slap.

The stranger grabbed Decima's wrist, halting the blow within millimeters of her face. "Now, is that any way to treat somebody who's just done you a big favor?"

"What do you want, childe?" Decima spat as she jerked her hand free, her features rigid with rage. She was angry, but her voice held a great deal of uncertainty and a little fear, too. She did not like this strange vampiress, but she was unwilling to challenge her. Until she got a handle on the stranger's abilities, she could not risk being bested in front of the humans.

The stranger smiled, tilting her head so that the mirrored lenses of her sunglasses reflected Decima's angry face. "I heard you were hiring."

♋

"Who goes there?" barked the perimeter guard, bringing his riot gun to bear on the figures emerging from the shadows beyond the checkpoint. Those stationed at the checkpoint considered themselves Esher's elite guard, and they tended to take their job seriously. Decima made no effort to acknowledge the challenge. The guard tensed for a moment, then relaxed as he recognized Esher's field lieutenant. "Oh, it's you, milady."

Decima did not bother to respond to the Pointer's flowery sobriquet, brushing past him as if he did not exist. The stranger followed in her wake. The Pointer's gaze tracked her for a few seconds, but when she turned her mirrored eyes in his direction, the guard quickly looked away, returning his attention to the darkness beyond his post. When it came to their fellow humans, the Pointers were as aggressive and vicious a group as anything this side of a wolf pack, but they automatically deferred to Kindred.

The House of Esher loomed over the blasted landscape like a mammoth tombstone. The stranger focused her attention on the building, dropping her vision into the Pretender spectrum. She had to bite her tongue to keep from swearing out loud. The energy fields surrounding the stronghold pulsed and vibrated with considerable power.

There was magic involved—which confirmed the rumors she'd heard of Esher being a Tremere blood-wizard. She had dealt with vampires of great power before—but their strengths had lain in the disciplines of the mind, not the occult. She had knowledge of magic through her business arrangements with such alchemists-for-hire and spell-slingers as the *kitsune* Li-Lijing and the *petit daemon* Malfeis—indeed, it had been Malfeis who'd given her switchblade the Kindred-destroying enchantment it now possessed—but she had never done more than dabble in the dark arts. Still, it was clear from the braided chains of etheric energy surrounding the House that Esher had access to some serious supernatural connections. This was going to be tricky. Very tricky, indeed.

The Pointers lounging outside Esher's stronghold snapped to attention upon sight of Decima. The vampiress did not bother to look in their direction as she glided up the stairs. She paused on the threshold of the front door, her hand on the ornate brass knob fashioned to resemble a roaring lion's head.

"This is the house of my prince, the heart of his domain. It is his power made manifest. I will warn you but once, childe—do not stray from the central corridor. If you do so—then you are doomed." Having issued her ritual warning, Decima pushed the door open and motioned for the stranger to step inside.

The floor of the building abruptly fell away like the bottom of a carnival Gravity Barrel, and the interior spun in a dizzying circle. Pinned to the wall by centrifugal force, the stranger glimpsed numerous doors that turned into lizards, then into birds, then into doorways again. Some of the doors were over her head, others under her feet, while still others hung suspended in empty space.

Decima's voice came from nowhere and everywhere: "Do not move. Do not try to open any of the doors you see before you. Only the corridor is safe. The corridor leads to Esher, no matter where he may be. Close your eyes. Do you see it?"

The stranger did as she was told. The dizzying carousel of doors disappeared, to be replaced by the image of a perfectly ordinary corridor, the hallway decorated with tasteful wallpaper and gilt-framed portraits. As she focused on the corridor, Decima appeared before her, motioning impatiently.

"Hurry up! I haven't got all night to waste on you, childe!" she snapped.

The stranger stepped forward, her eyes tightly shut. She followed Decima, keeping to the corridor as it snaked its way through the house. At times the hallway turned in on itself and she found herself walking back the way she came. She battled a surge of vertigo as the corridor twisted into itself, turning the floor and ceiling into a Möbius strip. Still, she had to admire the skill and knowledge necessary to create such an impressive magical construct. It took a great deal of power and effort to bend space so deftly. Esher's stronghold made the spirit-house called Ghost Trap look like a shoebox dollhouse.

At last Decima stopped before a huge oaken door on which was carved the symbol of the Tremere. She paused to glare over her shoulder at the stranger. "This is the audience chamber. The master awaits within. Tell me your name and bloodline, so I can announce you into his presence."

The stranger shook her head. "If he wants to know what's my name and who's my daddy, he'll have to ask me for himself."

Decima's jaw twitched. "You dare much, fledgling! I will enjoy breaking you under my heel."

"Just open the fuckin' door, bitch."

Decima's eyes flashed crimson—but she pushed open the door all the same.

The audience chamber was hung with black velvet drapes and blood-red tapestries with occult symbols and sigils embroidered in gold thread. The room was lit by several cathedral-style candelabra, each weighing as much as a man, whose curving arms held over a hundred candles apiece. The prince of this domain was seated in a fifteenth-century Savonarola chair, behind which hung an exact replica of Notre Dame's famed Rose Window, suspended by steel cables and lit from behind by artificial light. Curled about his feet like a dozing cat was Nikola, her eyes half-lidded as the vampire lord caressed her hair.

Esher was learning forward, speaking to the two Pointers who served as Nikola's guards—the Anglo with the spiderweb tattoo and the Haitian called Obeah—using a quiet, but authoritative, tone of voice.

"I don't care *whom* you pick—although I would prefer it to be one of the lesser lights, if you understand me. No one who will be greatly missed or might prove useful later on." Esher glanced up at the sound of Decima's approach, then motioned for the Pointers to leave. "Go, now. Do as you must."

The stranger eyed the duo as they passed by her. The one with the tattoo, unlike the perimeter guard, openly returned her stare and sneered as he exited the audience chamber. Apparently not all of Esher's human servitors were fully conditioned.

Esher leaned back in his seat, his hand resting atop Nikola's silken head as if she were a faithful hound at his heel. "Have you anything to report, lieutenant?"

"Three of Sinjon's get were destroyed tonight. They were looking for me, to retaliate for the Black Spoon I took down."

"Good job, Decima."

"She didn't snuff 'em—*I* did."

Esher straightened, his gaze focusing on the stranger. "Who is this fledgling, Decima? Why did you not announce her?"

"She would not permit it."

Esher lifted an eyebrow and turned his gaze on the vampiress with the mirrored sunglasses. "Indeed? Who are you, childe? Which bloodline do you claim?"

"My sire was Sir Morgan, Lord of the Morning Star—Ventrue, I suppose you'd say—but he abandoned me shortly upon Embracing me. I claim no clan."

Esher leaned forward, staring at the stranger with interest. "You are anarch?"

"*Ronin* might be a better word for it, milord," she smiled crookedly.

"You claim to have slain three of my enemy's brood—why?"

The stranger shrugged. "As I told the lady with the fishhooks through her tits—it was a case of mistaken identity. They jumped me—I waxed them. It's that simple."

"Why are you here?"

"I heard it on the grapevine you were looking for muscle. Rumor has it there's a *jyhad* brewing between you and Sinjon."

Esher stood up abruptly, forcing Nikola to scoot out of his way. "*Jyhad?!?* There is no *jyhad* going on in Deadtown, my dear! I am merely protecting my interests! It would be foolish of me not to, considering the known aggressiveness of my opponent, don't you agree?"

"Absolutely, milord."

Esher's boots rang against the hardwood floor as he paced in a circle around the new recruit, eyeing her speculatively. "It is plain even to human eyes that you are a woman of great strength and ability. It radiates from you like heat from a freshly forged sword. I would like you to join my enclave, stranger. To be clanless is no great virtue amongst the Kindred, childe! No doubt you have already learned this sad truth! You shall have much to look forward to in the years ahead. Deadtown is but a stepping stone; I have great plans for this country! Cast your lot with me, my dear, and you may very well find yourself in charge of a whole city—perhaps an entire region—come the new millennium!"

"Sounds tempting. What do I have to do to join?"

"You must swear fealty to me as your liege-lord through the taking of a blood oath."

The stranger stiffened. "You would place me in thralldom?"

Esher smiled and held up a hand in appeasement. "You misunderstand me, friend! I ask merely for an oath—I do not wish to bind you to me! No, I desire that your service to me be of your own free will. Only through mutual agreement will we benefit from our arrangement! The taking of a blood oath is a mere formality, if you will. I am a great believer in ritual and tradition amongst our kind; it is what separates us from the more bestial species."

"Very well. I'll do it. I've gotten tired of being harassed by every punk with fangs I run into. It's time I belonged to something besides myself."

Esher smiled, clapping her on the shoulder. "I'm pleased to hear it, my dear! You have made a wise decision." He snapped his fingers and Nikola got to her feet, swaying like a reed. "Nikola! Bring me the claive!"

The dancer ducked behind the Savonarola and retrieved a dagger holstered in an ornately jeweled scabbard. Moving like a sleepwalker, she brought the knife to the vampire prince. Esher smiled indulgently and caressed Nikola's pallid cheek with one of his fingers.

"Is she not exquisite, my friend?"

"Yes, she's quite—lovely."

Esher fixed the stranger with a hard stare. "She is *mine*, and mine alone. Is that understood?"

"Perfectly, milord."

Esher rolled up his left sleeve, exposing an impressively muscled forearm. He pulled the dagger from the scabbard. The hilt was made of pure platinum, with a large bloodstone set in the pommel, the blade glinting like ice in the reflected candlelight. With a single stroke, he opened his inner forearm from the elbow to his wrist. The lips of the cut pouted, then opened wide, revealing several layers of skin. Had he been alive, Esher's life would have come gushing forth in a crimson geyser, but instead he was forced to grab the underside of his elbow and squeeze, milking the wound so that it would bleed. After several long seconds a viscous red liquid, looking more like molasses than blood, welled from the cut.

"Partake of this, my blood, Daughter of Morgan. Drink of my essence and swear your loyalty to me, Esher, Prince of Deadtown. Drink and be of my blood," Esher intoned, his voice echoing mightily.

The stranger knelt before the prince. "I swear my fealty to you, Esher, Prince of Deadtown. By your blood my existence is dedicated to your service and glory," she responded. She pressed her lips to wound, sucking the blood offered her. Esher's lids fluttered as his eyes rolled back in their sockets and a groan, like that of a man on the brink of orgasm, escaped from his throat. With a sudden shuddering gasp, he jerked his arm away and stepped back, blinking like a man shaken from a dream.

"Enough!"

The stranger nodded and got to her feet. Esher rolled his sleeve back down, looking somewhat unnerved. "Go, now! From this night on you are under my protection and bound to my service. My only request is that my newer recruits stay close by."

The stranger bowed, placing her left hand over her heart. "As you wish, milord."

Esher clapped his hands, summoning a vampire who wore the tattered clothes and grizzled beard of a wino. The vampire bowed nervously before his master. "What is your wish, milord?"

"Show the new recruit the catacombs, Torgo. See that she is made comfortable."

"Yes, master."

The stranger followed the shuffling servant out of the room while Decima stared after her with unveiled hostility. The moment the audience chamber closed, Esher's lieutenant turned to face him, her body trembling with anger.

"Why did you accept her? I don't trust that mirror-eyed bitch any farther than I can spit!"

"Jealous, my dear?" Esher smirked, as he returned to his seat.

"There's nothing to be jealous of!" Decima sniffed. "She's just some smart-ass Caitiff, out to cause trouble!"

"You know that's not true, my dear," Esher chided. "You could feel her potential, just as I did. Whatever else this stranger may be—she's a walking weapon."

"She's dangerous, Esher! You're playing with sunlight, bringing her into the enclave! I say we're better off killing her!"

"You worry overmuch, Decima. I would be a fool to allow an agent as powerful as this one to wander into Sinjon's service! Besides, I believe in keeping my friends close—but my enemies closer. That is why I insisted she bunk in the catacombs. I fully intend to keep track of our new recruit's comings and goings. Besides, should she prove bothersome, I will either place her under full Blood Bond or cast a spell that boils her brain like a cabbage."

"Are you sure *you're* the one in control? I didn't like the way you looked when she drank from you."

The back of Esher's right hand caught Decima on the side of her face, sending her flying against the wall with enough force to snap the spine of a human woman. "You forget your place, childe! Something you've been doing too much of late! If you weren't my progeny, you'd be truly dead by now! "

Decima staggered to her feet, wiping at the blood oozing from her nostrils and mouth. "Forgive me, sire."

"Perhaps. But first I want you to send a message to the Black Lodge. Tell him that there have been some grave misunderstandings of late between his troops and my own. Tell him I'm interested in calling a truce and that I would parley with him at the Dance Macabre this midnight."

"As you wish, milord. Is there anything else?"

"Leave us," Esher snapped, extending his blood-smeared hand to Nikola. "I would be alone with my bride-to-be."

"As you command, my prince," she whispered, backing out of the audience chamber.

As she closed the heavy oaken doors behind her, Decima silently swore that she would see to it that both the human and the anarch bitch would pay with their lives for what they were trying to do. Esher had been hers for decades—and now she was being cast aside for a pallid music-box ballerina! And it was clear the stranger hungered to take her place as Esher's lieutenant—and the bastard was smitten enough to let her do so! Well, the bitch could plot all she liked.

She'd find Decima ready for her.

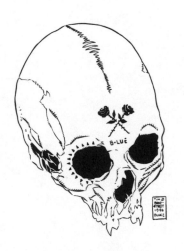

A FISTFUL OF ROSES

Cry "havoc!" and let loose the dogs of war,
That this foul deed shall smell above the earth
With carrion men, groaning for burial.

— William Shakespeare, *Julius Caesar, act 3, sc. 1*

Keep not your roses for my dead, cold brow
The way is lonely, let me feel them now.

— Arabella Smith , *"If I Should Die To-Night"*

Chapter

5

Eyes closed to the swirling chaos around her, the stranger followed the vampire called Torgo into the bowels of the House of Esher. "Pretty fancy digs," she said as they climbed down an inverted spiral staircase. "How do you find your way around this joint?"

"Once you become used to it, it ain't too hard, milady," Torgo replied. "Prince Esher is the heart of the House, no matter where he may be. Once you find him, gettin' round the House is simple enough."

"Find him? How could I possibly find him in this madhouse?" she snorted.

Torgo looked over his shoulder at her. "You took his blood, didn'tcha? Blood calls to blood. All you gotta do is listen."

The stranger stood still for a moment, turning her attention inward. She could feel something vibrating within her, the way fine crystal responds to a tuning fork. The sensation was faint but persistent—and vaguely menacing. "I see what you mean," she muttered uneasily.

They continued their downward climb until they came to a large cellar with stone walls and a dirt floor. The underground room was huge, easily occupying twice the space of the building above it. The catacomb was crowded with discarded sofas, old couches, tossed-out mattresses, and stained futons, making it look like a subterranean homeless shelter. A network of tunnels, some shored by brick lintels, others little more than oversized gopher holes, could be glimpsed radiating from the central chamber like spokes from a wheel. Save for a few rats and silverfish, the place was deserted.

"This is the main catacomb," Torgo explained. "The master's recruits stay here."

"Looks pretty empty."

"Come the dawn it will be full enough. I'd recommend finding a place to doss down before it gets too crowded."

"What if I decide I don't want to sleep here?"

"You heard the master—you are to remain nearby, with the rest of the recruits!"

"Then I guess that's just too bad—for you, Torgo!" She shot out her arm, catching the vampire in a headlock. Although Torgo was far stronger than he appeared, his earlier life as a wino and his fondness for battening on his former drinking buddies left him no match for a vampire of the stranger's vigor. He yowled like a cat as the silver switchblade slipped between his ribs and found his heart, then collapsed like a bag of wet laundry. The stranger wedged the dead vampire's already putrefying corpse under an aged red velvet sofa that reeked of mildew and urine, where he would go unnoticed for awhile.

She sprinted down the tunnel that looked the most heavily traveled. She had no intention of remaining in Esher's barracks, and the sooner she was out of his reach, the better. The vampire lord was a powerful, charismatic personality; staying in close proximity to him would only strengthen the bond between them—something Esher was keenly aware of.

She had not planned on having to take a blood oath, but there had seemed no way around it. To refuse would have made him suspicious of her. As it was, she was having a hard time keeping herself under control. For decades her gut response when confronted by other vampires had been to kill them on sight. Having to play along with their rules and head games was an onerous task. But at least she'd succeeded in locating Ryan's mother. Getting her away from Esher, on the other hand, was going to prove tricky. The bastard had her heavily tranced—and no doubt doped to the gills. It made unwilling brides far more tractable, after all.

After a few minutes she emerged from the tunnel into one of the open cellars that ringed the House. The pit was littered with broken bottles, discarded rubbers and mummified rats and dogs drained dry of blood. A ramshackle flight of wooden stairs in the corner led topside. As she headed upward, she could hear voices. She instinctively switched into overdrive—what these Kindred fools called Celerity—stepping sideways through the door of human perception. It was energy-intensive and physically draining, but at her level of mastery it effectively rendered her invisible to the untrained eye.

She flitted up the stairs like a moth, moving so fast her feet didn't touch the ground. To her eyes the three humans gathered around the burning trashcan at the lip of the cellar were frozen in place, like tableaux in a wax museum. The air pulsed with a sound which resembled the underwater serenade of humpback whales more than human speech. She recognized the Pointer with the spiderweb tattooed on his skull and the man Obeah, and decided it might be worth listening in. She located a patch of darkness nearby and pulled the shadows tight about her; she had learned long ago the vampire's trick of remaining unseen while in plain sight. Satisfied she was properly camouflaged, she eased herself out of overdrive.

The frozen gangbangers suddenly leapt into motion, their voices returning to normal speed. The Pointer with the tattooed head was speaking.

"You with us on the gig, cuz?"

"I'm with you, Webb!" grinned the third Pointer, a tall Anglo with spiky hair and BORN 2 LOSE tattooed onto his left forearm.

"I don't want anyone skitzing on me when the shit goes down. You pull that on me, I'll pop a cap in your skull, dig? I ain't gonna shit you, man— we might not make it back from this stunt. But if we do, we're set for life. Maybe longer. Esher can be *very* generous when the mood strikes him, homey."

Born 2 Lose nodded his understanding. "I'm in, Webb. Just tell me what you need me to do."

Webb grinned and nodded for Obeah to hand him the knapsack. "Seems one of the Borges Brothers is waiting for the Spoons at the docks tonight. Only the Spoons don't know it. Esher figured out the code they were using to set up their drug buys. So Borges is expecting to do a deal tonight, only he thinks he'll be dealing with Sinjon's boys." He opened the duffel bag and pulled a leather jacket out—on the back of which was the Jolly Roger emblem of the Black Spoons. "And who are we to let him down, right?"

Born 2 Lose frowned at the rival gang jacket. "You want me to wear Spoon colors?"

"Just for a little while."

"I don't get it—why don't we just show up, wack the asshole and take his stash?"

" 'Cause Lord Esher doesn't want the Borges Brothers down on *him*! Haven't you ever heard of divide and conquer, cuz?"

"No."

"Well, that's what Esher wants, so that's what he's gonna get, okay? Now put on the fuckin' jacket and let's get this damn show on the road!"

Grumbling under his breath, Born 2 Lose did as he was told, removing his Five Points jackets and pulling on the Black Spoon gear.

The stranger watched them from her hiding place with keen interest. What did Esher have up his sleeve? Whatever was going down tonight sounded important—and far be it from her to miss what promised to be the pivotal social event of the season.

"Where's Pico?" growled Dario Borges, eyeing the youth tricked out in Black Spoons colors. "Pico usually handles the buys."

"Pico had hisself an accident a few nights back," replied the Black Spoon with the spiderweb tattooed onto his shaven head. "It was very sad. We're still broke up about it."

They were standing in Warehouse 69, on the riverside boundary between Deadtown and the city. The place smelled of coffee beans and machine oil.

The Spoon representative stood with his back to a pile of arabicas in burlap bags, an attaché case clutched in one hand. Borges, a small man with a neat mustache and a middle-age paunch, stood opposite him, carrying a gym bag. He was flanked on either side by two massively built men in dark suits with bulges in their armpits.

Borges shrugged. "My condolences. Do you have the money?"

The Spoon grinned and opened the briefcase, holding it so Borges could see the neatly bundled bills. "Two hundred grand for four kilos, as per the agreement. Would you like to count it?"

Borges smiled tightly and shook his head. "No need. I trust Sinjon. At least when it comes to this." He snapped his fingers and motioned for one of the bodyguards to take the attaché.

Webb yanked the case away, taking a step back. "That may hold true for you—but not Sinjon. No sugar without snow, amigo."

The bodyguard began to reach inside his jacket, but Borges stopped him by placing a neatly manicured hand on his elbow. "The Freemason trains his servants well," he said ruefully. "Very well—as you wish." He stepped forward, holding out the gym bag. Webb smiled and did likewise, reaching out for the proffered bag with his free hand—then fell to the warehouse floor.

The first bullet caught Borges square in the heart, dropping him like a stag at a watering hole. The bodyguards were sprayed with bullets before they could clear their holsters. Webb picked himself off the bloodied floor and grinned up at his compatriots hidden among the coffee beans, giving them a victorious "thumbs-up."

Obeah and Born 2 Lose came sliding down from their hiding places, laughing and whooping their war cries.

"Like takin' candy from a fuckin' baby!" Born 2 Lose crowed, kicking the still-bleeding corpse of one of the bodyguards hard enough to flip it over onto its back. Webb kneeled and yanked the dead man's gun free of its holster, studying it casually.

As the flush of adrenaline dissipated, Born 2 Lose glanced at the bodies and scratched his head. "What I can't figure is how come you needed me to pull this job? Looks like you and Obeah could have jacked the sucka on your own, no sweat."

"You know something? You're right," Webb agreed, and fired the dead man's gun point-blank into his companion's stomach.

Born 2 Lose stood there for a long moment, mouth hanging open, staring in dumb surprise at the hole in his abdomen, before dropping to the ground. Webb leaned over and put the gun in the dead bodyguard's hand, then stood up, surveying the carnage as he dusted off his knees. "Yo! Obeah! Time for the voodoo that you do so well," he grinned.

Obeah nodded and reached into his knapsack, retrieving a machete wrapped in oiled cloth. Webb watched as the conjure-man handled the weapon with ritualized care.

"Is it true you chopped off a hundred hands with that thing when you was Tonton Macoute?"

Obeah laughed. It was a rich, dark sound. "Hell, no! It was two hundred!" With that, he drew back his right arm and brought the machete blade down on Borges' neck, severing the head in one blow. He carefully wiped off the blood and rewrapped the weapon, returning it to the knapsack. He then pulled out a large Tupperware container, which he tossed to Webb.

Webb grinned and stuck a blunt in his mouth as he peeled open the rubber lid of bowl. Obeah scooped up Borges' head by the hair—what little there was of it—and dropped it inside. Webb dug around inside his purloined gang jacket's breast pocket and pulled out a pair of metal spoons. Chuckling to himself, he set the Tupperware bowl down between his feet while Obeah produced a disposable lighter. Webb's grin grew even wider as his friend lit his cigar, then held the butane flame beneath the spoons for a few seconds, blackening their undersides. Webb dropped the spoons inside the Tupperware container, then knelt to replace the rubber lid.

"You gotta burp these in order to lock in freshness," he told Obeah. "We wouldn't want our friend here to go stale when we mail him home."

They laughed all the way to the car over that one.

♋

From her vantage point high in the rafters of Warehouse 69, the stranger thought about what she'd witnessed. She had to give Esher his due—the bastard was cunning. He knew that an open *jyhad* between himself and Sinjon would attract unwelcome attention, from Kindred and human society alike. He would not hazard an open declaration of war until he knew he could take his enemy down fast and hard—and with a minimum of personal risk. And what better way to destroy someone than to arrange for others to do it for you?

Chapter

6

Decima anxiously scanned the floor of the club from her vantage point in the balcony. "Do you think he will accept the invitation?"

"Of course he'll accept," Esher replied confidently. "He has no choice! Ventrue etiquette requires him to respond. Besides, the old reptile is curious to see what I'm up to. I'm more concerned about the Pointers. Are you certain they're disarmed?"

"I stripped them of firearms myself. But I can tell you they don't like it! The idea of Sinjon and a phalanx of Black Spoons waltzing in here at midnight really pisses them off. I've got five recruits guarding the arsenal, just in case."

"If they feel threatened, then they can mark their turf with piss," Esher sniffed. "I've got too much riding on this to have it spoiled by a feeble mind and an itchy trigger finger!" Esher's gaze drifted across the floor, then paused. "Ah! I see the new recruit has arrived! Have her sent to me, Decima. I would speak with her."

"As you wish, milord."

♋

The stranger stood among the mixture of vampire and human clubgoers, eyeing Dance Macabre's layout. Although there had to be close to four dozen young males on the floor, there was only a handful of women in evidence— and most of those were either chained to the wall or undead. She could feel the Pointers' eyes on her, but none dared speak, much less make a move. No doubt they'd learned the hard way not to fraternize with Kindred females. Still, the room reeked of testosterone and the madness that infects crowds that have surrendered their free will. The odor reminded her of a cross between a gym and an insane asylum. No doubt Nazi-era Berlin and Jonestown once smelled much the same.

She turned to find herself face-to-face with Decima. The vampiress was glowering at her with open hostility. "Esher wants to see you."

The stranger glanced up at the balcony overlooking the dance floor. She could see the vampire lord seated in what looked like a wooden throne, Nikola hovering by his side. "What does he want?"

"That is beside the point. He wants to see you. You will be seen."

The stranger followed Decima to the back of the club and up a spiral staircase that led to the balcony. The vampiress tried to trip her as she reached the upper level, but she deftly avoided her outstretched foot.

"You'll have to do better than that, girlfriend," she whispered. "I'm not some doped-up fan dancer you can pinch and poke when daddy's not looking!"

Decima's fangs clicked like dice in a cup, but she managed to keep her voice neutral when she spoke. "The new recruit is here, milord. Now, you must forgive me—I must see to security."

The stranger watched Decima storm off, smiling crookedly. "I don't think your progeny likes me very much."

Esher laughed. "There's not much Decima *does* like! I fear she is a possessive creature."

"She said something about security—what's going down?"

"I have invited Sinjon here this evening. He is to arrive at midnight."

"Sinjon? But I thought you and he are worst buddies!"

"We have indeed been at odds in the past."

"So what's the deal?"

"I have decided it is time to declare a truce between our houses. Neither of us can afford a *jyhad* right now. We waste too much time in petty squabbles and territorial disputes. I have decided to try to mend fences, so to speak."

"Do you think Sinjon will buy into it?"

"He is a reasonable man. Or was so, when he lived."

"So what did you want me for?"

"I want you to be present at the parley, my dear. I think you will work well as a liaison between the House of Esher and the Black Lodge—don't you agree?"

"I don't know—do you think that's such a good idea?"

Esher's eyes flashed as he spoke. "What do you mean?"

"Don't get me wrong, milord! It's not that I don't want the job—and I appreciate the trust you've placed in me—but don't you think it might be a little, I dunno, impolitic? I mean, I *did* snuff three of his progeny earlier tonight. He might still be a tad sore about it."

"You're right—I'd forgotten all about that! Perhaps it would be better for all concerned if you made yourself scarce. I'll bring you into play once Sinjon has had time to forget the incident." He smiled, flashing her some fang. "I can see you'll be a useful addition to the enclave already, my dear—? I'm sorry, but I don't seem to have gotten your name?"

The stranger opened her mouth, but before she could speak, Esher's attention was drawn to one of the television monitors. "Aha! Sinjon's car has just arrived outside the club!"

"I'd best be going then, milord," she said.

The canned music thundering from the club's speakers came to an abrupt halt. Warily, the patrons of Dance Macabre turned their eyes to the red-vinyl front door. A phalanx of Black Spoons, walking with the caution of tigers in a lion's den, entered the club, forming a human corridor. The rival gangs glared at one another, their body language screaming hostility, but neither side spoke or made a threatening gesture.

And, at precisely the stroke of midnight, Sinjon entered the building.

Compared to his leather-clad bodyguards, the vampire lord cut a peculiarly genteel figure. He was dressed in a high-waisted double-breasted royal blue cutaway coat, with a high-standing collar and pointed lapels. Cut square across at the waistline, the coat's skirt sloped into tails. A cambric ruffle showed from the cuff of the coat sleeves. Underneath that he wore a shorter cutaway blood-red waistcoat with the front extending downward in two V-shaped points. About his neck he wore a jabot, the double frill of silk spilling as white as snow from the front of his vest. He wore tight black satin breeches that extended to just below the kneecap, and long white silk stockings. About his waist was tied a blue-and-white silk apron boasting gold fringe, on the front of which was embroidered the symbol of the Freemasons—the eye in the pyramid. On his head was a powdered wig, the pigtail bound with a red ribbon, and a tricorn hat. On his feet were elaborate diamond buckles that could support a small town for a year. In one hand he carried a cane with a large amber knob and a tasseled cord. All in all, Sinjon was quite the clothes horse—circa 1776.

Esher greeted his rival in the middle of the dance floor, flanked by his elite guard. "Welcome to my club! I am pleased you are here, Sinjon," he smiled.

"I could not ignore such a gracious invitation, Esher. You are right; there is much we must discuss."

Esher nodded and motioned for Sinjon to join him. "Come—let us retire to my private box. We can talk undisturbed there."

"I trust your men are unarmed?"

"Indeed. I trust yours are as well."

"Of course."

The stranger watched the elaborate charade of cordiality between the two rival lords. Despite their viciousness—or perhaps because of it—the ruling classes of the Kindred observed rigid rules of conduct when dealing with one another. One of which was ritual politeness. Since she had come of age on her own, she had never been absorbed into Kindred society and did not accept its labyrinthine codes of behavior. But she had learned to exploit it for her own uses.

One thing she knew from past experience was that while they were eternal, the Kindred were not creatures of change. Most were like Sinjon—elders who preferred the garb and customs of centuries long dead to the age in which they currently dwelt. Given time, most would succumb to such anachronistic eccentricities. After all—who could bother keeping up with human fashions? Those who remained in the past too long eventually found themselves out of touch—and under the heel of the younger, more vital Kindred.

As she watched Sinjon and Esher exchange their ritual pleasantries, she knew at once which of them was the stronger. Doubtless, so did Sinjon. That's why he had come in the first place.

The stranger turned away from the stage and headed for the exit. She already had a good idea of what Esher was pulling—or trying to pull—on his rival. Now it was up to her to see if she couldn't put her own personal spin on the situation.

Father Eamon sat in the bell tower of St. Everhild, nursing his bottle of no-name bourbon as he watched the lights of the city glitter on the river's dark surface. He had to marvel at how close and yet so far the rest of humanity was from Deadtown. He felt a certain hot excitement, not unlike that kindled by pornography or self-abuse, when he thought about how easy it would be for him to walk out the front doors of St. Everhild and through the blasted streets and enter once more the world of stockbrokers, housewives, shopping centers and fast food. His exodus would have to occur during the day, but still it could be done. All it took was the determination to leave St. Everhild behind.

Of course, that would never happen. He was tied to Deadtown as tightly as a mother to her unborn child. He could no more walk away from his church than he could fly from the bell tower. He was bound by chains of guilt and sin just as Christ was nailed to the cross.

Still, there was a certain titillation to be had from fantasizing about leaving—

Father Eamon's attention was drawn to a shadow flickering across the street below. When he looked again he saw that the shadow was actually a creature of substance. He felt his skin crawl with the realization that he was watching one of the demons that wandered Deadtown after dark. Although he had seen several of the monsters during his years as St. Everhild's curate, he had yet to lose the sense of horror that came from spotting them on their unholy rounds. Some, like the thing below, took the shape of comely women, while others wore the flesh of handsome young boys—but Father Eamon knew them for what they truly were: the living dead.

The vampiress paused for a moment, the dim light reflecting off the mirrored sunglasses she wore, but it was long enough for Father Eamon to get a good look at her. At first he'd thought she was Esher's witch, but now he could see that that wasn't the case. As he watched, the female vampire ducked down the alley that led to the rear of the Black Lodge. Whoever the stranger was, she certainly wasn't one of Esher's minions.

♋

"Relax, Sinjon," Esher said, holding out a cordial glass filled with blood. "Help yourself. It's from my private cellar."

"You're too kind," Sinjon replied, accepting the drink with a gracious nod. He sniffed the proffered liquid as a connoisseur would a fine wine, nodding his approval. "Ah! This one shows fine breeding! **Xg**, if I'm not mistaken? I'm suitably impressed!"

"I'm honored." Esher's smile never made it to his eyes.

Sinjon set aside the cordial glass, crossed his leg at the knee and placed his steepled hands in his lap. "Now that we have observed the niceties, Tremere, let the talking begin. Why have you invited me here?"

"I would like to propose a truce."

Sinjon lifted an eyebrow but remained silent.

"Despite what you may believe, I have no desire to be the crown prince of Deadtown, nor do I wish to engage in a *jyhad* with you, Sinjon."

"You certainly have a strange way of showing it, then! I have it on good authority your progeny slew one of my Spoons at my very doorstep!"

"Decima? You must be mistaken! She would not do such a thing without my knowledge! As it is, rumor has it the death was a retaliation for the murder of one of my Pointers. I suspect this to be the handiwork of mortals, Sinjon. You know how foolish these boys can be."

"Yes," Sinjon murmured, glancing down at the Black Spoons standing in a clot on the floor below, glowering at the Pointers surrounding them. "I'm afraid I do. They're worse than the gypsies ever thought of being."

"You see, Sinjon—that is part of the problem I wish to solve! The bad feelings between your camp and mine arise from our mortal servitors. You and I are, at heart, businessmen. Our business is survival. Yet our mutual distrust and resentment of one another have led to constant clashing and skirmishing. I spend as much time and effort outfitting my men with weapons as I do selling them! That's bad for business. We spend too much of our time scheming and plotting against one another. And it is not necessary! I have no interest in moving in on your rackets, Sinjon! It is a shame that we have not come to an understanding until now."

"I'm not so certain we understand one another even now," Sinjon replied. "You are an ambitious man, Esher. Am I to believe that you have no interest in what is mine?"

"Yes. I *am* ambitious. But since when has that become a sin in the eyes of the Ventrue?"

"I have my position to consider, wizard. I was prince of Deadtown when you were still sperm swimming in your father's balls! Deadtown is my domain, and you have blatantly challenged my control of it! I cannot allow such an affront to go without reprimand. You know this as much as I."

"I am aware of this. That is why I propose a ritual appeasement that will prove my good will."

Sinjon's eyebrow crept up even further. "Appeasement? Of what sort?"

Esher smiled, spreading his hands in a magnanimous gesture. "I'll allow you to decide that."

Sinjon stroked his chin, looking pensive for a long moment. Then he smiled and pointed at Nikola, who was draped about the back of Esher's throne like a silk cape. "I'll take the girl."

Esher's face went rigid. "Not the girl! I'll grant you anything else!"

Seeing his rival's discomfort turned Sinjon's smile sharp as broken glass. "No. It's *her* I want! Give me the girl, or I'll know you're lying!"

"You call me a liar?"

"Let us say, wizard, I doubt you speak truthfully. Now, if you'll excuse me, I have other matters to attend to this evening."

"But what of my offer?"

"I will consider it genuine only if you give to me that for which I have asked—your toy dancer. Until then, we have nothing to say to one another." Using his walking stick, Sinjon rose from his seat, bowing slightly at the waist and touching the brim of his tricorn. "*Adieu*, my upstart friend. You have been a most gracious host."

Esher watched his rival climb down the spiral staircase and, flanked by his bodyguards, stroll the length of Dance Macabre unharmed. He tried his best to conceal the rage inside him as Sinjon exited the club. Physically attacking the old turtle would not be wise. There was a cracking sound and he glanced down to see that his clenched fingers had reduced the wooden armrests of his throne to kindling.

Decima left her place in the shadows and came forward, lowering her head so that her lips were next to his ears. "Why didn't you give him the girl?"

"The old bastard is canny—I'll give him that! You don't get to be his age and not know some tricks. He had no intention of agreeing to a truce—yet he had to make it look as if he was the affronted party, not I! So he asked as a boon the one thing he knew I would not part with. He's a clever fox indeed! But it does not matter. The truce would have made it easier to arrange his demise without the messiness of an actual *jyhad*. That way he wouldn't be expecting trouble when the Borges Brothers moved against him. Now I have to step up my dealing with the cartel. Did you notify the authorities as to the location of the bodies?"

"Yes, milord. I have no doubt it'll make the morning news. Possibly even CNN."

"Did you send them Dario Borges' head?"

"I sent it overnight express. It should arrive in Miami by ten a.m."

"You didn't pack it in dry ice, did you? I want them to get the full effect." Esher glanced up at Nikola, who was hovering at his elbow, looking confused. He took her pallid hand in his, caressing the outline of her veins with the tip of his tongue. "You needn't worry, my darling," he whispered. "I would never let you go. Not even to death eternal."

The Dussenburg pulled up to the curb in front of the Black Lodge. A youth in a Black Spoons jacket scuttled forward to open the rear door. Sinjon emerged from the back of the vintage automobile, smiling like the proverbial cat.

"D-did everything go okay, master?" stammered the boy.

"Swimmingly," Sinjon replied. Met with a blank stare, he took a deep breath and said, "Yes, everything went okay."

The boy smiled and nodded. "That's very good, master! Very good!"

Sinjon brushed past the Spoon with a disgusted sigh. He wasn't sure if it was drugs or the gene pool, but the quality of servitors nowadays was genuinely appalling. Granted, the gypsies had hardly been towers of intellect, but compared to what he had to use in this, the end of the twentieth century, they seemed proverbial Renaissance men. He shuddered to contemplate what the new millennium would bring in the way of humankind.

Then again, Americans had always possessed a wide streak of thickness. He should know—he'd watched the nation evolve from a conglomerate of ill-conceived commercial ventures into the sole remaining superpower. Indeed, he had been a participant in the birthing of the nation.

Before his resurrection, he'd been the third son of a minor nobleman. His elder brother claimed what wealth and title there was to be had, and the fool sank a great deal of the fortune into Sir Walter Raleigh's Roanoke Island Colony—on the condition that one of his family go along in order to keep watch over the investment. The unlucky task fell to Sinjon—who had recently disgraced the family name. Truth be told, he was wanted for murder and his choices were either to leave England or end up in the Tower. So, in 1587, a nineteen-year-old Sinjon set out for a new life in the New World.

The Roanoke Colony proved worse than hell. In the summer it was hot and fetid. In the winter it was bitterly cold and damp. In between those seasons it was assailed by fierce coastal storms that snapped the trees like kindling. Insects, poisonous snakes, alligators, and other bothersome fauna existed in abundance. Disease was constant, as was hunger—since few of the colonists knew the first thing about farming. After all—they were gentlemen.

Most of the colonists were ill-suited to the privations and rigors of such a primitive place. Indeed, those of the upper classes sat about and waited on those of the lower order, or the few surviving women, to do for them. However, Roanoke was not London, and the supply of social inferiors was finite. When the Englishmen attempted to make slaves of the local natives, the Croatoans, the savages had the bad manners to resist, adding warfare to the colony's tribulations.

Sinjon watched as the colony gradually shriveled up and died over the course of two years. Some colonists dropped dead of disease and malnutrition, while the women were invariably claimed by childbirth or peripatetic fever. Some wandered too far afield and disappeared into the surrounding swamps, no doubt the victims of alligators or snakes. And still others fell into the hands of the Croatoans; their wretched screams echoed through the forest for days on end. Sinjon prayed for the day Raleigh's ships would return with provisions and he could escape the green hell to which his brother had banished him. Anything—even the gallows—was better than the horrid place called America.

But it was not to be. One moonless night in 1589, a ship arrived at Roanoke Island, but it wasn't Sir Walter Raleigh come with fresh provisions.

That night Sinjon was awakened by screaming and the sound of people running about in a panic. His first thought was that the Croatoans had mounted another attack. He grabbed his sword and charged outside in his nightshirt, to find the village overrun with pirates!

The invaders seemed to be everywhere at once, dragging the few surviving colonists from their homes by their hair. Sinjon leapt forward, swinging his sword at one of the pirates, running him through the liver. Instead of dropping to the ground dead, the bastard merely laughed—revealing fangs as white and sharp as a wolf's and eyes the color of fresh wine. Before Sinjon could react, the vampire gave him the back of his hand—which rendered him unconscious for some time.

When Sinjon awoke, it was to find himself in chains, along with the remaining colonists and a handful of captured Croatoans—about twenty in all—in a large metal cage lashed to the deck of a ship with black sails. He soon learned that the name of the ship was *The Osiris*, and that its crew was composed almost entirely of the undead. During the day a handful of human servants tended the ship, but come evening a host of Kindred declaring allegiance to Clans Lasombra, Ventrue and Brujah swarmed from the holds to take their places on deck and in the rigging.

The captured colonists' fate was indeed cruel. One by one, they were dragged from their prison and bled dry by the ravenous crew. Once they were drained, the bodies were turned over to the human servants, who either jerked them for their meat or fed them to the sharks that followed *The Osiris* like faithful hounds. Such would have been his fate—if he hadn't been lucky. His luck came in the form of Captain Blood, the fierce leader of *Osiris'* crew. Perhaps the pirate king looked into the frightened twenty-one-year-old's eyes and saw the murderer that lurked within, but in any case he took a fancy to Sinjon and decided to make him his new cabin boy.

Captain Blood, who claimed to have sailed alongside Odysseus in his day, dressed all in red and wore his dark hair in a single plait that hung down to the middle of his waist. Although he had at first been terrified, Sinjon soon learned to respond to the captain's cold caresses. It wasn't long before he was helping his master plot raids on the European colonies scattered about the New World.

In 1591 Captain Blood rewarded his loyal cabin boy with the gift of the Embrace. And when Sinjon arose, reborn, into the ranks of the Kindred, he was made first mate of *The Osiris*. And so it went for the next decade—until *The Osiris* finally met its match at the hands of a Papal man o'war crewed entirely by Inquisitors under direct orders from Innocent IX to eradicate the inhuman menace on the high seas. The warrior-priests were armed with a battery that fired cannonballs cast from blessed silver, and their cutlasses and musket shot were likewise blessed.

Captain Blood was high in the rigging, bellowing his defiance, when he was felled by a consecrated musket ball. Sinjon watched as his lover's body plummeted into the water below, where it was savaged by the sharks that churned the sea foam to crimson froth.

Sinjon saved himself that night by tossing overboard one of the waterproofed coffins in the hold and climbing in, closing the lid tight behind him. Two days later he made landfall on the coast of France. For two years he wandered the great cities of Europe, drifting in and out of Kindred and human society alike, until he received news of the Virgin Queen's demise. Sinjon then returned to England and murdered the brother who had sent him off to Roanoke nearly twenty years before. His brother's heirs met equally quick and mysterious ends, which enabled Sinjon, posing as a distant cousin, to claim the ancestral title and lands for himself. Thus camouflaged, he emerged once more into high society, where he became well known as a nobleman who favored London's nightlife.

Over the next century Sinjon orchestrated a series of identities for himself, being careful to drop out of various social circles before his perpetual youthfulness could draw undue attention. Often he would have his human servants pretend to be him as an older man, while accompanying them in public as his own look-alike son or grandson. Occasionally, as during Cromwell's rule, he was forced to leave England for the Continent for years on end, only to return as his own offspring.

It was a time of great change, both political and social, what with the Counter-Reformation and the Enlightenment. Religion's chokehold on the minds of humanity started to weaken, and the centuries-old superstitions gradually began to give way to science. As rational thinking began its rise in popularity, more and more people stopped believing in such creatures as vampires and werewolves, making it easy for Sinjon to mingle in human social circles without fear of discovery.

Although the dogma that had given birth to the Inquisition was fading away, human society was still unprepared to stride naked into the cold, stark light of the Rational Universe. During this time there was a growth in "secret societies," unprecedented since the days of the mystery cults that infested Rome during the time of the Caesars.

Sinjon, and many other fellow Kindred, saw the emergence of the Rosicrucians, Freemasons and other quasi-mystic fraternities as a unique opportunity to do what they had always done with human society—run it from behind the scenes, but this time using the complicity and subterfuge of other humans as their cover.

In 1717 Sinjon joined the Grand Lodge of London, whose Master was Desaguliers, the founding father of modern Freemasonry. Not long after, he became a member of the notorious Hell Fire Club, a secret society composed largely of free-thinkers, libertines and philosophers, who played at Satanism and enjoyed the occasional orgy. It was through these two organizations that he became familiar with the American inventor and diplomat, Benjamin Franklin.

Franklin was fifty and Sinjon nearing his second century when they met in 1757. The printer was representing the Pennsylvania legislature in London, petitioning for the right to tax the lands of the Penn family in order to raise revenue for the colony, which had suffered financial setbacks following the French and Indian War. Six years earlier he had published *Experiments and Observations on Electricity*, where he detailed his adventure of flying a kite in a thunderstorm, and won international fame for being one of the world's leading scientific thinkers.

Normally Sinjon considered American colonials bumpkins of the worst sort—upstarts fancying themselves cosmopolitan. But Franklin possessed a quick wit and quiet dignity and genius that affected the vampire unlike any other human before him. He found himself enjoying the American's company and relishing their conversations. One thing Franklin enjoyed talking about most was his home, Philadelphia. The more he spoke of the colonies and the activities going on there, the more Sinjon came to realize that America was on the verge of becoming a brand-new nation—one in which the potential for advancement and success for those brave enough to realize their dreams was boundless.

The more Sinjon thought about it, the more he liked it. Europe was old. Not as old as Africa, where the Antediluvians were rumored to lie, but there were still plenty of Kindred wandering about the Continent who could date their origins back to Troy or beyond. Competition among these older, more powerful Kindred was keen, as they jockeyed for positions of prince or duke or margrave. There was little opportunity for a vampire as relatively young as himself to make his mark in Kindred society. Unless he went someplace where the competition had yet to establish a foothold.

Sinjon knew how slowly the elders acknowledged change. America had been on the map for over three hundred years, but he was certain they were just now noticing it. It might take them another fifty years to decide to attempt to make it part of their Hidden Empire. And though Sinjon had heard rumors that the Camarilla's rival sect, the Sabbat, had established a beachhead in America, he harbored little fear of those night-fiends.

Utilizing his Masonic connections, Sinjon once again abandoned the gay nightlife of London for the New World. This time around he found the accommodations far more pleasant than those on Roanoke Island, even if he was surrounded by colonial bumpkins. Franklin was quite eager to introduce his well-born expatriate friend to his social circle, which included the likes of Washington, Jefferson, the Adams brothers, Hamilton and Revere. Jefferson eyed Sinjon far too sharply for his taste, but otherwise he found his way into America's power elite as easily as he had Europe's.

The upheaval of the Revolutionary War was a convenient excuse to kill his former identity yet again and emerge, phoenixlike, as his own heir. He left Philadelphia and went in search of a city where he would not be so easily recognized. He ended up in a seaport that sat at the head of an estuary, a stone's throw from the huge bay that had welcomed many of the original settlers who came to this strange new world. It was there that he came up with the idea of Deadtown.

Using different names and various dummy companies, Sinjon set about buying up property. It wasn't difficult. The neighborhood that would become

Deadtown was seedy and rundown, even back then. Once again using his Freemason connections, combined with prodigious bribes, Sinjon arranged it so special provisions concerning the area were written into the city charter—provisions none but a handful of mayors and aldermen would ever lay eyes on. In the long decades since then, Sinjon's human agencies had made sure the proper amount of money got into the proper hands at the proper time, effectively keeping Deadtown "under radar" for over two centuries. It was this arrangement, sealed with Masonic handshakes, that kept the lights running and the water flowing in a part of the city that, officially, didn't exist.

Deadtown was Sinjon's finest achievement. He had been its lord and master for generations. Those who dared challenge his supremacy in the past tasted Death Everlasting. Now he was confronted by the upstart blood-wizard, Esher—and for the first time in his four hundred and thirty-five years, Sinjon was afraid.

Not that he would show it. If his human servants though he was intimidated, they would abandon him in droves. Unlike the gypsies of old, who could be counted on for their tribal loyalty, the Black Spoons followed the bastard with the most power, the hardest heart, and the coldest blood. Any sign of weakness was cause for a vote of no confidence.

These were Sinjon's thoughts as he walked through the Black Lodge. He headed up the grand marble staircase to the second floor, where his favorite's boudoir was located. He thought about Esher's fragile little ballerina and shook his head. He had no desire for Esher's pet—he'd merely asked for her to embarrass the wizard and force him to show his true colors. He couldn't blame his rival for being so attached to a human lover. After all, it is in the nature of the Kindred to fall in love with the living.

Sinjon pushed open the boudoir door, tossing his tricorn onto the canopied bed's purple satin coverlet. "Vere—Daddy's home! Where are you, my pet?"

There was a stirring from behind the Chinese screen in the corner of the room and a sixteen-year-old boy with the face of an overripe Cupid stepped out from behind it.

"There you are! What were you doing behind there, you silly boy?" Sinjon chuckled. "Were you hoping to surprise Daddy, eh?"

"No," replied a female voice. "But *I* was."

Vere took a second hesitant step, revealing the vampiress standing behind him, one hand clamping his arm while the other held an open switchblade to the back of his neck. Sinjon's eyes blazed and he advanced on the intruder, fangs bared, hissing like a basket of angry cobras.

"Keep back!" barked the stranger, twisting the boy's arm so he yelped. "Stay your distance or so help me, I'll take his head off where he stands!"

Sinjon drew back, glowering at the intruder. "Who are you, woman, and what are you doing in my lodge? Are you one of Esher's wretched thralls?"

"That's what he'd like to think—but no, I'm not one of his. I've come here to do you a favor."

"Somehow I doubt your sincerity."

"Maybe this will prove I mean you no ill-will, then," she snapped, shoving the frightened Vere at Sinjon. "Here, take your lapdog back! And by the way—Esher's set you up big-time!"

The boy stumbled but recovered his balance before he could fall, turning to give her the finger. "Fuck you, bitch! Kill her, Daddy!"

"Shut up and sit down, Vere," Sinjon replied. "I would talk to our visitor."

"But, Daddy—!"

"*Sit down and shut up!*" the vampire hissed, flashing his fangs. "Now—as you were saying, milady?"

"Earlier this evening, about the time you were being invited to Esher's little club, I followed three of his goons out to the waterfront. Funny thing was, they were all wearing Black Spoon colors. Imagine that. They were there to meet with a friend of yours called Borges. The goons smoked him and his bodyguards and made it look like the Spoons did it. It's a pretty sweet frame-job, dude. You should be hangin' in the Louvre."

Sinjon's face was perfectly still as he lowered himself into a nearby armchair. "I see," he muttered, his voice so quiet it was little more than a whisper. "What else do you know?"

The stranger moved to stand in front of the fireplace, leaning against the mantelpiece. "Very well: I know that Esher's men took Borges' stash when they whacked him—it comes to at least a half-mil, street. Esher's sitting on it, for now. He's arranging a get-together with Borges' bereaved siblings. He figures they'll want to avenge their brother's death, but might be unwilling to go up against you without some Kindred muscle on their side. Once you're out of the picture, he'll give 'em back their rock candy, tell them he pried it from your cold dead fingers, and then he'll end up with both the arms and the hard drug business for the East Coast, and Deadtown will be his and his alone."

Vere leaned over and whispered into Sinjon's ear, keeping a cautious eye on the stranger. "How can we be sure she's not lying about all this?"

"Because I *know* she's not!" Sinjon growled. "You don't get to be as old as I am without learning to feel the truth when you hear it. And what she says—I feel the truth of it in my bones. It explains a lot of things—especially that ridiculous attempt at creating a truce! Esher is hardly the type to fear the censure of the Camarilla. But what I don't understand, my lovely, is what do *you* get out of all this?"

The stranger shrugged. "The pleasure of coming to the aid of my clan."

Sinjon frowned and tilted his head to one side, squinting at her as if trying to identify a peculiar breed of butterfly. "You are *Ventrue*?"

"My sire was Morgan, Lord of the Morning Star."

"Morgan?" Sinjon's frown deepened. "Wasn't he slain recently? Rumor has it he was consumed by one of his own get. Diablerie most foul."

The stranger tried to look saddened. "It was horrible. I miss him greatly. That is why I have decided to help you, Prince Sinjon. We Ventrue must stick together in these uncertain times."

"Yes. How true."

"I will arrange to notify you as soon as I know when and where Esher plans to rendezvous with the Borges Brothers. My messenger will be a small boy named Ryan. I want it made clear to your followers, Kindred and human alike, that the boy is not to be harmed in any way. If they see any of Esher's minions trying to hurt the child, they're to intercede—is that clear?"

"Perfectly. But what is this child to you?"

"Nothing. He is the son of Esher's bride-to be. Esher wants the boy dead."

Sinjon grinned, exposing his fangs. "Say no more, my dear! If the child's existence is a thorn in Esher's side, then I shall see to it that he makes old bones! But what do you suggest we do?"

"I will attack Esher during his rendezvous with the Brothers. It will, by necessity, be outside of Deadtown, and therefore he will not be able to escape to the safety of his wizard's den quite so easily. While you keep him and the Pointers busy, I will search the House for the stolen drugs. Only by returning the cocaine can you hope to clear your name with the Brothers. If anything, they are even less trusting than vampires when it comes to these situations."

Sinjon stood and joined the stranger at the fireplace. "When do you think Esher will rendezvous with the Borgeses?"

"Did you agree to the truce tonight?"

"No."

"Then it will be soon. Possibly as early as tomorrow evening. Esher is moving fast—as if he's fearful of detection."

Sinjon gave a humorless laugh. "Are you saying he's afraid of being found out? As I said, he's not one to fear the Camarilla!"

"Come now, Sinjon! For someone who spent so much time immersed in secret societies, haven't you figured out who he's really worried about?"

Sinjon's eyes widened. "Of course! The Council of Vienna!"

"Exactly." The stranger smiled, tapping the side of her nose. "He's afraid his family will find out what he's been up to."

The sun was already brightening the morning sky when Cloudy answered the door. Actually the sawed-off answered it for him, thrusting its abbreviated double-barreled snout between the doorjamb and the security chain like a suspicious animal.

"Who th' fuck is it?"

"It's me, Cloudy."

The sawed-off was quickly withdrawn. The door closed again for a moment, then reopened, allowing her to slide inside. Cloudy stood in his book-cluttered front parlor, dressed in a pair of tattered jeans and a bowling shirt that hung open to his waist, his wispy white hair still tousled from bed. Along with the sawed-off, there was a Buck knife tucked into a holster on his hip. There was no such thing as sleeping easy in Deadtown.

"Where's Ryan?"

"He's asleep. He usually crashes an hour or two before dawn. He might as well be nocturnal, for the hours he keeps." Cloudy motioned to the kitchen. "C'mon, I'll fix us some coffee. Oops—sorry! I forgot. You can watch me drink my coffee, then."

The stranger eased into the spare chair as Cloudy busied himself with filling the teakettle and lighting the pilot light. Ryan's bed under the sink was curtained off by a piece of discarded drapery, giving the boy a little privacy.

"How did it go?"

"I got inside both Esher's and Sinjon's strongholds. Of the two, Esher is definitely the more dangerous quarry. He is young, as Kindred judge such things, and exceptionally ambitious."

"A 'lean and hungry look', eh?"

"Exactly. And those are the most dangerous vampires to contend with. They have much to win—and much to lose. Sinjon, on the other hand, is what could be called 'a reasonable monster.' He has what he wants, but fears losing it. It makes him easier to manipulate. He is a museum piece, but is loath to admit it. I've dealt with many of his breed: anachronisms clinging to the era that saw their greatest glory. Still, I would be a fool to underestimate him. Elder vampires such as Sinjon came of age during times far harder and more punishing than any born of this century could possibly know. His foppery hides a will of iron and a heart of coal."

"Sound like real sweethearts." Cloudy lowered his voice, glancing over at Ryan's sleeping nook. "What about his mother? Did you see her?"

The stranger tried to keep her face neutral. "I saw her."

"Is she okay?"

"She's alive."

Cloudy raised an eyebrow, but before he could say anything, the kettle began its shrill wail. He quickly snatched the pot off the boil, not wanting to wake Ryan. He spooned instant coffee and powdered creamer into a cracked mug that read WORLD'S GREATEST GRANDMA, then sat down opposite the stranger.

"She's bad, huh?"

"Do you want it straight?"

"Do I have a choice?"

The stranger ran her fingers through her hair, and for a split second Cloudy glimpsed the utter weariness inside her. It was the kind of deep-down tired you see in veterans of trench warfare. "I think I can get her away from Esher. But to tell the truth—it might not do any good. She's heavily tranced. Plus I think he's been drugging her—and not with the usual street crap either. He's got a *bokor* working for him."

"A what?"

"Voodoo witch doctor. A mean-ass motherfucker named Obeah that carries a machete. He's a displaced Tonton Macoute. Nasty customer."

Cloudy paled and his coffee mug trembled slightly. "I know the bastard you're talking about. But what's that have to do with drugs—?"

"Esher's got Nikola strung out on zombie dust."

"Zombies—? Aw, c'mon, man! You're pulling my leg, right?"

"Look, you're living in a neighborhood swarming with the living dead, and you can't swallow zombies? Besides, it's not like the crap in the movies. Witch-doctors use the stuff from blowfish. The shit's a neural toxin. Normally it'll paralyze you so thoroughly your heart can't beat and you can't breathe. But in the right amounts it's a powerful drug, and under certain circumstances it can be used to induce a deathlike state.

"Let's say a *bokor* gets crossed by some schmuck, and he puts a curse on him in public. Then he manages to slip the zombie dust into the poor schmuck's Wheaties. Next thing you know, there's a dead schmuck—but he's not really dead. He just looks it, right? So he gets stuck in the ground, and the *bokor* hauls ass to the graveyard, where he digs up the schmuck and feeds him the antidote. Next thing you know there's a dead man walking around—except he's not really dead. But he *is* a zombie now.

"Usually they suffer from a hell of a lot of brain damage, what with the oxygen deprivation from being underground, so they end up a little slow—hell, they're actually a *lot* slow! They can't feel much in the way of pain, nor can they communicate very well. About the only things they want out of life from that point on—if you can call it life—are food and zombie dust. I guess they're the only pleasures they can still feel. And they'll do anything to get those two things. And since the *bokor* pretty much has the zombie dust thing sewn up, they end up becoming his personal slaves for the rest of either his or their lives, whichever comes first."

"And this is what Esher's trying to do to Nikola?"

"Not exactly. He's got her messed up on it, but he doesn't want to zombify her. He's trying to turn her."

"Turn?"

"A lot of the lords, when they decide to take a bride or companion, select a human they feel has the potential for evil and corruption. Sometimes the human's dark side responds eagerly. Other times it may be buried so deep that a rigorous campaign, lasting years, is necessary to nurture its growth and encourage its ascendancy. However, not all of these turnings are successful. Some humans refuse to let their dark side win out and die at their own hand. I suspect that may be the case with Nikola—it's why she's being drugged. Esher wants to keep her susceptible to his influence, but he fears what she might do to herself when he's not there to control her."

"Then if that's the case—there might be some hope for her, after all," Cloudy pointed out.

"Perhaps. But as long as Esher is nearby, she's completely and utterly his creature. That kind of mind control does serious damage. If I get her away from him, she may very well remain—how shall I put it?—highly susceptible—to those with a stronger will. And at this point, Skippy the Kangaroo has a stronger will than she does."

"You don't exactly paint a rosy picture, do you?" Cloudy grunted.

"You asked for it straight."

"Yeah. I did, didn't I?" he sighed, draining the last of his coffee. "So what do you propose doing?"

"The only way both Ryan and his mother will be safe is if Esher is well and truly dead."

Cloudy lowered the mug, eyeing her as if she'd suddenly grown a second head. "You planning on killing him?"

"That was my intention from the very beginning, even before I met you and Ryan."

"Honey, you don't happen to have an army I might have missed stashed in that gym bag of yours, do you?" Cloudy chuckled in spite of himself.

The stranger stifled a yawn as she stood up, stretching like a cat. "Killing him will be easy. Not getting myself killed in the bargain—that's the tricky part! Now, if you'll excuse me—it's been a long night, and I'll need my rest if I'm to keep on top of what's going down tonight. Are there any other squatters in this building?"

"Not anymore. Since things started jumpin' round here, most of the squats moved to the outer fringes of Deadtown. No one wants to be in the thick of it."

The stranger gathered up her belongings and headed for the door. "I'll bunk down in the attic, if it's all the same to you. I like being close to rooftops. They're handier than back doors, when you have unexpected visitors."

Cloudy frowned and fidgeted with the keys. "It's daylight out there—!"

"I'm well aware of that," she replied.

"But the sun's up!"

"It usually is when it's daylight. So?"

"Are you sure you wanna go out right now?"

"Cloudy, I appreciate the concern, but open the fuckin' door, okay? I'm not gonna bust 'n' bake."

Cloudy looked unconvinced, but he unlocked the door anyway. The stranger patted his shoulder as she slipped past the threshold into the morning sunshine. "Don't worry about me," she chided. "I've got my sunscreen on."

♋

The attic smelled of dust, rat turds, dry rot and mildew. The middle of the room was tall enough for a man to stand upright in, while the far corners would make a mouse hunchbacked. It wasn't the Taj Mahal, but it was far from the worst place that she'd ever dossed down for the day in. She dragged a stained mattress out from under the eaves, displacing a pile of discarded needles and empty crack vials. The mattress reeked faintly of piss and other secretions, but it would do.

The only window in the attic was an oculus set on a hinge, so that it could be tilted open for ventilation. As she dropped onto her haunches to root through her gym bag, she glanced out the window—and found herself staring at the bell tower of a church.

Although it was at least a block or two away, the view was unobstructed; the surrounding tenements were only three or four stories tall, as opposed to the one she was in, which dwarfed its neighbors at six stories. She dimly remembered passing what might have been a church on her way to the Black Lodge the night before, but she hadn't realized it was so close to Cloudy's squat.

Although strong light proved bothersome, if not painful, her eyesight was still five times sharper than the average human's. As she squinted against the sun, she could see that the church bells had been removed. While God might not have turned a blind eye to Deadtown, his earthly representatives were another matter.

Something moved in the deep shadows of the belfry—something too large to be a bird or a bat. This made her look closer. She knew someone trying to avoid being seen when she saw it. At first she thought Esher had discovered her duplicity and sent one of his minions to spy on her, but she quickly discarded the idea. She was sure she had not been followed, certainly not by any human agency. And the skulker in the belfry certainly couldn't be Kindred. No, whoever it was watching her was probably one of Deadtown's hapless human citizens.

She was too tired to let the problem of the peeper's identity occupy her for more than a few seconds. Although she could move around during the day and was immune to sunlight, that didn't mean she relished it. She needed to go to ground in order to recharge her energy stores and allow her body to repair whatever damage may have been done to it. Besides, she'd put in a long, exhausting night's detective work, and she needed her rest.

As she dropped onto the mattress, her blood pressure plummeted like a stone, as did her respiratory and heart rate. To all outward appearances, she was dead.

At least until the sun went down.

Chapter

7

In the dream, she can see herself get into the car.

Only, it's not really her; it's the person who existed before her creation and gave birth to her as she died, raped into oblivion by a demon prince. Denise Thorne.

In the dream, she watches Denise get into the car. She is but a ghost; mute and intangible, observing as her former self steadily plods toward her fate, unable to change the course of events. Surely this is a taste of what Hell must be like.

For the thousandth time she watches as the dashing and debonair gentleman playboy Lord Morgan metamorphoses into a leering vampire, red of tooth and claw. She watches as the pallid, ruby-eyed monster takes the terrified Denise's young mind and body and rapes them with cruel abandon. She watches as he slakes his unnatural lusts by violating and biting her at the same time, flooding her womb with dead sperm and contaminating her bloodstream with the taint of the undead.

She watches as Denise Thorne, her mind shattered and soul destroyed, disappears behind a wall of shock—and she is born, emerging like Athena from the forehead of Zeus. She watches as Morgan tosses her naked and abused body from the back of his vintage Rolls-Royce as if she were an empty fast-food wrapper, leaving her for dead in the gutters of London's East End. She is only moments old, but already she is beginning to learn the name of the game: Survival of the Fittest.

Her surroundings warp and time speeds up, as it tends to do in dreams. Although she cannot see what is transpiring during the time lapse, she knows what is occurring behind the scenes. After all, it happened to her, didn't it? Now she is standing atop the Empire State Building. Decades have passed. She is there with Lord Morgan—only he is no longer the dashing debonair playboy who seduced Denise Thorne so long ago. His face is scarred. His lips are pulled into a permanent, disfiguring sneer, the left eye white as a boiled fish's. The stranger watches as she caresses the vampire lord's ruined face as gently as a lover's—then buries her fangs in his throat. Morgan looks surprised—then scared—as she drains him of his life force. He struggles and tries to escape her embrace, but it's no use—his limbs have already begun to wither. He screams and flails his wasted arms and legs in protest as she reduces him to an animated scarecrow.

Above them, the sky turns the color of a ripe bruise and lightning stitches the bellies of immense thunderclouds. Sated, she lets the desiccated remains drop. He looks more like a puppet than a man. Although he has been drained of his very essence, the vampire prince still has enough life force remaining to plead for mercy. The stranger watches as she brings the heel of her boot down on her sire's skull, snuffing out a malignancy that has stretched more than seven centuries.

She knows she should feel exaltation, joy—at least a perverse pleasure. After all, she's spent over twenty-five years searching for the bastard who stole her humanity. But instead of feeling a sense of closure, there is only rage: the churning fury of the whirlwind. In the dream she looks up into the rippling sky, with its ominous thunderclouds, and suddenly she is no longer watching herself. She stares up into the heart of the coming darkness, and in it she sees a pair of eyes. The eyes are blood-red and without pupil or white—just huge, blood-filled eyes. And she knows then, as dreamers always seem to know things that go unspoken in dreams, that she is looking into the eyes of the Other—the vampiric side of her personality; the part of her that revels in the pain of others, that delights in the suffering of enemies, that relishes cruelty. It is the side of her she fears and yet needs if she is to survive.

The Other looks down on her and its voice shakes the heavens.

"Beware."

The stranger claps her hands to her ears, even though she knows she is dreaming.

"Beware the blood-wizard."

Crimson wells from under the Other's lids and begins to spill from the skies. Wherever it strikes it hisses and steam rises, like water boiling over in a pot. Some of it splashes onto her hand, scalding it. She cries out and draws back in pain—

Only to find Ryan's pale face before her, his eyes wide with fear. With a gasp of shocked surprise, she let go of his throat. "Sorry, kid," she rasped, trying her best to conceal the shuddering that racked her body like a junkie. "I—I must have been having a bad dream."

The boy scuttled over to the window, watching her cautiously as he massaged his throat. She groaned under her breath and wondered if there was a way to possibly feel worse than she did at that moment. She rolled off the mattress in a single, fluid moment, picking up her leather jacket.

"I thought you said you aren't like them." Accusation and hurt rasped in his voice. Despite his street-toughness, Ryan was still only a child. And a sorely used one, at that.

The stranger sighed and combed her fingers through the unruly tangle of her hair. "Most of the time I'm not, Ryan. I try to keep the bad part of me under control—but sometimes it gets out. And when that happens, I don't want anyone around I care about, because I'm afraid I'll hurt them."

Ryan tilted his head and looked at her. "Do you care about me?"

"Yeah. Yeah, I guess I do. 'Cause I sure don't want to hurt you, Ryan. Not now, not ever. That's why I'm going to get your mother back for you."

The boy darted forward, wrapping his arms about her waist, burying his face into her stomach. Despite his slight build, the boy had a grip like an anaconda. It had been a long time since a child had hugged her like that. Too long. She smiled as she stroked the boy's head.

"Hey, don't get your hopes up just yet, okay? It's still not a sure thing! I've got a lot of strings to pull on this one—and I need your help to make sure everything works out."

"I'll do anything you tell me to!" Ryan said, tilting his head back to look up at her.

The stranger caressed the boy's chin with the ball of her thumb and ruffled his hair. "I don't doubt it. You're a brave kid, Ryan. And you'll need every last ounce of that bravery if you want to get your mother away from Esher. Tonight I've got to send a message to Sinjon about what Esher is up to—and I need you to take it to him. Don't look so worried—I got Sinjon to promise to give you safe passage. You're under his protection now, which will keep you safe while I'm not around. But to be sure, I'm going to give you this to wear."

She reached inside the neck of her T-shirt and withdrew a thin silver chain from around her neck. At the end of the chain hung a silver crucifix, the cross lengths made to resemble briar thorns. She looped the necklace about the boy's neck twice so that it dangled at his chest and not his crotch.

"This is an enchanted crucifix, specially warded against Kindred. Vampires fear it above all else. None will dare touch you while you wear this."

Ryan moved to the circular attic window, to study the necklace in the last of the dying light. The stranger glanced past the boy to the church bell tower, and remembered the shadowy figure she'd glimpsed shortly before going to ground.

"Ryan—what is that building over there?"

The boy looked to where she pointed, then shrugged. "It's some kind of church. It's got a weird name. Saint Ever-Ready or something."

"Does anybody live there?"

"There's an old guy who stays in there. He wears a long black dress with a white thing sticking up in front. Cloudy says he's a father, but I never see any kids with him. The only time he comes out is to go to the liquor store.

I think he's kind of crazy, but not bad crazy, like the homeless guys kinda are. He used to leave me scraps, back when I was sleepin' on the street."

The stranger returned her gaze to the bell tower and tapped one of her fangs, momentarily puzzled. A priest? In Deadtown? Interesting. Her train of thought was interrupted by Ryan tugging on the belt of her leather jacket, holding up the thorny crucifix.

"Did this cost a lot?"

"I suppose. I don't really know. My sire gave it to me."

"Will he get mad if he finds out you gave it to me and I lost it or something?"

"It's okay. He won't mind. I killed him."

Reentering the House of Esher proved just as disorienting as it had the first time. She wondered how many times she would have to traverse the diabolical funhouse before she got used to it. Or perhaps only those completely in thrall to the vampire lord were truly immune to its magic.

As she strode through the House's twisted corridors, she could feel its master draw her toward him, as a magnet does an iron filing. She had neglected mentioning the blood oath to Cloudy, partially because she knew he wouldn't grasp the significance of the act, but largely out of fear that it would erode what trust she'd built with him. While she was secure in her own willpower, she had to admit that Esher was indeed a charismatic lord. It was easy to see why the weaker, less secure vampires flocked to him.

She found Esher in his audience chamber, holding court with several of his new recruits. Most of them looked to have once been drifters or unwary commuters—the easiest prey for today's urban vampire. Unremarkable in life, they remained so in undeath. Without clan or class, they needed someone like Esher to provide their new existence with focus. They watched his every nuance avidly, like starving men outside the window of a bakery. Esher was seated on his portable throne of office, with Decima standing to one side. Nikola was nowhere to be seen.

"I called you before me, my friends," Esher said, his voice ringing like a bell, "because we are on the cusp of great change! In two hours' time, I am to meet with the representatives of a powerful human drug cartel. The results of this meeting will be far-reaching—both inside and outside Deadtown. I have every reason to believe that the humans are interested in eliminating Sinjon and the Black Spoons once and for all—and that they would enlist my help in the matter!"

There was muttering among the gathered Kindred. One of them, a vampire dressed in the skin of a junior executive, spoke up. "But, milord— wouldn't that lead to *jyhad?*"

The gathered recruits muttered even louder among themselves. They all knew that a declaration of open war between princes was indeed serious. Although covert warfare was standard among the competing vampire clans existing in the urban demesnes of the twentieth century, full-fledged *jyhad* was increasingly rare. In the olden days, *jyhads* between vampire lords had been extremely common, but the invention of communication satellites, personal computers and video cameras made such traditional activities exceptionally risky. To make things even chancier, *jyhad* was frowned upon by the Kindred governing council, known as the Camarilla, which saw to it that the existence of the various clans were kept hidden from the human world on which they fed. Those who transgressed against the Camarilla's codes of conduct were dealt with quite harshly. And permanently.

"Technically, this is not the same as a *jyhad*." Esher said, smiling patiently. "If an outside agency, such as—in this case—human druglords, declares war on a Kindred prince and formally elicits the help of other Kindred against their enemy, then it is not a true *jyhad*. A true *jyhad* between Kindred is signaled through the ritual delivery of a bouquet of a dozen black roses.

"Now, I want to have some of you with me tonight, when I go to meet the human druglords. Not because I fear them, but because I wish them to see that I am what I claim to be—a prince of the Kindred!" The recruits fell to talking among themselves again, but Esher silenced them with a clap of his hands. "Decima will notify you as to which of you will be part of my entourage. Until then, await my arrival at Dance Macabre!"

The recruits bowed as one, placing their left hands over their throats in deference, and turned to leave. The stranger moved to follow them, but Esher's voice rang out, stopping her in her tracks.

"A moment, if you please. I would talk to you."

"As you wish, milord," she replied, forcing a smile.

Esher leaned forward, his chin resting on his fist, and eyed her intently. "I am told you were nowhere to be found in the barracks during hibernation. Nor has Torgo been seen since I sent him down to the catacombs with you. He was in thralldom to me, and I have called to him, blood to blood, but he does not respond."

The stranger shrugged. "I'm not big on slumber parties. And as for Torgo, the last I saw of him, he was tottering down an alley in search of a buzz."

Esher sighed and shook his head. "That is highly likely. A lush is a lush, whether he gets his alcohol from the neck of a bottle or that of a wino. I wouldn't be surprised if the drunken fool got caught out in the sun. But that still does not excuse your insubordination. Watch your step, stranger. I am quick to reward those who serve me well, but I am quicker to punish those who displease me. You don't want to get on my bad side."

She bowed, placing her hand over her throat. "Your will is law, milord."

"Don't think you've escaped being disciplined, childe," Esher said as he shook a finger at her, his voice stern. "I'll see to you later. But first I have more pressing business to attend to this evening."

"The druglords are actually coming to Deadtown to meet with you?" she asked, changing the subject.

Esher barked a dry laugh. "They don't dare set foot here even during the day! They are superstitious fools, born of dirt-ignorant peasant farmers. Still, just because they fear us doesn't keep them from trafficking with devils. No, I am to meet with them in a restaurant that serves as a front for one of their operations."

"Do you trust them?"

Esher shrugged. "What have I to fear from humans? They are tools in my hand, nothing else."

"Am I to accompany you, milord?"

"No, you are to remain here. I have sent for Nikola. She is to await my return in my private chambers. Since Decima will be accompanying me to the rendezvous, I need you to guard her against Sinjon."

"But I thought Webb and Obeah guard her at all times."

"They do. But they are mere humans. I need a Kindred sentry to back them up, in case Sinjon sends his progeny to attack. And I have every reason to believe that Sinjon is interested in stealing my precious dancer from me!"

The stranger lifted an eyebrow. "How so?"

"I was foolish enough to offer the old reptile any boon he desired—and he claimed Nikola! Of course I denied her to him, and now he claims I have breached Kindred etiquette!"

"Technically, he's right, milord…."

"I don't care if he's in the right! I'll see him to Hell first!" Esher snapped as he got to his feet. "You are to keep watch until I return, is that understood?"

"Perfectly, milord."

"Ryan? Where are you?" whispered the stranger, her eyes flashing back and forth.

"Down here," the boy replied.

She glanced down at her feet and saw the boy's pale face peeking up at her from underneath a sewer grating. The stranger dropped down on her haunches, pretending to adjust her bootlaces, and passed a piece of folded paper to him. "I'm supposed to be patrolling the perimeter, so I don't have much time to talk. You're to take this to Sinjon."

"What about you?"

"Esher's ordered me to stay here and watch after Nikola."

"You're going to take her away, aren't you?"

"I'll try. She'll have Obeah and Webb with her."

"You can kill them easy!"

"Look, kid—just deliver the note, okay?"

She straightened up and headed back in the direction of the House. She shouldn't have told Ryan about his mom. Now the kid was going to expect the rescue to happen tonight. As she neared the checkpoint, she noticed the area was sparsely manned. Esher had ordered the Pointers to hang at the Dance Macabre that evening, so Sinjon's forces wouldn't notice the decrease in numbers in front of the club. As she trotted up the steps to the House of Esher, the door opened and Decima stepped out.

"I was about to go track you down," the lieutenant said icily.

"I was just finishing the perimeter check. The zone's clear."

"Lord Esher will be exiting from one of the auxiliary tunnels in five minutes, as he does not wish to be seen leaving Deadtown. You are to await the arrival of his bride, then see that she is safely escorted to Lord Esher's private chambers. You are to remain on guard outside the doors of the chamber until Lord Esher's return. Is that clear?"

"I suppose."

"It better be crystal-clear, bitch!" Decima snarled. "If anything happens to Nikola, you are to answer for it!"

The stranger flipped the bird at Decima's back as she checked her watch. Webb and Obeah were scheduled to leave the safe-house with Nikola in five minutes. She would be cutting it close. Possibly to the bone. She only hoped the boy didn't run into too much trouble trying to reach Sinjon.

Ryan leaned cautiously out of the dark doorway, scanning the street. He glanced down at his chest, at the silver-thorn crucifix. It was heavy and tended to swing quite a bit when he ran. After a moment's deliberation, he carefully rearranged it between his ragged jersey and his undershirt. He clutched the stranger's note to his chest like a life preserver. Taking a deep breath, he darted from his hiding place in the direction of the shadowed alleyway across the street. He'd learned that the trick was to keep his head down and shoulders hunched and make himself as small as possible, so if one of the Pointers spotted him out of the corner of an eye, they'd mistake him for a stray dog. Not that there were many strays wandering the streets in Deadtown, nowadays.

He was still holding his breath as he cleared the curb and made the entrance of the alley—but it escaped him in a single gasp as he ran headfirst into a pair of legs. Although the collision sent him sprawling, he did not relinquish his grip on the note.

A heavyset African-American wearing a Pointer jacket and sporting the letters "BMF" shaved into the hair on the side of his head glowered down at Ryan. He held a 40 of Olde English in one meaty hand and a blunt in the other. "You tryin' t'fuck with me, punk?" BMF growled. His frown deepened. "Hold on—! You that kid—!"

Ryan scrambled to his feet and began to run. He could hear the big man swear and toss aside his malt liquor as he gave chase. Ryan was younger and faster, but BMF's legs were easily three times as long as his. His only hope was to find a broken basement window or an old coal chute to scoot down.

As he turned the corner, he realized he was opposite the church. That meant he was close to the Black Lodge—he was almost there! But as he turned to glance over his shoulder to see where his pursuer was, he tripped and fell headlong onto the cobblestones hard enough to scrape his knees and bloody his nose.

His first instinct was to cry—but the tears were not those of a child who has hurt himself while playing. They were tears of grief. He'd failed to get the message to Sinjon. And because of his failure, he was never going to see his mother ever again. His eyes swimming with tears, he lifted his head to look at his killer face-to-face. But instead of BMF's dark features, he found himself staring up at the face of a boy who looked to be little more than sixteen.

Although the teenager's skin was corpse-white, his lips were as red and full as ripe tomatoes. "What have we here?" purred the vampire youth. "Squab?"

A second, equally pallid face, seemingly even younger than the first, loomed into view. "Tristan! Look! He's *bleeding!*" the second one said with breathless excitement.

"So I see, Ethan. Such a yummy little boy! I could eat you right up!"

"Back off, motherfuckers! The punk's *mine!*"

Tristan and Ethan glanced up at BMF, who was standing twenty feet away, pointing a .45 semiautomatic in their direction.

"Don't try an' mess with me, assholes, cause I'm packin' phosphorus clips in this baby!"

Tristan smiled, exposing his fangs, and raised his hands. "Don't shoot, Mr. Gangbanger!"

Ryan lay on the hard cobblestones, looking from Tristan and Ethan to BMF and back again—then Ethan wasn't there anymore. It was as if someone had thrown a switch and he simply disappeared. A second later BMF screamed as his gun arm was turned completely around in its socket. His arm made a noise like a balsa-wood airplane being crushed. Then Ethan was back, only this time he was standing behind BMF, holding the Pointer's gun. The vampire youth's snide smile disappeared, to be replaced by a look of genuine anger as he placed the muzzle of the .45 against the letters shaved into BMF's head.

"Lesson Number One: Humans don't threaten Kindred. Especially if they're outnumbered."

Then he pulled the trigger. The Pointer's head disappeared in an explosion of flame. Ethan stepped over the gangbanger's body while dusting off his hands.

"Now—where were we?"

Tristan returned his attention to Ryan, leaning close until his unnaturally red lips were all the boy could see. The vampire's tongue darted out and licked at the blood smeared across his cheek. His breath reeked like a dog's. Suddenly Tristan gasped and recoiled, making a noise like an angry cat.

"*Magic!*"

Ryan glanced down at his chest and saw that the crucifix the stranger had given him had worked its way free from his clothing.

"This is the one Sinjon told us about!" Ethan said, pointing at Ryan. "We are to bring the boy to him!"

Tristan regarded Ryan with open distaste. "What would our prince want with such a wretched child?"

"All I know is that he is under Lord Sinjon's protection." Ethan bent over and grabbed Ryan by the back of the collar, careful not to come in contact with the silver crucifix or the chain securing it around his neck, and yanked him onto his feet. Two minutes later, Ryan found himself being hurried through the corridors of the Black Lodge. Other vampires, curious to see what a child was doing in their midst, stuck their heads out of various doors as Ryan passed by, but the moment they caught sight of the talisman around his neck they visibly flinched and quickly withdrew.

Finally they came to a room where a vampire dressed like the man on the dollar bill sat on a big golden chair. Seated at the vampire's feet was a boy who bore a strong resemblance to Tristan and Ethan, except that he was still human.

Sinjon smiled and held out an elegantly manicured hand. "Welcome, small one. I am Sinjon, Prince of Deadtown. I believe you have something to give me—?"

"I don't like this," Obeah mumbled from the back seat of the Batmobile. "Much as I hate that vamp bitch, we need her riding shotgun." He glanced over at Nikola, who was seated between him and the driver's-side door, gazing at her reflection in the heavily tinted window. If she heard him, she gave no signs of doing so.

"Esher said he'd have someone waiting for us on the curb. It'll be cool, man. Don't sweat your balls," Webb laughed. He was sitting up front with the driver, literally riding shotgun.

"Sweatin' my balls what's kept 'em on me all this time," Obeah snapped back. "Who's he got waitin' on us?"

"I dunno. I think it's the new chick. The one with the shades."

"Fuck! She's even worse than Decima!"

Webb turned around to grin at Obeah. "Whatchoo talkin' bout? Hey, I'd fuck her in a New York minute! The bitch is fine!"

"Yeah, if you like dead meat."

"Shit! Pussy's pussy, whether it's body temperature or not!" Webb laughed. He was still laughing at that particular witticism when the hand punched through the front passenger-side window and grabbed the collar of his jacket, yanking him out of the car.

The driver swore and grabbed for the Glock resting on the Caddy's dashboard, but before his fingers could close on the butt of the gun, something cold and sharp touched his throat. Then there was a sudden spurt of warmth as blood sprayed from his jugular, splashing the windshield.

As Nikola watched the driver's blood turn the inside of the car bright red, it occurred to her that something was wrong. She turned to look at Obeah, who was trying to climb into the front seat and grab the steering wheel as the Batmobile bounced over the curb and headed straight for a brick wall. At least it looked like a brick wall. It was hard to tell with all the blood coating the windshield.

There was a loud crash as the vintage Caddy smashed into the wall, sending Obeah hurtling through the windshield in a shower of glass. He bounced off the hood of the car as if it were a trampoline and landed hard on the sidewalk. Nikola was thrown against the back of the front seat hard enough to bruise her shoulder, but was otherwise unhurt. She sat on the floor, motionless, listening as the Batmobile's radiator hissed. She remained still as the back passenger door was wrenched off its hinge and tossed aside. Only then did Nikola finally react, cringing at the sight of the woman she assumed was Decima.

"Nikola? Are you okay?"

Whoever the stranger was, she wasn't Decima. The vampiress could care less if she was hurt or not.

"Nikola, can you hear me?"

Nikola nodded.

The stranger groaned something under her breath, reached in and grabbed the dancer's wrist, pulling her out of the wrecked car. Nikola gazed placidly at the sight of Obeah sprawled alongside the car, his hair full of busted safety glass. Although there was blood coating his face and clothes, he was still breathing. Webb, on the other hand, wasn't so lucky. His skull was split open from landing headfirst on the curb, his brain oozing through the spiderweb tattoo like toothpaste squeezed from the middle of the tube.

"Bonk-bonk on the head," Nikola giggled.

The stranger hustled her into a nearby alley, then took the dancer by the shoulders and turned her so they were face-to-face. She removed her sunglasses, exposing eyes the color of fresh blood. "Nikola, *listen to me.*" Nikola twitched and blinked, but did not pull away. "Tell me where it is."

"Tell you where what is?" she whispered, her voice as tiny as a child's.

"The cocaine Webb and Obeah took from Borges. Where is it?"

"Esher's room."

"*Where* in Esher's room?"

"The Chinese chest."

"Good girl, Nikola." The stranger leaned forward and pressed her index finger against the back of the dancer's neck. "Go to sleep." She quickly snatched Nikola up as she went limp, tossing the woman over her leather-clad shoulder like a load of wet laundry. It didn't look as if she had any choice now but to drop back into overdrive—and take Nikola with her. She was uncertain as to how this might affect her traveling companion; after all, ghostwalking, or Celerity as assholes like Esher called it, was physically stressful even for vampires. At this stage, though, there was no other option.

Taking a deep breath, she centered herself and took a step sidewise in time and space. To the naked eye, it appeared as if she'd simply winked out of existence, but she was still there as a flicker of dark at the corner of the eye. Normally she moved at leisure in overdrive, but even in this time between time she was in a hurry. The stranger darted down alleyways and jogged along side-streets, doing her best to avoid areas she knew to be trafficked by Esher's thralls. She didn't drop out of overdrive until she was at the door of the Black Lodge, blinking into existence in front of a startled Black Spoon guard.

"Sinjon is expecting me," she said brusquely, pushing past the youth before he could bring his AK47 to bear on her.

She found Sinjon in his private chambers, watching Ryan gulp down chocolate milk and Hostess Sno-Balls with the morbid fascination usually reserved for people who watch boa constrictors feed. Vere, Sinjon's favorite, was seated on an ottoman in the corner, looking much put-upon. The moment Ryan saw the stranger ease Nikola off her shoulder and onto a nearby chair, he forgot about his treats and jumped to his feet, spilling chocolate milk on the eighteenth-century Persian rug.

"*Mama!*"

Ryan shot across the room, burying his face in Nikola's lap, smearing chocolate and creamy filling on her white satin skirt. Nikola blinked suddenly, as if shaken from a dream, and looked down at the boy clinging to her. She reached out with a trembling hand and lightly touched the crown of his head, smoothing the prematurely gray hair they both shared.

"*R-ryan?*" she whispered.

"You said my name!" Ryan beamed at his mother. However, his smile flickered as he looked into Nikola's face. He looked to the stranger, confusion in his eyes, then back to his mother.

"Ryan. Your name *is* Ryan. I knew that, didn't I?" Nikola said, oblivious to her son's reaction. "I knew that from before Esher, didn't I?" She turned and smiled at the stranger, revealing a face much like the one she'd woken up with that day. Except that it was ten years older.

The stranger cringed inwardly but nodded and returned the dancer's smile. "Of course you know Ryan, Nikola. He's your son."

Sinjon drew the stranger aside, smiling crookedly. "You are proving quite an ally, my dear. First you alert me to Esher's double-cross, now you deliver his little lap-dancer to me! Now if you can only recover the drugs…"

The stranger shook her head. "No can do, kinsman. He's got them on him. He's going to claim one of his minions took them off one of your couriers, then give them back to the Brothers as a sign of good faith."

"Damn his eyes!" Sinjon spat.

"Looks to me there's only one way you can clear your good name—and that's to break up his little *soiree* with your former business partners. You got the note?"

"Yes. And I know exactly which restaurant you mean."

"So what are you waiting for?"

"Nothing, now. How about you, my dear? Are you coming with us?"

She shook her head. "If it's all the same to you, milord, I think it best I not show my hand as to where my sympathies lie. Should things not go well, you'll still need someone on the inside."

"What about them?" Vere pointed at Ryan and Nikola, seated on the divan near the fireplace.

"They are to remain under my protection!" Sinjon announced as he picked up his tricorn and his walking stick. "The woman may not prove much of a bargaining chip once Esher sees her in good light—but then, he has no way of knowing that, does he?"

A decade ago, the neighborhood was nothing but crumbling warehouses, greasy spoons, and missions, but a couple of years back it had been christened by realtors as an "art district." The warehouses had been renovated and turned into "artist lofts" no artist could afford; the greasy spoons became chi-chi eateries specializing in nouvelle cuisine, southwestern cooking, or sushi; and the missions were replaced by boutiques and overpriced knick-knack shops.

The restaurant that served as a front for the Colombians was a converted wooden camel-back called L'Emeraud. Downstairs boasted a general dining room and bar, while upstairs was reserved for large dinner groups and special occasions, such as wedding receptions, birthday parties—and meetings between drug kingpins and vampire lords.

The upstairs banquet room was tastefully appointed in sea-foam green and off-white, with three French windows opening onto a widow's walk that, weather permitting, allowed the diners a view of the city lights reflected in the nearby bay. But tonight the curtains were drawn tight, and heavily armed men in cheap suits stood guard beside the windows. The service stairs that led to the kitchen were also heavily guarded.

The Borges Brothers sat at one end of a long table, flanked by several armed men. Their leader was Antonio Borges, a squat man with hair graying at the temples and a long ponytail hanging down the back of his Armani suit. While his cartel's power had its roots in Cali and the surrounding area, he handled operations out of Miami. Seated at the other end of the table was Esher, accompanied by Decima, four members of his enclave, and a half-dozen Pointers.

"I am honored that you have agreed to meet with us, Lord Esher," Borges said.

"The honor is all mine, Señor Borges," Esher said, smiling without showing his teeth. "And my condolences on the untimely death of your brother."

"Dario was not just my brother—he was an integral part of the business. But then, you know more than most the value of blood."

"Yes. Yes, I do," Esher agreed. "What is it you would propose, Señor Borges?"

"An alliance between your enclave and our cartel. We want you to help us against Sinjon."

"And when you say 'help', you mean—?"

"To destroy him."

Esher stroked his chin for a moment, then leaned over and whispered something to Decima, who shook her head. Esher returned his attention to Borges. "What do I get out of the deal?"

"The death of your enemy."

The vampire lord laughed, this time making sure the drug dealers could see his teeth. "If that were motivation enough for me to act against the Freemason, he would have been dead years ago! No, Señor Borges. You know the Kindred do not interfere with the concerns of humans unless it benefits us in some way. Come, amigo, what pretty bauble do you have that can entice one such as I?"

"We'll supply you with enough cocaine to make you twice as rich as Sinjon."

Esher's smile widened, grew even sharper. "My that *is* pretty. I believe you have yourself a deal, Señor. However, there are a few—formalities— we must observe." Esher produced a folded piece of parchment and an old-fashioned fountain pen, its barrel fashioned of obsidian, from his breast pocket. The nib gleamed as sharply as the edge of a razor.

"Formalities?"

"I like to get things down in writing."

Borges frowned. "You want me to sign a *contract?*"

"I prefer to call it a pact, my dear fellow," Esher explained as he strolled the length of the table to where Borges sat. He unfolded the parchment and slid it across to the druglord with his fingertips.

Borges picked up the blank sheet and muttered something in Spanish to his companions, who fidgeted nervously. He looked up at Esher, doing his best to conceal his revulsion. "Th-this isn't paper."

"Ah! I appreciate a man who can identify human skin when he feels it!" Esher held the pen out to Borges, who, after exchanging glances with the others, reached out his hand to take it.

Moving with the speed of a cobra, Esher rammed the nib into Borges' thumb, drawing blood. The druglord yanked his hand back. "*Madre de Dios!* What are you playing at, you crazy bastard!?!"

"I play at nothing, Señor! Not now, not ever! If you want my help against Sinjon, then do as I say—sign your name in your own blood on this parchment. If you do not, then—well, heaven help you. Because I know where *my* help will be coming from."

The look on Borges' face was that of a man who has seen his damnation, but knows salvation has long since ceased to be an option. With a trembling hand he took the pen from Esher and signed his name at the bottom of the blank sheet of human skin.

"*Excellent!*" the vampire smiled. "I'll have it notarized later."

As he moved to fold the document and return it to his breast pocket, there was a sound like the rising of a sudden wind, and the French windows abruptly flew open, allowing Sinjon, in all his foppish glory, to stroll in, accompanied by several vampires and a dozen or more Black Spoons.

"Good evening, one and all! It looks like someone forgot to send me an invitation to this little *soiree*. I hope you don't mind if I gate-crash?"

Borges' men, the Pointers, and the Black Spoons drew their respective weapons. There was a tense moment as the Black Spoons pointed their guns at the Pointers and Borges' muscle, the Pointers aimed at the Black Spoons, and Borges' men, uncertain, tried to cover both gangs.

"You miserable bloodsucking freak!" Borges bellowed at Esher, pushing himself away from the table. He pulled a chrome-plated .38 from his Armani jacket. "You set me up! Nobody sets up Antonio Borges! *Nobody!*"

Borges fired point-blank, but the vampire turned into a dark blur, reappearing a heartbeat later on the other end of the table. However, the bullet intended for Esher did not go entirely to waste, as it found a target in the waiter who had just stepped out of the service stairwell, bearing a tray of coffee sent up by the management. The hapless L'Emeraud employee hit the ground in a crash of flame and crockery, his blood mingling with the scalding hot liquid.

Outrage flashed in Esher's eyes. "*Phosphorus?* You brought *incendiary bullets* to a parley?"

"You better fuckin' believe I brought 'em!" Borges retorted. "You think I was gonna fuck with monsters like you and not cover my ass?"

"That tears it! The deal's off!" Esher snarled, wadding the parchment in a ball.

Borges' eyes started from his socket as he clutched at his chest. Blood drooled from the corners of his mouth. He collapsed to the floor, crimson leaking from his nostrils, ears, mouth, tear ducts, and anus.

Borges' men opened fire on both Sinjon and Esher's gangs, and within seconds the room was filled with incendiary bullets. Esher, roaring his anger, overturned the parley table, pinning one of Borges' lieutenants underneath. The air seemed to grow tight, like the skin of a soap bubble before it bursts, and as one the vampires disappeared, leaving only their human servants behind.

The Pointers and Black Spoons knew exactly what the mass exodus meant and drew closer together, so that their backs weren't exposed. Borges' men, however, merely blinked and looked around, confused. Then one of them screamed as his arm was broken by unseen hands. Then another's head suddenly came detached from his body and bounced across the floor. Within seconds, all twelve of the druglord's men were scattered about like the remains of chickens after a weasel-raid on a henhouse.

While in overdrive, the vampire combatants could easily sidestep any bullets whizzing through the air. The vampire princes' human servants, however, did not have such an option. Pointers and Black Spoons alike littered the floor, clutching smoking wounds as they died. It was hard to tell, but Sinjon's forces seemed to be gaining the upper hand.

Decima winked back into view. She was standing in one of the French windows, and she had Sinjon's favorite, Vere, in a chokehold, the point of a crossbow bolt shoved under the boy's chin.

"Daddy!" wailed Vere. *"Stop!"*

Sinjon, his powdered wig askew and waistcoat stained with blood, signaled for the others to drop out of overdrive. He took a step toward his lover, but Decima growled and shook her head.

"Stay put, old man, or I'll spear his brain like an olive!"

Esher's forces reappeared. While the blood-wizard himself was unharmed, the same could not be said for his recruits. Although Esher's enclave was larger than Sinjon's, its members were mostly young, untried Kindred. Sinjon's brood, on the other hand, were older, more experienced fighters, who had spent decades dwelling in the hell of Deadtown, and their seasoning showed.

"Good work, Decima," Esher said. "I knew I could rely on you!"

"Let the boy go!" Sinjon snarled. "He's of no use to you!"

"On the contrary, my dear Sinjon," Esher replied. "He serves a useful purpose—as a shield! Order your minions to stand down, or I'll have Decima do something decidedly unpleasant to your little boy-toy!"

"You heard the man!" Sinjon barked at his troops. "Stand down!"

The Black Spoons exchanged uncertain looks, then lowered their weapons. Decima dragged Vere past the elder vampire, pausing to let him take one last look at his lover's face.

"Don't you dare hurt the boy!" Sinjon warned. "Or you'll be sorry, wizard! Mark my words"

"How so, old man?" sneered Esher.

Sinjon fixed his enemy with a cold stare, and, grinning nastily, replied;

"Ladybug, Ladybug,

Fly away home!

Your house is afire

and your children alone!"

Esher's triumphant smile disappeared as if wiped off with a rag. The sound of police and ambulance sirens caused both vampire lords to hiss in displeasure. They had grown used to Deadtown, and were unaccustomed to humans meddling in their affairs.

Moments later, the police thundered upstairs, followed closely by paramedics. They found over a dozen partly charred bodies, some of them bullet-riddled, others apparently rent limb from limb. And, to make matters even more confusing, some of the dead seemed to be, well, far from fresh. Even as they watched, the corpses withered and collapsed inward, like pumpkins rotting on the vine. The police and paramedics muttered among themselves, and some of the older hands glanced about warily. If anyone noticed the shadows flickering at the corners of their vision, they did not speak up.

Chapter

8

The stranger lurched uncertainly along the topsy-turvy corridors of Esher's stronghold. She had to hurry. Esher would be back any time now. If he found her searching his private chambers, then it was all over; she'd be forced to duke it out *mano a mano* with not only the blood-wizard but his entire enclave. She was willing to take risks now and again, but she wasn't a fool. Still, as difficult as navigating the House might be while Esher was in residence, it was even worse when he wasn't. All the doors seemed both familiar and strange at the same time, mocking her sense of direction. Some of the doors she'd tried opened onto relatively prosaic rooms, while others seemed tied to a menacing intradimensional void. These doors she wasted no time in slamming shut. Who knows what lurks in the corners of a house where space has been folded in on itself like a child's paper hat?

She tried yet another doorknob, expecting it to open onto blank nothingness, but this time she found herself gazing into a room that had to be Esher's personal suite. The rooms were spacious and decorated similarly to the audience chamber, with tapestries draping the walls and candelabra scattered about for light. A bewildering hodgepodge of antique furniture, varying from Empire to Jugendendstil, cluttered the room, which made finding the Chinese box Nikola had mentioned more difficult than she'd originally thought.

She found it tucked inside an alcove, hidden behind a curtain of multicolored glass beads designed to resemble a snarling tiger. It was a black lacquer chest shaped like a pagoda, with bronze dragon's feet and a grinning dragon's head decorating the lid. Lifting the lid of the box, she saw two five-pound bags of Jack Frost brand sugar. She smiled and shook her head. She had to hand it to Esher—he'd wasted no time in repackaging the stolen drugs. She quickly stashed the purloined drugs in special pouches sewn into the lining of her jacket. She'd done her fair share of smuggling over the years, although the contraband she dealt in was far more esoteric than mere narcotics. When dealing with demons and other unsavory supernatural elements, the body parts of convicted murderers and similar dark totems were considered far more valuable than money.

After making sure the packages were secure, she pulled a perfumed lace handkerchief from her back pocket. The hanky was unremarkable, except for its distinctive scent and the Masonic emblem embroidered in one corner. Careless of Sinjon to leave such personal items lying about. With a smirk, she dropped it into the Chinese box and closed the lid.

Now she had to hurry back to the audience chamber and await Esher's return. One thing was for certain—he probably wasn't going to be in the best of moods when he got home.

The doors to the audience chamber flew open, slamming against the walls so hard they made the very House quake as the stranger moved to greet Esher.

"Where is she?!?" Esher thundered. *"Where is Nikola?!?"*

"She's not here, milord."

Esher's right hand moved inhumanly fast, clamping tight as a vise around her throat. The stranger's body went rigid as she battled an overpowering urge to plunge her switchblade into the vampire lord. Physically attacking Esher would be personally satisfying, but far from wise. She was locked into an elaborate quadrille with both vampire princes, and deviating by a single step could prove disastrous. She could feel the Other stir, deep at the bottom of her brain, responding to the aggression and hostility radiating from Esher as a hibernating serpent would to the first signs of warm weather. The last thing she needed was to have the Other become ascendant, ruining all her carefully laid-out plans with its psychotic rage. She told herself she would have Esher's blood soon enough—but for now she needed him alive. Or at least not dead.

"I can't tell you with a broken neck!" she gasped. She reached up and tried to pry Esher's fingers from her throat. Esher let go, leaving her to stagger backward, massaging her larynx. When she spoke, her voice was hard and cold as black glass. "Don't touch me like that."

"Are you threatening me, childe?" the vampire lord growled.

"I'm not threatening. I'm telling."

His lip curled in derision, revealing a glimpse of fang. "I do the telling around here, woman! You'll do well to learn that if you wish to keep your head on your shoulders! Now where is Nikola? "

"Sinjon has her."

"How!?! How did this happen?!?"

"I did as I was told—I waited outside for the Batmobile to arrive. When it didn't show, I went looking for it. I found it halfway along the route. It had swerved off the street and into the side of a house. The driver and Webb were dead. Obeah was alive, although injured and unconscious. Nikola was nowhere to be found. I brought Obeah back here and got some of the Pointers to look after him. I figured you would want to interrogate him as to what actually happened."

"Is he conscious?"

"I believe so, yes."

Esher stomped angrily across the floor and climbed the dais, standing before his chair of office. "Bring him to me."

A minute later, Obeah arrived, escorted by a couple of Pointers. His broad, dark face was crisscrossed with red welts, and shards of busted safety glass still glinted in his thick dreads. He leaned on a makeshift cane made from a length of lead pipe, favoring a stiff right leg. His nose was broken and his left eye was swollen nearly shut, but aside from these injuries he was in surprisingly good shape for a man who'd gone through a windshield and bounced off the hood of a car.

"You have failed me, *bokor*," Esher said grimly.

"It's not my fault, milord!" Obeah explained. "Whatever moved on us wasn't human! Normally that wouldn't be a problem, since the Lady Decima rides with us, but tonight—tonight we were driving without protection! There had to be two, maybe three of 'em! First thing I know, Webb's gone—yanked right out of the fuckin' window like we was standing still! Then they go for the driver. I'm in the back seat, right? So I try to grab the wheel, but it's no good. Next thing, I'm flyin' through the windshield! When I wake up I got busted glass in my hair, my face, even in my fuckin' mouth! This mirror-eyed bitch here, she's shaking me, wantin' to know where the hell Nikola is. I told her Sinjon snatched her."

"Are you certain it was Sinjon's minions who did this?"

"They were ghostwalking, so I didn't get a good look. All I know is one minute I'm riding in the back seat, next minute I'm bouncin' off the hood of the fuckin' car! But it has to have been Sinjon—I mean, who the hell else could it be?"

Esher seemed lost in thought for a long moment, then motioned for the Tonton Macoute to step forward. Although his eyes were bright with fear, the other man obeyed. Esher leaned forward, resting his hand atop Obeah's. His voice was soft, almost sad. "Regardless of your excuses, you have still failed me, Obeah. And those who fail me—must suffer for their mistakes. It is a matter of discipline—do you not agree?"

"Y-yes, milord."

"I'm glad we understand one another, *bokor*," Esher said, with a small smile. He snatched the length of pipe from Obeah, bringing it squarely against his kneecap. The voodoo man shrieked in pain and collapsed to the floor, clutching his leg. Esher snapped his fingers and the Pointers lifted the injured Obeah by his armpits and removed him from the audience chamber. "See that he's tended to. Give him some heroin to shut him up. But not too soon," he called after them as he dropped down into the seat, his face set into a fierce scowl. "The old reptile has bigger balls than I thought if he was able to uncover my meeting with Borges and snatch my bride from under my nose! I underestimated the Freemason—but it won't happen again! Still, he is not as clever as he would think—after all, he made the mistake of taking his lapdog along with him when he crashed the tête-à-tête at L'Emeraud."

"He did what—?" the stranger said, looking confused.

Decima entered the room, dragging Vere behind her on a leather leash attached to a spiked dog collar. The youth's hands were secured behind his back by a pair of hinged wristcuffs. Vere's eyes widened when he saw the stranger, but he kept silent—largely because he had a rubber ball gag shoved into his mouth.

"I want you to take a message to Sinjon," Esher said, pointing at the stranger.

"Me?" She tried to keep the suspicion out of her voice.

"Sinjon knows Decima and does not trust her. You, on the other hand, are a *tabula rasa* as far as he's concerned. He has no reason to doubt your word. Tell Sinjon that I will exchange Vere for Nikola in an hour's time on The Street With No Name. No weapons. No tricks. If he fails to show up— or if I see any guns—I send his boy-toy back to him piecemeal."

The stranger glanced back at Vere. This was screwing up her plans, big-time. She had hoped to smuggle Nikola and Ryan out of Deadtown come dawn, but now that was being shot down in flames. And, if she didn't move fast, she had no doubt that Vere would spill the beans about her. Doing her best to hide her frustration, she bowed and touched her throat in deference. "Consider the message as good as delivered, milord."

Sinjon was highly agitated when the stranger returned to the Black Lodge. He was pacing back and forth in his drawing room, hands clutched behind his back. He glanced up at her as she entered, his eyes flashing like polished rubies.

"Esher has Vere!"

"I know. I saw him."

"Has he been harmed?"

"Not as far as I could see. But that might end soon. Esher sent me here to arrange a hostage exchange."

"He doesn't suspect you, does he?"

"Possibly. But if he does, he's keeping it to himself."

"What are the terms of the exchange?"

"It's to occur an hour from now, on The Street With No Name. No weapons. No funny stuff. Vere for Nikola. By the way—where is she?"

"She's well enough, don't worry," Sinjon replied. "I had a couple of my boys lock her up for safekeeping. The little guttersnipe was let go. Tell Esher I agree to his terms."

"Sinjon—you promised me the girl."

Sinjon dropped into a French Rococo chair, crossing his legs at the knee. He plucked a perfumed lace hanky from his sleeve and daubed his upper lip. "So I did. But that was before. This is now. You're not getting her."

"Is Vere that important to you?"

"*All* my boys are important to me," the vampire replied. "After all, I'm their sire, aren't I?"

In an hour's time The Street With No Name was jammed. Pointers and Black Spoons lined the sidewalks outside their respective headquarters, milling among their compatriots and glowering at their rivals, flashing gang signals and trying to look as tough as possible.

At the appointed time the doors of Dance Macabre and Stick's opened simultaneously. Sinjon, resplendent in his powdered wig and diamond-encrusted shoebuckles, stepped out of the pool hall. Esher, outfitted in a black leather duster, the chrome infant-skull glinting on his belt, strode from the bar. The assembled gangbangers turned to their respective leaders, like daisies following the sun. As Esher and Sinjon stepped forward, the Pointers and Black Spoons parted before them. The two vampire princes met toe-to-toe in the middle of the street.

"I believe you have something of mine," Sinjon sniffed.

"Put up or shut up, Freemason," growled Esher.

Sinjon pulled a perfumed lace handkerchief from his coat sleeve and patted his upper lip. This was the signal for the vampire youth, Tristan, to step out of Stick's, leading Nikola on a stainless-steel choke-chain.

"Satisfied, upstart? I've shown you yours, now show me mine."

Without taking his eyes off Nikola, Esher snapped his fingers. The red vinyl door to Dance Macabre swung open a second time and Vere emerged, still gagged and bound, Decima's crossbow pointed directly at his back.

Sinjon nodded in approval. "Very well. Let the exchange begin."

Esher pointed in the direction of the assembled Black Spoons. "I warn you, Sinjon—if I see a weapon of any kind—even so much as a toothpick— Decima will spear your precious boy-toy's heart like a ripe olive! That's a promise."

"And let me hasten to remind *you*, Esher. If your Pointers try anything, Tristan is under orders to garrote your beloved dancer. It should only take one tug on the leash to snap her neck, don't you agree?"

"I believe we understand each other," Esher replied stonily. He motioned to Decima, who gave Vere a sharp nudge with her crossbow. The terrified youth took a hesitant step forward. Sinjon nodded to Tristan, who moved forward, Nikola trailing after him like a lovely, sad-eyed hound.

Just as the hostages were within a few feet of the exchange point, a commotion erupted from Sinjon's side.

"Mama!"

Ryan, his face streaked with tears, darted past the cluster of Black Spoons and headed straight for Nikola. The pale-skinned dancer turned in his direction, and the sadness in her eyes melted.

"Ryan! Baby!" she cried.

Dodging the gangbangers' grasping hands like a broken field runner, the boy threw himself at his mother, wrapping his thin arms about her waist and burying his head in her skirt. Nikola tried to bend down to embrace him, but was brought short by the choke-collar about her throat.

"Decima! Get rid of that child, once and for all!" Esher snarled.

Decima pushed Vere out of the way and grabbed Ryan's shirt collar with her free hand, lifting the kicking boy off the ground and holding him at arm's length like a lice-ridden wolf-cub.

"*My baby!*" Nikola wailed, trying to snatch Ryan away from the vampiress. "Don't you dare hurt my baby!"

"Shut up, cow!" Decima snapped, backhanding Nikola with the hand that held her crossbow. Nikola staggered backward, struggling desperately to keep her footing and avoid strangling.

"*Don't you hurt my mother!*" Ryan shrilled.

"Or you'll do what, kid?" Decima smirked, drawing the boy close to her face, saliva dripping from the corners of her mouth.

Ryan grabbed the enchanted crucifix the stranger had given him and, with a strength born of fear, snapped it free of his neck with a single yank, shoving it in Decima's face.

The vampiress screamed as the silver burned her flesh, dropping both boy and crossbow to clamp her hands over her wounded face. Ryan hit the ground running, trying his best to dodge the fists and boots aimed at him. He was fast and determined, but there were just too many of them. A heavyset Pointer grabbed Ryan by the back of his pants and turned him upside down, holding him by the ankle like a champion-weight fish.

"I got 'im! I got 'im!" the Pointer grinned triumphantly, displaying missing front teeth. "I got—" Suddenly the rest of the Pointer's teeth disappeared— along with his head. The gangbanger's body dropped to the ground, revealing Cloudy, the smoke rising from the barrel of his sawed-off. Ryan scuttled behind his friend and peered out from behind his legs.

"Leave the boy be!" Cloudy shouted. "Any of you try to lay a hand on him, you gotta go through me!"

Esher stood and laughed, his hands on his hips. "You're a fool, old man! You're hopelessly outnumbered! Besides, I can take that shotgun away from you and shove it up your ass before you could bat an eye!"

"Why don't you try it then, sucker?"

A leather-clad arm snaked around the old hippie's neck from behind, locking him in a chokehold. Cloudy cried out in surprise, the shotgun discharging into the air as he was yanked off balance. Ryan yelled his friend's name as he was grabbed by a taloned hand.

"Good work, my dear," Esher smiled. "Be a pet and destroy them for me, would you?"

"Sure thing, boss," grinned the stranger, as she dragged the struggling humans away.

"Ryan!" screamed Nikola, yanking against the choke-chain hard enough to turn her lips blue.

"Obeah!" Esher snapped.

The *bokor* hobbled forward, his damaged leg strapped into a temporary splint, and produced a mojo bag from one of his pockets. He poured the contents of the leather pouch into his cupped palm, blowing the fine powder directly into Nikola's face. She coughed violently, then went limp. Esher quickly caught his errant bride and lifted her in his arms so she would not strangle. Nikola moaned as her head lolled back, and Esher saw clearly for the first time the crow's feet about her eyes and the lines about her mouth.

"What trickery is this, Sinjon?" he snarled. "What have you done to her?"

"Don't blame me if your precious can't take life in the fast lane, Esher," Sinjon sneered. There was a plucking at his sleeve, and he turned to glower at Tristan standing at his elbow, holding Vere on a leash. "Oh. It's you. What is it?"

"Do you want me to set him free, sire?"

Sinjon eyed the trembling youth for a long moment, then smiled. It wasn't a pleasant sight. "No. Leave him like that. That's what he gets for letting himself be captured. I'll deal with him later."

The Pointers parted before the stranger and her charges, but none of them seemed particularly interested in following her. Once they were clear of the crowd, she dodged into a nearby alley, roughly pushing her captives ahead of her.

"*What the hell did you two think you were doing?!?*" she hissed. "Ryan I'd expect something like this from—but you, Cloudy? Shit, you know better than to pull a bonehead play like that!"

"I was just trying to look after the boy. I knew he was going to try and see his mama. I couldn't let him go out alone."

The stranger glanced around quickly, then reached into her jacket and pulled out the bags of "sugar" from the hidden pockets. She handed the parcels, plus a folded piece of paper and a hundred-dollar bill, to Cloudy. "There's not much time! Things are coming down fast. I need you to take this with you back to the crib."

"No prob. What is it?"

"About ten pounds of uncut cocaine."

"Shit!"

"Stash it the attic with my things. Something will be by for it later."

"Don't you mean someone?"

"No. I also need you to contact the number I've written on this piece of paper. Everything you need to know is already written down. You'll have to go pick the order up yourself. The dead president should cover that and the cab ride. Take Ryan with you—I don't want him getting loose again! Remember—you and he are supposed to be dead! Now beat it! I gotta get back soon or they'll get suspicious."

Ryan caught her sleeve as the stranger turned to leave. "What about my mom?"

She smiled and smoothed the boy's hair. "I'm doing the best I can. I'll get your mom back, Ryan. I promise you that. But you have to do as I say and go with Cloudy. Understand?"

"Yes."

"Good. Now scat! I've business to attend to!"

She watched as Cloudy took Ryan's hand and the two hurried from the alley. The wheels were turning and there was no going back. Hopefully she wouldn't get crushed by the juggernaut she was setting in motion. Then again, it wouldn't be the first time.

♋

The payphone had seen better days. It stood outside the liquor store, which seemed to be the only legitimate business on The Street With No Name. The change box had been jimmied open a long time ago, and hung open like the drawbridge on a ransacked castle. Not that it mattered. No one in their right mind would ever put a quarter in it. The metal shell was covered with gang tags, the metal cord that tethered the receiver to the box had been severed with a pair of bolt-cutters, and the earpiece was cracked in two.

The stranger picked up the dead phone and stabbed at the keypad. There was a sound in the receiver like the wailing of lost souls, then a gruff male voice picked up on the other end.

"Monastery Bar and Grill."

"Hey, Grendel. Put Malfeis on, would ya?"

The bartender grumbled something, then was replaced by a young man's voice. "Girlchick! How's it hangin'?"

"I can't waste time playing, Mal. I got a deal for you."

The young voice became as thick and gravelly as a chainsmoker's. "When is it not business with you, girly-girl? I didn't think you called just to shoot the breeze. What have you got for me?"

"Four kilos of snow. Uncut."

"My-my," the demon on the other end of the line chortled. "Slumming, are we? To tell you the truth, I thought you'd have something far more interesting for me, lovey. That dust from the Oklahoma City bombing was killer!"

"This particular shipment of cocaine is responsible for at least a dozen or more deaths."

"Really?" She could tell by his voice that Mal's ears had pricked up. No doubt his tail was starting to lash back and forth like an anxious cat's.

"I need cash and I need it tonight—tomorrow morning by the latest."

"I'll send one of my apprentices along."

"You got me on radar?"

"Of course! We pride ourselves on being full-service. However, I'll need an exact address for the exchange."

"Okay. But remember: no eating anyone this time!"

"Very well, if you insist," Malfeis sighed.

As she hung up the receiver, she experienced a peculiar sensation. It felt like the gentle, but persistent tug of a weak magnet. It was Esher, calling to those bound to him by blood. She could turn her back on the summoning, but there was no way she could ignore it.

Dance Macabre was jammed full of humans and Kindred alike. She knew Esher had recruited a sizable enclave, but until that moment she did not realize just how large it truly was. She'd never seen so many vampires together under the same roof. The sight of them made her palms twitch. Most of them were the younger, unaffiliated vampires the Kindred referred to as Caitiff. Of course, 'young' had a different meaning among the undead than it did the living. While some wore the skins of runaway teenagers, others were outfitted in the bodies of decrepit street-people. None of them had been undead for longer than a year or two. They had all been created by careless predation, probably by Kindred no different from themselves, and left to wander the urban jungle alone and untutored, much like she had been, decades ago. Esher's enclave reminded her of a cross between Fagin's School for Thieves and the Manson Family, combining a ragged army of apprentice sneak-thieves and footpads with damaged souls drawn to, and manipulated by, a powerful, utterly amoral will.

As she moved through the crowded nightclub, she noticed how the Pointers were huddled together in one section of the room, eyeing the assembled Kindred uneasily. Although the gang had sworn itself to Esher's service, apparently things sometimes got a little too hairy even for them. There was a definite lions-at-the-watering-hole vibe going down as the vampires squabbled over the available feeders chained to the walls.

She watched as two Kindred—one wearing the skin of a junior executive, the other a street hustler—got into a hissing match over a tall, thin man. The feeder was so pale his veins resembled strands of blue yarn. There was very little juice left in that one, and the vampires knew it, hence the showdown. The junior executive's hair rose like the hackles on a cat's back, while the hustler growled like an angry mountain lion, unsheathing his fangs so far it looked as if his lips had been sliced away. After a few moments of this, the junior executive backed off and the hustler claimed the feeder as his own.

The stranger watched the winner drain the dying feeder, then quickly looked away. The sight and smell of the blood flowing around her were starting to make her edgy. She had not fed in a day or two. She usually carried a couple of units of whole blood in a special cryo-container in her gym bag, but preferred standard refrigeration when possible, so she'd left them in Cloudy's icebox for safekeeping. When she looked back, it was in time to see the club's bar back unshackling the empty feeder to replace it with a fresh one.

The industrial dance music blaring from the speakers began to fade, and the crowd turned to face the stage. Esher, stripped to the waist, stepped out from behind the blood-red curtains and gestured for the assembly to draw near.

"Come closer, my children."

The Kindred in the audience murmured to themselves and pressed closer to the stage and runway, their pale faces turned toward their leader.

"I call you my children, because even though you were not created by me, my blood flows through each and every one of your veins. You who have no family, you who have been cast aside—I gladly embrace you! You who are without clan, without place—find your place with me! A time of great tribulation is soon to be upon us, my friends! If we are to survive it, we must prove ourselves strong in the face of adversity—united in the face of doubt! That is why I have summoned you to my side this evening, my children—to solidify even further the bonds that tie us together."

Decima emerged from behind the curtains, carrying a ritual claive and a golden chalice. Ryan hadn't held the crucifix against her skin long enough to kill her, but it had done its damage. The wound on her forehead was red and angry, like a fresh brand. Although the stranger had been irked by the boy's foolhardy stunt, she had to admit she was proud of him.

Esher took the claive from Decima, pressed the point against his right wrist and sliced his inner forearm to the elbow. A maroon liquid—looking more like burgundy wine than blood—gouted forth. Although it was thicker than human blood, it still flowed faster than usual. Esher must have recently gorged for him to bleed so freely. Decima knelt before him, holding up the chalice in order to catch every drop of precious gore. Once the chalice was full, Esher took the vessel from Decima and held it up so all could see.

"Behold! My blood is your blood! Come forward, my children! Come forward and partake of that which is Life!"

The Kindred moaned as one and rushed the stage, tearing at one another in their eagerness to taste their liege's power. A celebrant tried to jump his place in line by climbing over the footlights; Decima kicked him in the head, sending him back into the crowd.

"Wait your turn, maggot-bait!" she snapped. "Try that again and I'll put a bolt through your fuckin' eyesocket!"

The stranger found herself standing between a drag queen and a tourist. The tourist-vampire looked exceptionally fresh, since he still had a Minolta looped around his neck and that glazed, shell-shocked stare common to the newly resurrected. She glanced about uneasily, but there was no way she could evade participating in the communion without drawing undue attention to herself. If any of the other celebrants were ambivalent about Esher tightening his Blood Bond, they certainly didn't show it. Most of them were shivering like junkies in anticipation of a fix.

When her turn finally came, Esher smiled as he offered her the chalice. "Drink this, so that we may be bound, blood to blood."

Steeling herself, she lifted the chalice to her lips. It tasted like the finest vintage wine and was as thick and nourishing as mother's milk. She felt it creep through her veins, spreading a warm glow as it went. Nothing could compare to it: not sex, not food, not drink. It was better than all those things, yet was the same as them as well. She closed her eyes and savored the moment, tempted to lose herself in the ecstasy of it all.

She started from her reverie as Esher removed the chalice from her hands and blinked in disorientation as the tourist eagerly took her place in line. She felt almost drugged as she left the stage and rejoined the others on the dance floor. She could feel Esher's blood inside her, humming to itself like a tiny dynamo.

The communion line was near the end when the door slammed open and a tall figure dressed in a scarlet cloak and hood entered the club. The Pointers did not challenge the new arrival, assuming it to be a member of the enclave late in arriving, but the newcomer's carriage made it clear that he was no mere thrall.

"Esher!" thundered a voice from inside the scarlet hood.

The vampire lord halted and peered into the crowd, frowning. "I know that voice. Who calls my name?"

The newcomer pushed back his cowl, revealing shoulder-length honey-blond hair pulled into a loose ponytail and features so classically perfect they could have been the model for a Greek statue. "Has it been so long that the student has forgotten his master?"

Esher stepped forward, his frown deepening. "Caul? They sent you?"

"Who else would they send? I was the one responsible for indoctrinating you into the guild—it is only natural that they should send me to bring you back to Vienna, apostate!"

"Apostate? Surely you jest, old friend! All I do here is for the greater glory of the Tremere!"

"Lie to yourself all you like, Esher! But don't lie to me! What you're doing is not in the name of our clan, Esher—it is a ploy to topple the Council and place yourself in power! You are on the verge of *jyhad*—if you declare war on Sinjon, his fellow Ventrue will feel honor-bound to retaliate against the Tremere in his name! This is neither the time nor the reason to do battle with one of the most powerful clans of the Camarilla, Esher!"

"I assure you, old friend, that was never my intention!"

"Be that as it may, you have broken a sacred tenet of the Tremere in creating the woman Decima. Do not deny parentage, Esher—I can read her lineage as easily as a book!"

"Ours is a long and lonely existence, Caul—and I have been separated from my clansmen for many years. I have created only one childe. Would the Council begrudge me the creation of a single mate?"

"You know the rules, Esher! None of the Tremere are to create progeny on their own! And as for the 'single mate'—what of the woman Bakil?"

A troubled look crossed Esher's face. He had not expected them to know of Decima's predecessor. "She is no more! I learned my lesson with her! I did not induct Decima into the mysteries, as I had Bakil: this I swear. She has no knowledge of the blood arts, so by rights she is not truly Tremere."

"And what of the mortal woman? The dancer called Nikola? Do you not plan to Embrace her as your bride?"

Esher's eyes narrowed and his frown became an angry scowl. "I weary of your questions, Caul! We were friends once—even more than friends—but those nights are gone! There was a time when you were the master, I the student, but I have gone on to claim the power you never dared to. Do not threaten me, Caul—for I will not stay my hand!"

"There is much you must answer for, whether you wish to hear it or not! The Council might overlook the creation of get, provided they are destroyed, but your hubris is another matter entirely! The Tremere value ambition and drive, this is true. But such a naked grab for power is dangerous not only to the clan, but to all Kindred throughout the world! You would risk exposing us all for the sake of making Deadtown your own? The altercation at the restaurant earlier this evening will not go unnoticed, I assure you! There are factions in the Holy See waiting for such evidence of Kindred activity to justify the reordination of the Inquisitors—and you may very well have given the witchfinders their new lease on life!"

"Let the Soldiers of the Question come!" Esher sneered. "They can prick me with their witch-pins all they like!"

Caul shook his head in dismay. "I had hoped that I would be able to talk reason with you, Esher. But I see you will have none of it! Very well—I have no recourse but to bring you back to Austria."

Esher laughed, but there was no humor in his voice. "I will not be judged, Caul! Not by you and not by the Council!"

"Very well," the blond vampire sighed. "Then you leave me no choice."

Caul leapt onto the runway, his movements as fast and smooth as those of a tiger, his hands glowing as if they held live coals. The Pointers and Kindred began pushing for the exits as Esher moved toward his former companion, his fangs bared and red energy crackling from his fingertips.

The blood-wizards lunged at one another, their hands locking onto one another's shoulders. To the uninitiated, it looked as if they were engaged in nothing more than a vigorous bout of Indian wrestling, but the look of pain on the combatants' faces told a different story.

The air inside Dance Macabre grew heavy as the stranger felt her skin prickle, as it does before a lightning strike. There was a crackling sound, like that made by an arc welder going full blast, as a tongue of red energy enveloped the battling wizards. The stranger swore and was forced to cover her eyes. The smell of burning blood clogged her nostrils, making her grimace in disgust. She had heard stories of the Tremere and their occult arts, but she had yet to see blood-magic in action. It was rumored that the adepts could boil their enemies' blood with just a touch, control others with a few drops of their life essence as a charm, or cause hemorrhages and clots with a whispered incantation. As a vampire, she knew the intrinsic power of blood—but she had never seen anything like what was transpiring on the stage.

As Esher and Caul strained against one another, crimson tears began to form in the corners of their eyes and run down their cheeks. As the blood-tears struck the wooden floor of the stage, they hissed. Then blood began to drip from their noses and bubble from their ears.

"Let go, Caul!" Esher growled. "Let go, or I'll boil you like a lobster!"

"Only if you agree to return to Vienna with me!"

Esher's response was to close his eyes, set his chin and push even harder than before. Caul cried out as he was hurled across the stage, sliding the length of the runway on his back. His eyes were gone, the sockets full of blood that bubbled like liquid sugar on the boil. Blood was pouring from his mouth and nose and ears, turning his face to a crimson mask.

There was genuine regret in the vampire lord's manner as Esher stood over his dying friend, wiping the blood from his own face with the back of his hand.

"Why you? Damn them, why did they have to send you? When they send their next proxy, he shall find me ready! I will not be stopped by a handful of ancients!"

Caul chuckled—it made a wet gurgling sound deep in his chest. "You fool," he gasped. "You blind fool. The Tremere need not raise a hand to swat you down. Your doom is upon you, but you cannot see it for what it truly is. You nurse a serpent at your bosom, Esher."

"What do you mean?" Esher glowered, but Caul was beyond responding to questions.

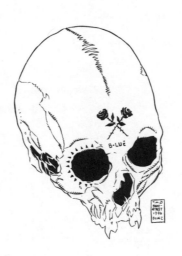

THE FALL OF THE HOUSE OF ESHER

*Suddenly there shot along the path a wild
light, and I turned to see whence a gleam so
unusual would have issued; for the vast house
and its shadows were alone behind me. The
radiance was that of the full, setting, blood-
red moon, which now shone vividly through that
once barely discernible fissure, of which I have
spoken as extending from the roof of the
building, in a zigzag direction, to the base.
While I gazed, this fissure rapidly widened—
there came a fierce breath of the whirlwind—
the entire orb of the satellite burst at once
upon my sight—my brain reeled as I saw the
mighty walls rushing asunder—there was a
long tumultuous shouting sound; like the voice
of a thousand waters—and the deep and dark
tarn at my feet closed sullenly and silent over
the fragments of the "House of Usher".*

— *Edgar Allan Poe*, "The Fall of the House of Usher"

Chapter

9

"Cloudy! Open up! It's me!"

The old hippie's eyes were wide and frightened as he peered past the security chain. "Man, this is getting fuckin' weird, even for Deadtown!" he whispered as the stranger slipped across the threshold.

"Did you get what I asked for?"

"Yeah—they're over there," Cloudy said, pointing to a florist's delivery box. "You've got some strange friends, lady. The woman who ran that freaky all-night flower shop—if I didn't know better, I'd swear she was *green* under all that makeup she was wearing!"

"Gaea's what you might call an Earth Mother," the stranger chuckled. "Has anyone come in or out of the building recently?"

Cloudy nodded, looking like he just swallowed a lemon. "Yeah. That's another piece of high weirdness! This dude was leaving just as me and Ryan were coming back from that errand you sent us on. Big guy. Had to be seven feet tall. Wore a bulky trenchcoat and porkpie hat. Funny thing was, he looked like he was missing an arm. And he had boar's tusks. Other than that, he looked pretty normal."

"Sounds like Mal sent Grendel. Did he say anything to you?"

"No, but he gave Ryan the fish-eye. Kind of like the way a dog does a piece of steak. Fucker gave me the creeps."

"Yeah, well, you should see his old lady. Excuse me a minute, Cloudy. I need to go upstairs and check on something."

Cloudy frowned and tugged on his beard. "You said things were gonna be comin' down fast—"

"The wheels of the juggernaut are in motion, Cloudy, and I'm doing my best to see that none of us are crushed beneath them, that's all I can tell you," she said as he unlocked the door.

She returned a few minutes later, carrying her gym bag. She knelt amid the jumble of books and removed several sheaves of neatly bound hundred-dollar bills, stacking them on the floor next to her.

Cloudy whistled in astonishment and bent to pick up one of the stacks. "Jesus Christ on a sea beach!"

"I need you to stash this for me until I get back," she said.

"No prob!"

The stranger removed the bouquet of black roses from their container. She frowned at the long stems for a moment, then used her switchblade to trim them back to a manageable length before stuffing them inside her gym bag. Several thorns punctured the flesh of her hands as she worked, but she did not seem to notice the blood dripping from her wounds.

"Where's Ryan?" she asked as she strode toward the kitchen.

"Here I am!" the boy chirped, sticking his head out from under the sink.

"You're supposed to be asleep!" Cloudy chided.

"But I might miss something!"

"That's the point," the stranger said as she opened the refrigerator. She took out one of the plastic plasma containers and shook it. She glanced down at the boy, who was watching her with rapt attention. "Kid, you don't want to see me do this."

"Yes I do!"

"*Ryan!*" Cloudy barked. The child's head promptly disappeared back under the sink.

The stranger snapped the seal on the container and upended it, chugging the chilled plasma like a blue-collar worker in a beer commercial. The blood was nourishing, but little else. Compared to life taken directly from the vein, the bottled stuff was bland and stale. The difference between the two was that between Dom Perignon and generic beer. When she finished, she licked her lips like a cat after a bowl of milk, then turned to find Cloudy watching her with ill-disguised disgust. Embarrassed, he quickly looked away. She pretended not to notice.

"There's less than an hour before the sun comes up," she said as she picked up her gym bag. "Look for me come the dawn."

"And what if you don't show up?"

"Take the money and the boy and get the hell out of Deadtown and never come back."

♋

Obeah sat and stared sourly at the TV set. Normally he played cards with Webb when things were dull, or they swapped sleep shifts. But Webb was no more—his brains now decorating the street he had spent most of his short life on—and Obeah was without anyone to talk to or play cards with. He grimaced as pain shot up his leg from his shattered kneecap. Cursing under his breath, he pulled a prescription bottle out of his shirt pocket and popped a couple of Dilaudids. Obeah hoped he could get a handle on the pain before his supply ran out.

The Pointers had knocked over a pharmaceutical warehouse a week or two back, to replenish the supplies in the gang's makeshift "infirmary." Unfortunately, most of the boys involved in the heist weren't rocket scientists, so they only made off with a few bottles of actual pills—the rest of the haul consisted of morphine sulfate suppositories. He could always dip into his mojo bag if things got to be too much, but he needed his wits about him, and besides—zombie dust could fuck you up bad if you weren't careful. Obeah picked up the remote and began channel surfing. One of the perks of being Nikola's bodyguard was satellite TV. He particularly liked Nick At Nite and the Sci-Fi Channel.

Another surge of pain made him curse Esher, but not loud enough for anyone—or anything—that might be lurking to hear. Esher was the only man he respected and feared more than he had Papa Doc. After all, Papa only played at being a servant of Baron Samedi, the Lord of Cemeteries. Esher was the real thing.

Although he had been in the Tontons Macoute, Obeah was not a native-born Haitian. He had been born and raised in New Orleans, the son of an illiterate dock worker. His mother came from Haiti as a young girl, to find her fortune in the white man's world. What she found was a job as a laundress. An intensely proud woman, she told her only son stories of the land she had left behind. In the mid-sixties Obeah received a draft notice inviting him to Viet Nam. Unwilling to fight the white man's war, he left the United States for his mother's homeland—and soon found himself embroiled in the voodoo societies, which in turn led to gainful employment with Papa Doc's secret police force.

In the years been 1968 and 1986, when Baby Doc fled his homeland for France, Obeah had been responsible for so many murders, mutilations, rapes and beatings he'd given up count. On one foray he and his fellow Tontons Macoute had stormed an opposition party meeting and hacked the arms off everyone in the house—men, women and children alike—then piled them in the street for the neighbors to see. He remembered how he'd laughed at the sight of the fingers on some of the freshly severed limbs twitching spasmodically, as if trying to wave bye-bye. Those had been good days.

Now he was in the country he'd turned his back on nearly thirty years ago. The last ten years had been rough—with Baby Doc gone, the citizenry of Port-au-Prince he had helped terrorize for so long suddenly found themselves free to exact revenge. The upshot of which was that Obeah discovered himself out of a job and his home burned to the ground. Although General Avril seized power in 1988, it did him little good, as he and Avril had clashed several times in the past. Fearing for his safety, Obeah fled Haiti—ironically enough, he had hidden among the thousands of boat people struggling to make it to Florida in leaky tubs cobbled together out of little more than desperation and sealing wax.

Things had changed quite a bit in America during his absence. His parents were dead, his father crushed by a runaway freight container and his mother from washing other people's clothes. There wasn't much call for a professional death squad leader, so Obeah became a professional killer—and a conjure man on the side.

Then, a few years back, he met Esher. The minute the white man walked into the *botanica* that served as the front for his death-for-hire business, Obeah recognized him for what he was. You didn't traffic with the Invisibles for twenty years and not come to develop a feeling for the Unseen World. The vampire lord was in the market for a human enforcer with knowledge of the occult, and Obeah came highly recommended. Two years ago he teamed up with Webb, and he and the younger white man did most of the dirty deeds that needed doing. Then, six months ago, Esher assigned them to be his new bride's bodyguards.

It was a cushy job, mostly. They spent most of their time in the brownstone that served as Nikola's safe-house, watching TV or playing cards or swapping bullshit. It wasn't like the bitch did anything. At least not anymore. The first few weeks she kept trying to escape, and when it became obvious she wasn't going to be able to do that, she tried killing herself a couple of times. That's when Esher told him to start dosing her with the zombie-dust. After that, their job became even easier than before. Which suited Obeah just fine. Webb, being younger, tended to get restless and resented the monotony, but Obeah was of an age where constant danger and action had lost most of its appeal. Still, Esher did send them out, now and again, on those errands he could trust no one else with, such as the business with Dario Borges.

He checked his watch and frowned. It was time for him to check on the bitch. He tried to lever himself out of the easy chair with the length of pipe he was using as a staff, but the pain shooting up his leg made him cry out and drop back. Fuck it. The bitch wasn't going anywhere.

He hoped Esher would find someone competent to replace Webb, but he doubted it. The Five Points Gang was the biggest bunch of scrambleheaded fuckups he'd ever dealt with. Compared to his homeys back on the island, they were a bunch of snot-nosed kids in baggy pants and expensive sneakers playing at being bad. Every now and again one of the punks would try and make his bones by messing with the witch doctor, to show everyone what a bad mother he really was. It always ended with the punk getting a taste of machete. If he was lucky he just lost a nose or an ear. The little fuckers were like a cottonmouth snake: you had to stand on their collective neck every second so they wouldn't whip around and bite you. Most of them were too whacked to be of any use except as cannon fodder. He didn't trust any of them to wipe their ass, much less watch his back. Webb had been more than a little nuts, but at least it had been bad-ass nuts.

He grimaced and took a swallow from the bottle of Olde English tucked between him and the upholstery of the chair. Things were going to shit and fast. Esher was losin' it, big time. He still had the juice to make things happen. If anything, he was more powerful now than he'd ever been. No, that wasn't the problem. The problem was pussy. Esher wasn't thinking straight on account of that bitch Nikola. And for what? Whatever happened after she got snatched, it sure as fuck did a number on her. Granted, she still was pretty fine in the looks department, but she wasn't twenty-five anymore. She couldn't even pass for thirty. Plus, it was clear there was no way in hell Esher was going to be able to scrub that kid out of her mind. If she responded that strongly tonight, after a steady diet of dust, then she was never going to give that part of herself up. If it was his call to make, he'd walk into that bedroom of hers and pop a cap in her fuckin' skull and get it over with. But that would be a fool thing to do. After all, he'd signed a contract with the vampire-wizard in his own blood. And he knew what happened to those who reneged on their contracts.

Fear for his life aside, Obeah prided himself on his loyalty. And despite the pain and humiliation he'd suffered at Esher's hands, he still held the man in awe. Besides, he had come too far to abandon his liege-lord now. He was too old to be anything except what he'd always been—a killer. A taste for brutality and an inborn obedience to the biggest dog with the strongest teeth had been part of him all his life. His soul was the devil's, part and parcel, just as his mama said, and it was too late to try and backpedal on the deal he'd made. He was in until the end—be it his or Esher's.

He glanced over to where Webb normally sat and shifted uneasily. There was something bothering him about the kidnapping, something that he couldn't quite put his finger on. Still, it nagged at the back of his brain like a popcorn shell wedged between his teeth. He couldn't shake the feeling that he was missing something. The last he saw of Webb was the soles of his boots as he was yanked from the moving car's window. But there was something else, wasn't there? Something he saw but did not see.

He'd always been in awe of and worried by the Kindred ability to ghostwalk. That was why Decima usually rode with them to and from the safe-house. Although humans normally couldn't see a vampire while it was ghostwalking, another vampire could. That was why the only time they were really bodyguards was during the drive in the Batmobile.

But Obeah had personally spoken with the *guede*, the spirits of the dead, and been ridden by the *loa*, the god-forces of ancient Africa. A man does not undergo such experiences and remain the same as other men. The gods leave something of themselves behind—a heightened awareness, a touch of second sight, that the *bokor* could call upon in times of need. He knew now that he had seen something in the moments just before and after the crash, but what?

Obeah reached down and caressed the handle of his machete. The weapon leaned against the right side of the chair, balanced on its edge so it was within easy reach. The handle was of finest mahogany and had been presented to him in a special ceremony by Papa Doc himself. It was Obeah's most prized possession.

There was a knock on the door. Obeah grimaced and glanced at his watch again. It was nearly sunrise, so whatever was on the other side probably was human. Grimacing in pain, he pulled himself out of the chair, doing his best to keep from losing his balance or blacking out. The makeshift splint did little to help his mobility. He hobbled toward the door as the pounding grew louder, his machete clutched in one hand, a 9mm semiautomatic complete with a clip of phosphorus bullets tucked into his waistband.

"I'm coming! Keep your shirt on!" he grumbled. Obeah put his eye to the spyhole set in the door and grunted in surprise. The visitor was Kindred—the new one with the sunglasses. Esher rarely sent vampires to the safe-house. It was kind of like posting bears to guard the honeycomb.

Scowling suspiciously, Obeah threw back the five deadbolts and opened the door, although he left on the two-inch-thick security chain.

"Whatchoo want?" he growled

"Esher sent me. It's an emergency!" She held up a gym bag at eye level. "I'm supposed to give her some elixir he whipped up that'll reverse the aging. She has to receive it before the dawn."

"How come he didn't call first to tell me you were coming?"

"Your cellular phone got trashed in the crash—remember?"

"Sorry. I forgot." Satisfied, Obeah removed the chain and let the stranger in. She glanced around the front parlor and kitchen as Obeah relocked the door.

"Where's Nikola?"

"Asleep in her bedroom," Obeah grunted, pointing at the door at the other end of the parlor.

"They find a replacement for Webb yet?" she asked as she moved ahead of him into the apartment.

"No. Not yet."

"Shame. You need a partner on a detail like this." She turned as she said that, and there was something in the way her body moved that triggered a memory deep within Obeah's brain. He was back on the street, sprawled among the busted safety glass. There was blood in his face, blood in his mouth, blood in his eyes. As he lay there, suspended between the boundary of the conscious and unconscious worlds, he looked up through a scrim of red pain—and saw something hovering over him. Something blurred about the edges, like a well-thumbed photograph. The impression he had, before the darkness claimed him, was that the thing had eyes of mirrored glass.

"*You!* It was *you!*" he bellowed as he swung the machete.

The stranger raised her left hand to block the blow, growling like an angered panther. She was on him in less than a heartbeat, knocking the machete out of his hand with her gym bag. Obeah screamed in pain as he fell to the floor, his injured leg pinned under him. The stranger quickly stood with one boot planted on the *bokor's* throat, the heel resting on his larynx. She plucked the 9mm from his waistband and checked the clip, then slapped it back into place.

She glanced down at Obeah, who was struggling to breathe and pray to his gods. She was tempted to drain him—the plasma she'd consumed earlier did little more than whet her appetite—but she didn't want to leave any evidence behind of a Kindred kill. It was better for Esher to think it the handiwork of a Black Spoons hit team.

She removed her boot from Obeah's neck and flipped him over onto his belly with a single kick. Although the pain must have been immense, all he could manage was a low, despairing moan. Obeah had been on enough death squads to know what would happen next. His last thought before the bullet entered the back of his skull was that he wished he could tell his mother he was sorry for disappointing her.

The stranger walked to the door of Nikola's bedroom. She tried the knob and found it was unlocked. "Nikola?"

No answer.

She entered cautiously.

The interior of the room was utterly dark, since the windows were painted opaque and all light-fixtures had been removed. Apparently Esher wanted his bride to grow accustomed to her forthcoming exile from the sun. The lack of light meant nothing to the stranger, since she could see as clearly as if it were high noon—even with her shades on. The darkened room was decorated completely in white—white plush rugs, white curtains, white vanity table, white dresser and chiffarobe. And curled in the middle of the circular king-size bed, with the white satin sheets and bedspread pulled around her like a cocoon, was Nikola.

The stranger set her gym bag down on the floor at the foot of the bed and nudged the mound under the sheets. "Nikola—? Wake up."

The lump under the covers made a noise and squirmed slightly, as if trying to crawl away, then went still. The stranger grabbed the edge of the mattress and tilted it, rolling Nikola out of the bed and onto the floor. She lay there, naked except for a pair of white lace panties, her head lolling back and forth like a doll's.

"Time t'dance awreddddy?" she moaned, peering groggily through sleep-swollen eyes.

The stranger grabbed her by the wrist and dragged her to her feet. "C'mon,

Nikola! It's time to go! I'm busting you out of here!" She strode to the chiffarobe, pulling the drugged woman behind her like a toy on a string, and began tossing clothes onto the bed. She let go of Nikola's hand and opened the gym bag, removing the dozen black roses. She tossed the bouquet onto the bed, so that it landed near the headboard. She stuffed a few pieces of Nikola's wardrobe into the bag, then turned to speak to the dancer— only to find Nikola slumped on the floor, curled in a fetal position. She knelt beside her and shook her shoulders vigorously.

"Nikola—c'mon! You can do better than this! You've got to! Do you want Ryan to see you this way?"

"*Ryan?*" Her eyelids flickered and she raised her head weakly. "Ryan's here?"

"No, but if you want to see him, you have to do as I say, Nikola. Do you want to be with Ryan?"

"*Yesss.*"

"Then prove it to me. Get up and get dressed."

The dancer struggled to her feet. She was wobbly, but otherwise focused. She pulled a one-piece white satin dress with a plunging neckline over her head, then stepped into a pair of white stiletto heels. Once she was dressed, the stranger took her by the hand and led her into the parlor. Nikola blinked at the sunlight flooding the room and raised a pale hand to her face. The skin around her eyes was puffy and purplish-pink, and tears streamed down her cheeks as she blinked rapidly. It was the first time she'd seen daylight in months.

The stranger steered her around Obeah's body and toward the door. If Nikola noticed her former bodyguard's corpse, she didn't respond. Nor did she show any emotion upon spotting the half-dozen Pointers sprawled on the sidewalk and stairs.

"Where's Ryan?" Nikola asked, looking up and down the street.

"He's waiting for you at a friend's house."

"Jesus," whispered Cloudy as he caught sight of Nikola. He stood aside and let the stranger tow her charge into the apartment.

"Mama!" Ryan squealed. He scampered out from under the sink and literally jumped into his mother's arms. Nikola staggered under the weight, but did not fall. She returned her son's hug, burying her face in his hair.

Cloudy leaned over and whispered, "Are you *sure* that's the right woman?"

"Sure as I'm standing here."

"What the hell happened to her? I mean—she looks like she's aged ten years!"

The stranger coughed into her fist and looked a little embarrassed. "That's because she has. I made the mistake of taking her with me when I went into overdrive. I knew Celerity was stressful on Kindred systems, but I never dreamed it would—anyway, the upshot was that she literally aged a year or more for every minute I spent ghostwalking. I wish I could undo the damage, but there's nothing that can be done."

"You lost me on that one, lady," Cloudy said shaking his head. "I thought living in Deadtown was strange enough—but since I've met you, you've introduced me to several new flavors of weird!"

"Cloudy! Cloudy! This is my mom!" Ryan held his mother's hand and reached out to his friend with the other.

Cloudy tried to smile and stepped forward, extending his hand to Nikola, who was staring at him like a doe at a watering hole. "Pleased to meet you, ma'am. Ryan's done nothing but talk about you since I met him. My name's Edward McLeod."

"You—you've been looking after my boy?"

"When he lets me."

Nikola smiled then, and something of the woman she must have been glimmered in her eyes. She took Cloudy's hand and leaned in to kiss his cheek. "Thank you for taking care of him. How can I repay you for what you've done?"

"You don't have to, ma'am. I did what I felt I had to, nothing more. Karma, y'know?"

"Look, I hate to break up the happy reunion, but there's not much time left," announced the stranger. "If we're going to smuggle you out of Deadtown, it has to be when the Kindred are down for the day and the majority of their human servitors aren't up and about yet. Which means we've only got an hour or two at the most." She turned to Cloudy. "Where's the money I left with you for safekeeping?"

Cloudy disappeared among the haphazard stacks of old books and returned a moment later, lugging an Oxford English Dictionary. He flipped open the cover to reveal the hollow interior and the money stashed inside. "I always figured a thief would never think of looking in a book—much less a dictionary," he grinned.

The stranger unzipped the gym bag and began stuffing the money in along with Nikola's clothes. "I got three hundred thou for the cocaine I ripped off from Esher. I'm giving you a hundred thousand cash. I figure that's enough to get you as far from Deadtown as possible and set you up in a new life. One where you won't have to worry about where your next paycheck's coming from for a long time and you don't have to work at night and leave Ryan by himself. I'm giving Cloudy fifty for his trouble—that okay with you, man?"

"You don't hear me complaining!"

"Didn't think I would. The rest I'm keeping for myself. I don't do this crap for free, y'know."

Nikola looked at the contents of the bag and back up at the stranger. She seemed stunned, but it was hard to tell if it was because of the money or the drugs in her system. She blinked and shook her head, as if trying to wake herself. "Why are you doing this? Why are you helping me?"

The stranger's mirrored gaze dropped to Ryan's upturned face, then to her boots. "Maybe it's because—you remind me of someone I used to know. Someone who needed help once—and there was no one there to give it."

Nikola looked at the stranger for a long moment, then glanced at her son, smoothing his hair back from his pale, wide brow. "I owe you my life, my soul—and my son. May God bless you for all you've done."

The stranger's smile was thin as a paper cut. "I'm afraid that's out of the question."

"Jumpin' Jesus—! When did you do that?" blurted Cloudy.

The stranger glanced down at her left hand—and noticed for the first time that she was missing her entire left pinkie and ring finger up to the second joint. She splayed her fingers, studying the wound. She had to give Obeah credit—the machete was so sharp and his slice so quick, she never even realized he'd landed a blow.

"Doesn't that *hurt?*" Cloudy asked, his face scrunched into a sympathetic grimace.

"Pain means different things to different people. In my case, my threshold is exceptionally high."

"No shit!"

"We don't have the time to waste on something as minor as this," she said with a dismissive wave of her maimed hand. We need to get this show on the road."

"But you're missing two fingers—!" Cloudy protested.

"It's nothing that won't grow back! What's important right now, however, is getting Nikola and Ryan out of Deadtown." She turned to Nikola, who was still staring at the money in the gym bag. "Do you have any idea where you want to go?"

"I-I have family in San Luis Obispo. My sister lives there."

"Good. San Luis Obispo it is." The stranger turned to Cloudy. "You should go with them. Deadtown won't be safe for you. There's a good chance it won't even exist after tonight."

Cloudy shook his head. "I can't leave. This is my home."

Ryan pulled away from his mother and grabbed one of Cloudy's big, callused hands. "You're going to come live with us, aren't you, Cloudy?"

The old hippie smiled sadly and knelt so that he and Ryan were eye-to-eye. "I'm really touched that you made the offer, kid. Really. But I can't go with you. This is where I belong. Maybe someday soon I'll come out and visit you and your mom—would you like that?"

Ryan threw his arms around his friend's neck and began to sob. Cloudy pulled the boy close to him, trying not to crush his frail body as he hugged him.

"Cloudy—the time," the stranger said, her voice soft but urgent.

He nodded his understanding and reluctantly let go of Ryan. "She's right. You better go, kid." He wiped the heel of his palm under his eyes, struggling to keep smiling in front of the boy. "But before you do, there's something I want you to have." He turned and dipped into the jumble of books that surrounded them with the unerring grace of a heron pulling a fish from a pond. He held out a much-thumbed hardback copy of *Make Way For Ducklings* to Ryan. "Here—something to read on the plane." Still sniffling back his tears, Ryan took the proffered book and clutched it to his narrow chest like a holy shield.

The stranger stood by the door, tapping her foot anxiously until Nikola and Ryan joined her. Then, with the simple turn of a deadbolt lock, they were out on the street. Nikola hesitated on the threshold for a long moment, clutching the gym bag as she blinked at the sun, until the stranger grabbed her wrist and pulled her out of the doorway.

In the early morning light, Deadtown almost looked normal. Or as normal as any other forgotten inner-city neighborhood. The Kindred who ruled its streets were curled up in their various underground burrows, while their human servants slumbered in their squalid squats, leaving the streets to those who had always called Deadtown home. Most of the residents were old— like the ancient woman in the shapeless raincoat and black babushka pushing a decrepit two-wheeled market-cart ahead of her. Others were junkies or alcoholics, shivering in the sunlight as they made their way to a rendezvous with their dealer or the nearest liquor store, like the rail-thin older man dressed in a filthy clerical collar—no doubt the elusive phantom she'd glimpsed haunting the bell tower. As the trio drew closer, the priest rapidly crossed himself and scurried to the other side of the street, clutching a paper sack under his arm.

As Nikola, Ryan and the stranger hurried along, those few citizens they happened across reacted in much the same way as the priest. At first they seemed surprised to see a child; then, upon spotting the stranger, the surprise became open fear, and they quickly averted their eyes, visibly shaken by the sight of a monster braving the sun.

Not that she was enjoying her little morning stroll. Although she could walk in daylight without fear of death, it wasn't a pleasant experience. She was tired and her body cried out for regeneration. The bright light was giving her a migraine and her skin felt as if an army of fleas were happily snacking on her.

But the further they got from the cancerous heart of Deadtown, the more people they saw on the street, as if the blight that afflicted the neighborhood weakened with every passing block. Without warning, they turned a corner and emerged into a busy downtown area, filled with bicycle messengers, honking cabs, and harried-looking men in suits and women in dress jackets.

Nikola shivered and turned to look back the way they'd come. "Was it always that easy to leave?" she asked.

"It's always that easy and always that hard to leave places like Deadtown," the stranger replied. "Come, you're not safe yet—not until we've gotten you to the West Coast." She stepped out into traffic and slammed her hands onto the hood of a passing taxi, bringing it to a full stop. The cabbie looked more spooked than angered, since he hadn't put his foot on the brake.

"Wh-where to, lady?" he stammered as the stranger, Nikola and Ryan climbed into the back seat.

"The airport," the stranger snapped.

"What airline?"

"Any of them. All of them. Just go!"

The ride to the airport was uneventful. Ryan sat with his nose pressed against the window, wondering aloud at landmarks he'd never seen before in a city he had lived his entire life in. When they arrived at the airport departure zone, the stranger paid off the driver with a hundred-dollar bill. The cabbie mumbled his thanks and peeled away as fast as he could.

"I don't think he liked what he saw in his rear-view mirror," the stranger said with a dry laugh. "But a fare's a fare, right?"

They entered the main terminal and scanned the bank of video screens until Nikola spotted a flight into Los Angeles that was scheduled to leave in a couple of hours. The stranger hung back and watched Nikola go to the ticket counter and talk to the booking agent. After a few minutes she came back, waving a pair of boarding passes. Although she was smiling, she still looked painfully wan, like Camille on a day-trip.

"I managed to get us on the next flight! They're first class, though."

"Hey, you can afford it," the stranger said with a shrug.

"I need to call my sister and tell her we're coming."

"I'll watch Ryan for you while you're on the phone."

The stranger waited until Nikola was at the payphone before turning to face the boy. She dropped down onto one knee and touched him lightly on the collarbone. "Ryan, you're going to have to look after your mom. She's been through a lot. She's going to need you to help her try and get back to how she was before—and that might take a long, long time."

"Is she gonna stay old?"

"I wouldn't call your mom old," the stranger smiled crookedly. "But, yes— she'll stay like she is. Which might be a good thing, really. They say the older you get, the wiser you become."

"Is that true?"

"For some people, yes. But I want you to remember, no matter what happens to you and your mom in the future, only one thing matters: Esher couldn't make her stop loving you. He did everything he could to scrub away her past and make her like him—but she wouldn't give you up. That's what kept her human all this time."

"I know," Ryan said, his voice so soft it was almost lost in the background noise of the terminal. He looked solemnly into the stranger's mirrored eyes. "Will I see you again?"

The stranger shrugged as she stood up, patting the boy on the head. "Who knows, kid? I've got a few good years left to me, and I travel quite a bit. Maybe someday I'll find myself in your neck of the woods. Look—here comes your mom."

Nikola was smiling even broader than before, her eyes gleaming with a manic sparkle. "I managed to get hold of my sister. I gave her our flight information and she'll be there to meet us at LAX! You've never met your Aunt Kate, have you, Ryan?"

The boy shook his head.

"She's got a son—your Cousin Jeremy—that's a year or two older than you that you can play with. He'll be your friend."

"Cloudy's my friend," Ryan said, glancing down at the copy of *Make Way For Ducklings* he was carrying.

"Well, he'll be your new friend," Nikola said, her smile suddenly growing brittle.

The stranger handed a fistful of quarters to Ryan. "You've got some time to kill before the flight. Why don't you go to that video arcade over there? Here, knock yourself out."

Ryan tucked his book under one arm and eagerly accepted the offered quarters, scurrying across the concourse much like he had the streets of Deadtown.

"He's a wonderful kid," the stranger said, as she watched the boy plunk his money into one of the video games. "You're very lucky, Nikola."

"I know."

The stranger turned so that her mirrored gaze was focused directly on the dancer. Her voice lost its previously easygoing tone, becoming as hard and unyielding as tempered steel. "Get this straight: I didn't do any of this for you. I did it for Ryan. And if word gets back to me that you've let that child down in any way—I'll come looking for you. You don't want that. Have I made myself understood?"

Nikola's face drained of what little color it possessed. She nodded dumbly, her eyes never leaving the stranger's sunglasses.

"Mom! Mom! Come look!" Ryan called out as he hopped up and down excitedly in front of the game controls.

The stranger glanced over the boy's shoulder at a pair of computer-animated dinosaurs kicking the shit out of each other, sending sprays of pixillated blood flying in every direction.

"Cool."

The stranger slid into the back of a waiting cab with a weary sigh. She'd done her duty. She'd seen Nikola and Ryan off to California. She glanced through the window at the 747 soaring overhead. She wondered if Ryan was preoccupied with the wonders of the first-class cabin or if he was staring out the window, trying to catch one last glimpse of the world he once knew.

She shouldn't have tampered with Nikola's mind like she did, but she really couldn't find it in her to feel that bad about it. So what if she reached inside Nikola's brain and tweaked the volume on her sense of responsibility a few notches? It wasn't like she was telling her to go out and become a highway sniper. The woman had the maternal instinct and genuine love to make a decent mother—but there was also her chronic poor judgment and tendency for weakness. Esher had recognized those traits from the beginning and preyed on them. Something told her he wasn't the first to do so—but he was certainly the most monstrous.

Come nightfall Nikola and Ryan would be safe and sound in her sister's home in San Luis Obispo. They'd be facing a new world, one free—at least on the surface—from bloodsucking monsters, while she, on the other hand, would be trying to drain the swamp while up to her ass in alligators.

She grimaced and fought the urge to scratch the stump of her left pinkie. The damn things always itched like hell when they grew back.

Chapter

10

Esher emerged from his hibernation, his thoughts racing at much the same speed as when he last closed his eyes against the coming dawn. The events of the night before remained fresh in his mind. He would have to move quickly if he was to secure his position against Sinjon and the Council. Of the two, the Council was his greater concern. Although he was confident in his abilities as a wizard, there was but one of him. However, he had crafted numerous spells and contracts over the years, and he was not without his friends in low places, so to speak. While he might not be able to overthrow the Council of Vienna, he had no doubt that he could successfully defy them.

These were his thoughts as he climbed out of his casket to greet the evening. The coffin was specially designed so that the side was on a hinge and would drop away when the lid was unlocked and lifted from the inside. As he climbed out, Esher reflected on how he would soon need to requisition a larger version, so that Nikola might sleep alongside him. Granted, her inexplicable aging had confused and angered him, but the passion he felt for the pale dancer remained as before.

He was at a loss to explain his obsession with the human, even to himself.

But that is how it has always been with Kindred and their consorts. The fascination burns bright and strong, and although it is not true love, it gives off enough light and heat to pass for the real thing. Only during these passing moments of mad fancy did Esher feel alive. There was a time, long decades past, when he had been similarly obsessed with Decima—and Bakil.

Esher did not like thinking about Bakil. She was his first progeny—and his greatest mistake. He did not like dwelling on the errors of his past. Perhaps what bothered him most was how her visage would sometimes come to him unbidden, in a moment's quiet. In life she had been a beer-hall songstress, singing for pennies in the Bowery's rowdy houses. Her name had not been Bakil then—that was the name she took upon her resurrection, to symbolize her break with the world of the living. In those days she went by the name of Black Nan. Her hair was black as a raven's wing; and her skin, when scrubbed of the coal-dust and filth of the Lower East Side, was as white as the flesh of an apple. It was her voice, however, that first drew him to her. He was walking down the crowded sidewalks, in 1879, searching for that evening's prey, when he heard what sounded like an angel lost among the damned. He went in and out of the myriad dives lining the street until he came to one with straw and sawdust spread across the floor to sop up the beer, vomit and blood that might be spilled. And there, amid the squalor, he found an eleven-year-old girl standing on the bar and singing for the pennies pitched her way by drunken miscreants, while her father stood by, drinking what meager wages she earned as quickly as he could. The sodden oaf was eager to pimp her to any taker for the price of a bottle of rotgut.

That very evening Esher killed the wretched father and took Black Nan as his bride-to-be. But he made the mistake of attempting to make her his equal. In the six years she spent with him, traveling the world, he taught her the mysteries of the Tremere, as Caul had once instructed him. It proved a near-fatal mistake, as Bakil—decades later—attempted to turn her magics against him. She'd become enamored of a human male and wished to make him hers, but Esher had forbidden it. She remained adamant, so he killed the human. Enraged, she challenged him. So he destroyed her, in much the same way he'd rid himself of Caul the night before.

That was 1910. It was sixty years before he dared try his hand at creating another offspring—the result of which was Decima. But he'd learned his lesson. Decima was reborn into the eternal world of the Kindred ignorant of the crimson mysteries that gave the Tremere their power. Decima had been a grubby little hippie chick when he first met her, a troubled young girl from a middle-class suburban family, on the run from—or to—something she could not describe. Under his ministrations she'd blossomed from a flower child into a moon child, and for a few years he was satisfied.

Until he saw Nikola.

Something about the way she moved when she danced triggered a possessive madness in him unknown since the night he first heard Bakil sing. Perhaps by Embracing those touched by the muse, he was Embracing that which was lost to him. But no. That would imply weakness. Regret. And a prince of the Kindred may never know such things. Or so he told himself.

Which is why he disliked thinking of Bakil.

Better to busy his mind with other, more pressing business. Such as how to repair the damage done by last night's misadventures. His original plan was to act as a mercenary for the Borges Brothers—thereby avoiding the proscriptions against *jyhad*. He had intended to present the druglords with the stolen narcotics tonight as a gesture of good faith, but with the Borgeses dead that no longer mattered. Still, four kilos of cocaine was not without its uses. He could easily convert it to pay for more weapons and ammunition. After all, incendiary bullets did not come cheap, even in volume.

He caressed the lid of the antique black lacquer Chinese box. The sides of the box were decorated by what at first looked to be red orchids, but on closer inspection proved to be ornately stylized bats—the Chinese symbol for luck and fruitfulness. Gripping the golden handle shaped like a grinning luck dragon atop the lid, Esher opened the box, and found himself looking into its empty interior. Empty, that is, except for a lavender lace hanky.

Esher's rage was so immense it exhibited itself as the utmost calm as he reached inside the box and removed the fragile handkerchief. He did not need to sniff its scent to guess the identity of its owner. The Masonic symbol embroidered in lieu of a monogram told him to whom it belonged. There was a knock on his door and Decima entered, the wound dealt her by the brat's crucifix still pulsing a raw, angry red. Esher quickly closed his hand about the handkerchief.

"Milord, the Batmobile's been repaired, as you commanded."

"Excellent. Go and escort Lady Nikola back here. I would like the enclave to assemble before me tonight!"

Decima raised an eyebrow in surprise. "So soon?"

"Do not question me!" he snapped. "Just do it! Put out the word!"

"As you wish, milord," she muttered, withdrawing.

Esher opened his fist and glowered at the hanky. He stuffed it inside his pocket as he strode through the contorted halls in the direction of the audience chamber. As he entered, a thin, nondescript vampire with lank hair and the clothes of an office worker awaited him, fidgeting nervously.

"Yes, what is it—?" he growled.

"Wilfred."

"Very well, what is it, Wilford?"

"We, uh, we found Torgo, milord."

"Indeed," he sighed as he dropped into his chair of office. "And what is his excuse for being gone these last few days?"

"H-he's dead, milord."

"Of course he's dead! He's one of us!"

Wilfred grimaced and trembled even harder than before. "No, milord— Final Death. We found him—or what was left of him—stuffed under one of the sofas in the barracks. He was pretty, uh, ripe before anyone discovered him."

"Torgo—dead? How?"

"We're not sure, milord. Like I said, there wasn't much left. But it looks like either Gangrel claws or some kind of enchantment."

Esher leaned back in his chair, his brow furrowed in thought. What was it Caul had told him before death claimed him one final time? *"You nurse a serpent at your bosom, Esher."*

"Milord!" The doors to the audience chamber flew open and Decima ran in, looking highly agitated. In her free hand she held a bouquet of black

roses, tied with a purple satin ribbon. *"Milord! Sinjon has taken the Lady Nikola!"*

"What!?!"

"I went to pick up Nikola, as you requested—but when the car pulled up to the curb I saw bodies. The Pointers assigned to guard the stairway were sprawled along the sidewalk and in the gutter! Judging from the flies, I'd say they'd been lying there all day. Inside the building I found Obeah dead as well—the back of his head blown off. The Lady Nikola was missing—and these were left on her bed!"

"So—it is to be *jyhad*, after all?" Esher said, taking the dozen black roses from her. "At least the old reptile has saved me the embarrassment of having to proclaim it myself! You see this, don't you?" He waved the bouquet at Decima. *"He* is the one who hurled down the gauntlet—not I! He is the aggressor—I am merely protecting myself!"

"Of course, milord."

"Was there anything else—a note of any kind?"

"There was no letter—but I did find something. They were under Obeah's body." Decima reached inside her leather jacket and retrieved a pair of neatly severed fingers—a left pinkie and half of a ring finger. She held them out to Esher, who took the pinkie and sniffed it like a cigar. He then licked the bloody stump and frowned.

"My blood runs through the veins of the owner. Whoever did this is Kindred."

"I could have told you it was an inside job," Decima sneered. "The door to the apartment wasn't forced. Obeah opened it of his own free will. Which means he recognized whoever was on the other side. Those fingers came from a woman—and I'm betting it's that mirror-eyed bitch you're so fond of."

Esher's frown deepened into a scowl. Decima was right. All the evidence fit. The stranger was the last one to see Torgo "alive"—she was the one trusted to watch over Nikola—she was the one left alone in the stronghold. He wondered how she could have pulled off the second abduction so close to sunrise, but apparently she was far more resourceful than even he had realized.

Esher took the fingers and wrapped them carefully in the lavender hanky, then tucked them in his pocket. He was calm and deliberate in his motions. Very calm. When he finished he looked up at Decima, who stood awaiting his orders like an eager hound.

"Bring the stranger to me," he said. His voice was very, very calm.

Decima licked her lips, displaying both her fangs and the surgical steel piercing in her tongue. "As you command, sire."

The stranger cursed her altruistic streak as she rolled off the filthy mattress. So this is what she got for trying to help somebody out—a head full of damp cotton and lead in her joints. She glanced down at her wounded hand and scowled. Her ring finger was back, but her left pinkie looked like a well-used pencil eraser. That what she'd been afraid of—she didn't get enough sleep to regenerate properly. She knew she was pushing herself too hard—but she had no alternative. She either had to keep pace or become caught in the gears of the machine.

As much as she hated admitting it, a little fresh blood would help wake her up and give her back that all-important edge. She could either prey on one of the myriad Pointers or Black Spoons that wandered Deadtown, or she could avail herself of the feeders at Dance Macabre. She would draw less attention to herself that way—but she could not bring herself to consider it a viable option. She wasn't like those giggling monsters flocking to Esher's banner. At least, that's what she kept telling herself. But then—she had his blood inside her, now. That's probably where the idea about the feeders had come from, in the first place.

Since she'd given Nikola her gym bag, she now kept what few possessions she had with her in a crumpled paper sack. She picked through the jumble of dirty and clean clothes, finally yanking a Stooges T-shirt out of the confusion. She discarded the shirt she was wearing—it had both her and Obeah's blood splattered on it—and pulled on the cleaner one. By now Esher would know of Nikola's disappearance. The bouquet of black roses—the ritual signature of open warfare between princes—was all the proof needed to tie the abduction to Sinjon. She had no doubt that Esher would wipe out Sinjon—thus saving her the trouble of doing so.

That would leave Esher for her to deal with—without fear of distraction or importune alliances between the vampire lords. She could dispose of them as separate, squabbling entities—but not united. Reuniting Ryan with his mother had not been part of her original plan—and now it was costing her. Well, it was over and done with—there was no going back and changing things now. Besides, it was too easy the other way—and she didn't trust easy.

She left the attic and climbed out a window on the deserted third floor that overlooked the alley, creeping down the face of the building like a black leather lizard. Careful to remain in the deepest shadows, she hurried along until she came to The Street With No Name. It would be easy enough to lure one of the Pointers away on some pretense or another. Despite their much-vaunted macho, they were exceptionally submissive to any dominant Kindred that presented itself before them. Like most humans drawn to serve the darker powers, they wanted the flame for their own, yet did not wish to burn to claim it.

She spotted three Pointers halfway up the street and quickened her pace. One of the youths noticed her approach and nodded in her direction. The boy standing with his back directly to her tossed his cigarette aside and began to turn, reaching for something tucked down the front of his jeans.

The stranger was already lunging to the side, rolling as she hit the pavement, as the Pointer spun and fired his 9mm, the weapon held to the side so that the spent cartridges flew away from him. Even if she hadn't read his body language from a mile off, she doubted the gangbanger could hit her with the butt of a bass fiddle.

She came out of her roll crouched low, snarling like a cornered wildcat, her fangs bared. The Pointer who had fired at her looked at his empty gun, swallowed, and took a step backward. With an angry growl, she pounced on the boy, taking him down hard enough to snap his back. The remaining Pointers stared, too stunned to react, as she crouched atop their companion. After a long moment the closest reached for the gun butt jutting from his own waistband, but he was too slow. The stranger came up off the sidewalk like a jack-in-the-box, ramming her skull deep into his solar plexus and tossing him over her back like a bull would a bothersome dog. The Pointer behind her fired his gun, but the bullet caught his friend instead of her.

"Damn it! I told you to hold your fire!" Decima shrieked, emerging from the mouth of a nearby alley. "She's needed for questioning! I don't want her dead!"

While she was far from fit enough to drop into overdrive, the stranger was fast enough to deliver a flying side kick that knocked the gun from the gangbanger's hand, followed by a forward snap kick that put the steel toe of her boot into his abdomen with enough force to rupture his grandmother's spleen. As she turned to face Decima, something slammed her against the wall. She tried to move, but a surge of pain nearly caused her to black out. She looked down and saw the last few inches of a crossbow bolt poking out of her right side, pinning her like a butterfly.

"Esher wants to see you," Decima said as she casually reloaded her weapon with another bolt from the quiver strapped to her back.

"Tough shit. I don't want to see him," the stranger grunted from between gritted teeth. She tugged on the arrow piercing her side, but the shaft was slippery with blood and less readily identifiable ichor, making it hard for her to get a secure grip. The pain was enough to make her swoon every time she pulled.

"Oh, you're going to see him, all right. Even if it's the last thing you do," Decima replied, leveling the crossbow directly at the stranger's head.

There was pain in her shoulders. Pain in her side. Good. Pain meant she wasn't completely dead yet. She opened first one eye, then the other. She seemed to be suspended by her wrists, the toes of her boots barely touching the floor. She was missing her leather jacket and her sunglasses. She did not know where she was and couldn't remember how she'd arrived. The last thing she recalled was Decima yanking the arrow free. There had been a *lot* of pain. Enough to bring her to her knees. Decima had then kicked her head while she was down—at least three times, possibly more. That's when things got dark.

"Seems like our little traitor is coming around."

She was in a room with thick stone walls and no windows. Esher leaned against the metal door, arms folded, studying her with evident distaste, like a man who had found a roach in his breakfast cereal.

"Cozy little dungeon you got here," she grunted, spitting a mouthful of blood onto the dirt floor. "You ought to dress it up a bit with some skeletons, though."

Esher smiled thinly and nodded to someone she couldn't see, and there was an explosion of pain at the base of her spine. Decima circled around to join her master, swinging a piece of lead pipe in one hand.

"Do you recognize the pipe Decima's carrying?" Esher asked, his voice surprisingly pleasant. He could have been chatting about the weather or his favorite TV show. "It was cut from the length Obeah was using as a cane. I thought you'd appreciate the irony."

"Yeah, you're a regular Oscar Wilde."

Decima moved to deliver another blow, but Esher stopped her with a small shake of his head. He pushed away from the door and stood inches from the stranger's battered face, looking into her unshielded eyes.

"You disappoint me, my dear. I thought you had better sense than to back a loser like Sinjon. But then, clan ties are strong. Your sire was Ventrue, was he not? I should have been suspicious from the start. I will admit that my enclave is a ragtag bunch of miscreants and loners. For such a specimen as yourself to wish to join was—unusual."

"I told you she was not to be trusted, even with your blood in her," Decima growled. "I smelled trouble from the very start."

"I am not unwilling to admit my mistakes," Esher said evenly. "I grant that Decima was far more intuitive than I was in this concern. Perhaps I allowed myself to be swayed by a pretty face—or the fact that I desperately need followers of your caliber. It does not matter—you have betrayed my confidence and will pay the price. But first I want answers—are you going to cooperate?"

At such close physical proximity to Esher, she could feel his blood within her stir. Being so near to the vampire lord gave her a strange thrill—almost like a hit of smack or the touch of a lover. For a brief moment she experienced a panic attack, fearful that he would go away and she would be left aching for him, bereft and alone. She felt her resolve begin to weaken. It would be so easy to tell him the truth. To give him what he wanted. If she gave him what he wanted, he wouldn't send her away.

Something dark stirred in the back of her skull, like a great serpent awakening from a long hibernation. The feeling had become a familiar one over the years—and always unwelcome. Until now.

What? Do I have to haul your ass out of trouble every fuckin' time? grumbled the Other. Its silent voice was deep and guttural, like that of a beast given speech. *Now you know why he's got these idiots hopping like fleas on a hot rock. He's not just their connection: he's their damn fix! So you're afraid you'll spill the beans to Studly here, is that it? Is that why you let me out? What a pathetic wuss you really are, woman!*

"I'll tell what you want to know."

"Where is Nikola?"

"At the Black Lodge."

"And the cocaine?"

"He has that, too."

"What does he plan to do with Nikola?"

"He's going to make her his. Forever. He said you'll have to bring down the Black Lodge stone by stone before you become Deadtown's prince."

"Sinjon said that, did he?" Esher's eyes narrowed. "Well, he shall get his wish!" He nodded to Decima as he turned to leave. "Do as you wish with her. Just see that she's dead when you're finished."

Decima's smile was slow and mean. "As you command, milord."

Marvin Kopeck sat huddled next to the tiny stove that heated his wreck of an apartment, a threadbare blanket draped over his shoulders. Someone was screaming on the street outside his window, but he did not look. He'd learned to ignore whatever happened after dark a long time ago. Kopeck served in Viet Nam twenty-seven years ago, but nothing in those distant jungles could compare to what stalked the streets of Deadtown once the sun went down. Still, the war had done its damage—driving him out of the familiar comforts of suburbia and into the inner city, until the day he found himself in Deadtown. It was as if the earth's crust had cracked to its very core, allowing a little bit of Hell to bubble up to the surface. What were nightmares of burning hooches and shrieking, napalm-drenched babies compared to this?

Ilyana frowned as the screaming began outside. She could remember a time when she did not live in Deadtown—but she could not remember a time when there had not been screams in the night. She survived both the Nazis and the pogroms, only to find herself living in one of her grandmother's folk stories. As if the *vrykolka* were not bad enough, the boys that served them were even worse! Hoodlums shackled to the devil, just like the gypsies had once been in the old country. Only worse. The gypsies never waited on her doorstep to demand a cut of her Social Security check.

"Come away from the window," Tommy whispered, his voice sounding much older than his thirty-three years. "You don't want to see what's going on out there."

"I can't help it," Janice said, hugging herself as she watched three Pointers kick an old man to death in the street. "Whenever I hear someone screaming like that—I have a need to look and see what's happening. To find out if it's someone I know. It's instinctual."

"So's self-preservation," Tommy grunted, not looking up from the spoon he was cooking. "Come sit down. You don't want to attract their attention." He stuck the needle into the sodden cotton, drawing the brownish liquid into the syringe with one deft pull. "Besides, I got a nice shot waiting for you here."

Janice shook her head, flipping the lank, greasy strands out her face. "I dunno. Maybe it's just me—maybe I'm just tweaking—but there's something different about tonight. My skin's all tight and tingly, like before a big storm. Can't you feel it?"

Tommy laughed dryly as he wrapped the length of rubber tubing around his forearm. "Baby, I gave up feelin' shit a long time ago."

♋

Father Eamon knelt before the altar, his rosary clutched in one hand, a bottle of yellow-label whiskey in the other. In the uncertain light cast by the votive candles, the faces of the plaster saints seemed leprous. He had been hearing things since the sun went down—what at times sounded like a baby's wailing on the steps to the church then became giddy, demonic laughter—but he was uncertain whether they were real or the DTs. He closed his eyes, but instead of prayer, he found himself reciting aloud: "*By the pricking of my thumbs…*"

♋

There are several different ways of killing the undead. One is fire. Another is exposure to sunlight. Decapitation works as well on them as it does on anything else. But all these methods are relatively quick. And Decima did not want that. She wanted her captive to suffer.

One of the enduring misconceptions about vampires is that because they are technically dead, they cannot feel pain. That is not true at all. Granted, their pain thresholds are extremely high by human standards, but they are perfectly capable of knowing pain. And Decima was determined that her captive become very intimate with every form of agony there was.

"Thought you were pretty smart, didn't you?" Decima jeered as she brought the length of pipe down onto the stranger's collarbone, snapping it like a green branch. "Thought you could fool our master! I knew from the beginning you weren't to be trusted!"

The makeshift club smashed into the stranger's left side, splintering her ribs and filling her lung with shrapnel.

"I saw the way he looked at you! Men are such fools! Even when they're dead! He saw you and wanted you. I could see it in his eyes!"

The pipe smashed against the stranger's spleen, rupturing it like a child's balloon.

"In a way I'm glad you got away with as much as you did! At least it got rid of that simpering cow he's been mooning over! How could he prefer her to me? After all this time—?!?"

The club came down on first the stranger's left, then her right kneecap.

"He's mine! I belong to him! She had no right making him love her! He's supposed to love me, not her!"

Decima delivered a backhand blow to the stranger's face, shattering her cheekbones and knocking her lower jaw askew. She was not worried about beating her captive to death—after all, she could not die from such wounds. A vampire's body can repair itself indefinitely, as long as it's properly fed. She stepped back to regard her handiwork. The stranger hung from her chain, looking more like a piñata than anything living. Blood dripped from her nose and mouth, and her right eye was swollen so tightly it was impossible for her to open it.

Decima spotted the stranger's leather jacket lying on the floor and bent to retrieve it. She'd been thinking about replacing her old one—and since they seemed to be the same size, it could serve a purpose other than that of a trophy. She patted down the pockets and felt something inside the inner breast. Reaching in, she pulled out an ornate switchblade. The handle was decorated by a gold-leaf luck dragon with a tiny ruby set in its eye. Curious, she pressed the stud—and six inches of silver blade, shaped to resemble a frozen flame, jumped from its hiding place, nearly spearing her hand. Decima dropped it like a baby rattlesnake. Though not technically Tremere, she had been around Esher long enough.

"*Enchantment!*" She turned to stare in simultaneous fear and horror at the stranger, who dangled limply from her chains, watching her silently with one blood-filled eye. "What manner of Kindred are you, that you would carry such a blade on your person?"

The stranger smiled. And smiled. And kept on smiling, until it looked as if her lips would meet at the back of her head. A sound resembling a cross between a lion's growl and the grinding of metal gears burbled out of her broken chest. It took Decima several seconds to realize it was laughter. The stranger tossed back her head and the laughter twisted in on itself and became a roar unheard from any but the deepest pit.

Purple-black energy crackled about her, like the halo of some dark saint. Decima raised a hand to her eyes as an arc of black light shot out of the top of the stranger's head and punched through the ceiling. The stink of ozone filled the room as a wind from nowhere began to blow.

The Other was free. And there was going to be Hell on Earth to pay.

Marvin Kopeck sat bent nearly double, his hands clamped over his ears to block out the screams. Tears streamed down his rigid face. Behind his eyes his best friend stepped on a mine and flew into bloody rags, a hysterical peasant woman clutched a roasted baby to her breast and wailed without end, a Viet Mihn officer stuck a rifle barrel up a terrified girl's vagina and pulled the trigger. The screaming inside him blended with the screaming outside him, and Marvin Kopeck finally decided he'd had enough. After twenty-five years, he was no longer afraid. In place of the fear was anger. He stood up, tossing aside the blanket, and walked over to the narrow cot that served as his bed. He pulled the footlocker out and opened the lid. Everything was still there, just as he'd left it in 1970.

Janice stared at the loaded syringe, then back at Tommy. He was slumped in his chair, already on the nod, a gout of vomit drying on his soiled shirt. She picked up the needle, frowning at the crust of old blood. She closed her eyes and readied herself for the plunge, but something made her stop and open her eyes.

"Fuck this!" she snarled, hurling the syringe against the wall.

There was a loud crack of thunder. Against her better judgment, Ilyana got up to look out the window. The hoodlums on the street below had stopped kicking their hapless victim and stood with their heads tilted back, like a wolf pack scenting a coming storm. Discarded newspapers and other bits of trash blew along the streets and gutters. The sky over Deadtown swirled like ink in an aquarium. Clouds the color of a ripe bruise boiled forth, their bellies lit from within by flashes of purple-white light. And the epicenter of the brewing tempest appeared to be Esher's stronghold.

From his perch high in St. Everhild's bell tower, Father Eamon pressed his rosary to his cracked lips, then took a swig from his bottle as a tongue of purple-black lightning leapt upward from Esher's house of evil, puncturing the ripe, overhanging clouds like a boil. Smaller fingers of dark electricity shot forth from the center, like the ribs of an umbrella, and zigzagged throughout the neighborhood.

Judgment had come to Deadtown.

If ever there was a neighborhood ripe for riot, it was Deadtown. Although such places of despair and hopelessness were magnets for the undead, only the older, more powerful Kindred could manipulate and feed off the negative energies generated by unhallowed ground. But the Other was nothing if not precocious.

There is a thin line between rage and madness. Every human has, at one time or another, experienced both emotions, in varying increments of strength. While gripped in rage's white-hot hand, an otherwise sane man may commit acts he would never dream of in calmer moments. But most do not succumb to passion-born madness because they fear the repercussions such actions might hold. Fear, more than virtue, holds humanity rigid within its social orbits. Fear of censure, fear of punishment, fear of the unknown, fear of changing things forever, and not for the better. But if the resentment and anger that lie boiling beneath the crust of an oppressed society are stoked high enough, the fear that keeps them lying prostrate while their enemy grinds his boot in their collective face will dissolve, triggering their sense of self-preservation. Timidity is replaced by fury. And the more desperate the community, the less they have to lose. And the less they have to lose, the more likely they are to succumb to the madness that lurks in the heart of even the most righteous anger. And the denizens of Deadtown were half-crazy to begin with.

♋

Jesse stopped kicking the old man yellow and tilted his head back, frowning at the rapidly swelling thunderheads filling the sky. He and Tuff Enuff and B-Jo had found the old lush cowering near a dumpster. The bum had risked leaving whatever dank hidey-hole he called home to score a bottle outside Deadtown, and now he was paying the price. Jesse liked kicking the drunk around, since he reminded him of his rat bastard old man. Judging how the others were going after the lush, he must have reminded all of them of someone.

Tuff Enuff paused to wipe the sweat out of his eyes and spotted the scowl on Jesse's face. " 'Sup, cuz?"

"Dunno. Something's not right." Jesse's scalp tightened as the sky overhead was split by a freak lightning bolt that seemed to splinter into a hundred smaller ones. "Jesus fuck! What was that?!?"

The answer came in the form of a moan. At first he thought it was the bum lying at his feet. Then he realized the moan was too loud to be coming from just one person. It was as if hundreds of voices were united as one, as when a stadium groans at the home team's loss, only a lot angrier. It was as if the very buildings were wailing. Jesse and the others exchanged wary glances. Weird shit went down in Deadtown nightly—but nothing like this had ever happened before.

There was a collective bang as dozens of doors were thrown open and the denizens of Deadtown came pouring out of the surrounding tenements like ants from a burning tree. Although Jesse, Tuff Enuff and B-Jo recognized their attackers, none of them could honestly say who they were. These were the nameless faces that usually cowered in doorways or hurried away when they walked down the street. These were the ones who disappeared behind barricaded doors at the first sign of dusk. These were the old, the deranged, the junkies, the alcoholics, the dispossessed and disowned—these were the children of exile who, through fate or design, found themselves with nowhere else to go but Deadtown.

Jesse noticed with alarm that while most wielded little more than sticks, some had conventional weapons. He pulled his semiautomatic out of his waistband, trying to decide whether to stand his ground or flee. Tuff Enuff and B-Jo looked equally uncertain.

"Jesse! What do we do?" B-Jo whispered, trying to keep his voice from turning into a frightened squeak.

"Fuck, man! Spray their asses!" Tuff Enuff barked, firing a volley at the approaching wall of flesh.

Ilyana could not tell if the young men firing at her were Nazis or Cossacks or Soviet Army Regulars. They seemed to flicker from one to the other and back again, as if glimpsed through the flames of a burning house. Then a bullet tore through her throat, dropping her to the pavement. She could barely feel the feet of the others as they trampled her, but she could see her blood coating their soles. As she gasped out her last feeble breath, the ghosts of her slaughtered family crowded her fading vision, like moths about a candle.

Jesse stared in numb disbelief at the mob surging toward him. They'd emptied a clip apiece into the crowd, but still they came, stepping over the bleeding bodies of their fellows as if they weren't there. The ragged wail grew louder, angrier. Closer.

"Shit, man! This is just like *Night of the Living Dead!*" Jesse moaned as he slapped a fresh clip into the butt of his semiautomatic. "The fuckers won't stop coming!"

"Fuck makin' a stand!" Tuff Enuff said, taking a step backward as the mob approached. "This is whack! We gotta run for it!"

"You want to be the one t'tell King Hell what's going down, feel free!" Jesse shot back over his shoulder at his friend. "Me, I'd rather take my chances with these fuckers!"

Marvin Kopeck stepped forward, dressed in the uniform in which he'd been sent home twenty-five years before. The Purple Heart and Bronze Star clinked and rattled on his chest like Christmas ornaments. The Pointer in front of him wavered, became a VC in black pajamas, then the laughing Viet Mihn officer waving his bloodied rifle barrel, then his platoon leader, holding up a baby by the ankle like it was a piglet. In the end it didn't really matter. They were all The Enemy. He opened fire with his M16.

Five rounds stitched across Jesse's torso, going from right hip to left shoulder, picking him up and throwing him into his companions like a ruptured sack of grain.

"Fuck this shit!" wailed Tuff as he turned to flee. M16 fire caught him across the back, effectively slicing him in two.

B-Jo stared at the bloody remains of his companions for a second, then tossed his gun onto the ground and put his hands behind his head. *"Don't shoot! Don't shoot, man! I give up!"* he wailed, sounding every day of his fifteen years.

The sea of angry faces surged forward, their outstretched hands tearing at the gangbanger's flesh. B-Jo began to scream. His cries for help were quickly muffled by the bodies of the mob as they pulled and tore and kicked and bit him like a pack of wolves worrying a deer to death. When the screams finally stopped, the group moved on, leaving the ravaged carcass where it lay.

As the crowd moved forward, Janice stopped long enough to remove the gun from Jesse's dead hand. She turned the Luger over, wondering if it still had any ammunition left.

"Janice!"

Tommy was standing on the top stoop of their building, tottering uncertainly in the doorframe. He looked confused and blurry-eyed, like he'd just woken up from a long nap.

"Janice—what are you doing out here? Come back inside where it's safe!" Tommy squinted at the Luger she was holding. "What you got there? A gun?" A sly, hungry look crossed his face as he licked his lips. "I know this guy who'll give us some White Tiger for it...."

Janice pointed the Luger at Tommy and squeezed the trigger. He staggered, then fell headfirst down the front steps, landing in a heap at the foot of the stairs. Yeah, it still had some bullets left.

Decima shielded her eyes from the strange glow that enveloped the manacled stranger like St. Elmo's Fire. The sourceless wind raging inside the interrogation room was close to hurricane force and it was all she could do to stand upright. Even though the storm was louder than a passing freight train in her ears, she could still hear the weird laughter rising above it.

The stranger's head and hands crackled with an eerie electricity that seemed to grow with each pulse. As Decima watched, the bruises and gashes covering her victim's face disappeared. With a shriek of maniacal glee, the stranger yanked herself free of her restraints, pulling her right shoulder out of its socket. Whatever the stranger was, she certainly wasn't a garden-variety Kindred. No novice had such control over the elements—nor could they regenerate so quickly without rest or blood.

The Other turned and grinned at Decima, and for the first time in decades the vampiress knew true fear. Not the fear of punishment that came from displeasing her master—but the fear that comes from seeing your Death in the eyes of another. The Other's grin grew wider as it moved toward her, its hair whipping in the maelstrom like angry black snakes.

Decima leapt forward, swinging the club with both hands, but the Other was too quick for her. It batted the length of pipe out of her grip. Decima swore and jumped aside, snatching up her crossbow from where she'd left it. It was already loaded and cocked, and she fired it at the stranger, striking her in the right chest and puncturing her lung. The stranger yowled in pain and toppled backward, clutching at the bolt jutting from her breast.

Decima pounced, landing atop her enemy and pinning her to the floor. Careful to keep her fingers clear, she pulled the switchblade she'd taken from the stranger's jacket and hit the trigger release. The silver blade leapt free and the stranger's eyes widened at the sight of it.

"*No!*" she cried out, lifting her hands to her face, as if to blot out the sight of her doom.

"Die, bitch, in the name of Lord Esher, Prince of Deadtown!" Decima shouted over the raging wind, and plunged the silver blade into the stranger's heart.

The stranger spasmed and voiced a strangled cry, then went still. The winds stopped as if someone had flipped a switch. The witchlight that cloaked her body faded and fizzled, like firecrackers tossed in a puddle.

Decima leaned back and studied her handiwork for a moment, then smiled. "See—that's what you get for fuckin' with me, bitch," she smirked.

The Other's eyes flew open and it grinned its too-wide grin as it plucked the knife from its chest. "I couldn't have said it better myself," it cackled, and plunged the switchblade into Decima's right ear.

The vampiress shot to her feet as if propelled from a cannon, clutching at her head. Her screams were so shrill they climbed into the ultrasonic register, like those of a bat. Her eyes began to swell, as if being inflated from within, until they literally sprang from their sockets. She trembled like a tuning fork as her brain and central nervous system liquefied and came pouring out her nose and ears. Decima tried to move toward the door, but her legs no longer worked and she crashed to the floor, where she landed on her right side with enough force to send the blade the rest of the way through her brain. As the point emerged from her left ear she went completely still and her eyes glazed over, becoming as white and milky as those of a baked fish.

The Other looked down at its enemy's carcass and grinned in triumphant glee. Then it coughed a lungful of blood. The spasm passed and the stranger, once more in possession of her physical self, kicked Decima's body over onto its back and bent to recover the switchblade, tugging it free from the vampiress' punctured skull with a grunt of pain. Straightening up, she snapped off the last few inches of crossbow that protruded from her chest. The pain was so intense her vision went monochromatic and everything sounded as if she were underwater. She staggered backward, fighting the instinct to curl up in a dark corner and regenerate. She had to get out of Esher's stronghold if she wanted to survive the night—and it was going to take every ounce of strength she had left.

She had no idea what madness the Other had tapped into in order to summon the necessary energy to break free and battle with Decima, but something told her it was big. The Other had siphoned off enough to effectively knit broken bones, but she was far from healed.

To her surprise, the door was unlocked and the hallway deserted. Then again, no one was ever expected to leave the room in anything but a body bag. She glanced back at Decima, her body lying twisted in on itself like an animal with its foot in a trap. She had to admit they did look a lot alike. It was like staring into a mirror and seeing what she would have become had Lord Morgan bothered to take her under his wing and tutor her in the ways of monstrosity. It gave her the creeps just thinking about it.

What the hell do you think you're doing? growled the Other. *Stop contemplating your navel! The skank's dead—get a move on!*

"Shut up!" she snarled, shaking her head in a futile attempt to clear it of the intrusive voice.

You can't get rid of me that easy! Now get us out of here! I didn't haul our collective ass out of the frying pan so you could wander around in the fire!

As much as she hated to admit it, the Other was right. She was suffering from severe internal damage, even by Kindred standards, and she was rapidly losing strength. She had to find a way out before Esher sent his minions after her. And in this weakened state, there would be no second chance for escape. She closed the door to the interrogation room behind her and headed down the darkened corridor. If memory served her, it led to the central vault, which was the barracks for the enclave. If her luck held, once she reached the subbasement she would be able to use one of the myriad tunnels that branched off from the main catacomb. Assuming she could stay a step ahead of the others. At present, she'd be satisfied with just a half-step.

Esher stood underneath the stained-glass oval suspended over his throne of office, arms folded, staring out at the sea of pallid, ruby-eyed faces turned toward him. The time had come. War was at hand, and these were his troops. He raised his hands and the room fell silent. When at last he spoke his words rang like a death knell.

"Tonight it begins, my friends! Tonight we wage war on our enemy! Tonight is the *last* night for Sinjon and his brood! The gauntlet has been thrown down! There is no other recourse but—*jyhad!*"

"*Jyhad!*" came the response, echoed by a half-hundred voices. "*Jyhad!*"

Esher smiled as the assembled Kindred thrust their fists into the air, pumping their arms vigorously. Most—if not all—of them would be dead come the dawn. But that did not matter. After all, they were cannon fodder, nothing more. And there were certainly more where they came from. Even Nikola's kidnapping could not spoil the exhilaration he felt: he was poised at the very cusp of success—come the sunrise he would be the undisputed master of Deadtown! As he basked in the glow of certain triumph, the doors to the audience chamber flew open and a badly frightened Pointer stumbled inside.

The enclave turned to stare in amazement at the human—it was forbidden for humans to enter Esher's presence unannounced or unbidden. The youth's clothes were disheveled and his face was bloodied and bruised from tumbling up stairs and colliding with flying doors. Esher snapped his fingers and the human was grabbed by a pair of vampires, who pinned his arms behind his back and dragged him to the dais.

"Impudent whelp! What is the meaning of this interruption?" he demanded.

"Milord!" the boy cried. "Milord—something's happening outside! The streets!"

"What do you mean—?"

"Deadtown's gone crazy! They're throwing bottles and rocks—some are setting fires—some of them even have guns and knives!"

Esher's frown deepened into a scowl. "Sinjon's minions are attacking?"

The Pointer shook his head. "It ain't Sinjon! I seen a bunch of old ladies tear apart some Black Spoon with their bare hands! It's bad out there! End-of-the-world bad!"

"What do you know of apocalypse, fool?" Esher sniffed.

"I ain't lying, milord—scope it out for yourself!"

Esher tilted his head to one side, like a bird listening for the telltale rustle of a hidden earthworm's passage. He could make out the distant din of screams and smashing glass and gunfire from beyond the thick walls of his stronghold, faint at first, but growing perceptibly louder—and closer—with each second.

"A riot—now, of all times? This *must* be Sinjon's doing!"

"I don't think so, sir," the Pointer said. "I mean—they're going after everyone—it don't make no difference! Some of 'em even go after each other!"

"You idiot! This is *jyhad*! The lives of humans mean nothing, no matter what their allegiance!"

"But what do we do?"

"*Do?* What does any army *do* in wartime? Break out the heavy munitions! Arm your men to the teeth and tell them to kill everything and everyone in their path! Is that clear?"

"Y-yes, milord!"

"Go do it, then!" Esher snapped. He motioned to the vampires holding the gangbanger to escort him out. "See that he leaves the building. I don't want him stepping into a wormhole and disappearing." As the trio left, Esher turned his back on his audience to glower at the stained-glass window, massaging his lower jaw as he thought. Without warning, there was a sharp pain in his chest, as if an unseen hand had driven a knife into his heart. He staggered a couple of steps, then dropped heavily into his chair, his limbs feeling as wooden and lifeless as a puppet's. He'd only experienced such abject emptiness once before, long years ago—when Bakil was destroyed. Kindred who sire numerous progeny eventually grow immune to the loss—much like sows that spawn vast litters yet routinely crush and smother their offspring by rolling atop them. But Esher was far from profligate. He had only one childe, and the bond between them was tight and keenly felt.

"M-milord?" one of the recruits whispered anxiously. "Milord, is something wrong?"

Esher's lips pulled into a grimace so frightful the assembled vampires instinctively cringed. "*The Lady Decima is dead! Avenge her, my brothers! Bring me the head of the stranger! Hunt her down and find her, before she escapes!*"

Without hesitation, the fifty vampires hurried from the audience chamber, their voices raised in an ululating cry, like a pack of baying hounds in pursuit of a fox.

♋

She was in luck. The barracks were empty. The collection of mildewed mattresses, rotting futons, and discarded sofas stretched before her like a subterranean Salvation Army drive. The reek was not unlike that of a snake den. All she had to do was pick her way across the vault and disappear down one of the tunnels that led to one of the exposed cellars that ringed the stronghold—although she was still blurry as to where exactly she could go after she was free of Esher's fortress.

The stranger was halfway across the main vault when a voice from behind cried out: "*There* she is!" She turned to see a pasty-faced vampire, his eyes gleaming like those of a rabid rat, standing at the foot of the central stairs that led to the subbasement, pointing in her direction. Behind him were crowded dozens of equally pasty, hungry faces. "*Get her!*"

"Fuck!" she groaned as she wheeled back around and resumed running toward the nearest exit. She tried to boost herself into overdrive, but it felt as if her insides were being taken apart. Still, at least she could see the ghostwalkers attacking her. Like the asshole that had zipped past her and was now positioned in the mouth of the tunnel she was headed for. He was tall and pale, with lank hair that hung in his gaunt face, a tight-fitting pair of leather pants, and a black net T-shirt. He grinned at her, exposing his dripping fangs.

"Outta my way, deadboy!" she snarled, driving her switchblade into his throat.

The vampire seemed surprised—perhaps even frightened—as he clutched his throat, but she pushed him aside without a second glance. As the stranger rushed down the narrow, unlit tunnel, the dying vampire cried out in agony, his death-scream echoing like the wail of a banshee. His fellow Kindred crowded the tunnel, snapping and slashing at one another with their fangs and talons in their eagerness to pursue their quarry.

She had to escape. She had to get away. It felt as if her gut was full of broken glass, and every step drove a barbed spike deeper and deeper into her back. Her arms felt like pieces of cold meat hanging from her shoulders and the numbness was spreading to her legs. Her right lung was full of blood and the left was swimming with bone splinters. She was lucky that most of Esher's recruits were so raw they were ignorant of how to ghostwalk, but luck always runs out sometime.

She only realized she was out of the tunnel because she could see something resembling a night sky above her. The exposed cellar was strewn with garbage, but the staircase had long since collapsed. The stranger flung herself at the wall, scrabbling at it with the frenetic tenacity of a cornered rat. Her pursuers boiled out of the tunnel like blowflies from a corpse, shrieking for her blood. As she reached the lip of the cellar a shadow loomed over her. The stranger froze as the figure raised its arm, revealing a Luger.

"Fuck you!" Janice screamed down at the pit of vampires. *"Fuck all of you!"* The gun she'd lifted from the gangbanger was loaded with phosphorus bullets. She opened fire, laughing as the white-faced monsters collided with one another, trying to dodge the lethal projectiles.

"Help me," the stranger rasped, plucking at the girl's pants leg. She was painfully thin, with hair that hadn't been washed in weeks, outfitted in threadbare bell-bottom jeans, a tank top emblazoned with a faded glitter-decal of a kitten staring at a butterfly, and busted-out high-tops. Her inner arms were pockmarked with needle tracks, some badly infected, but she seemed to be human. "Please—give me a hand up."

Janice glanced down in the direction of the voice at her feet, then raised the Luger and pointed it directly at the stranger's head. "Fuck you too, bitch," she said, her voice sounding almost dreamy. She pulled the trigger, and the hammer clicked on an empty chamber. The stranger blinked, surprised to find her head still attached to her shoulders, then grabbed Janice's gun hand and pulled, sending the junkie tumbling headfirst into the open cellar. The vampires yowled in delight as they pounced on the human that had landed in their midst.

She dragged herself out of the pit and staggered to her feet. The morsel tossed to her pursuers would distract them for a minute or two—but no longer. As she loped through the blighted no-man's-land of razed buildings that ringed Esher's stronghold, she could finally see for herself the madness the Other had unleashed on Deadtown.

Several tenements were on fire, blazing away like dry Christmas trees. Although she could hear screams and gunfire, the wailing of ambulance and firetruck sirens was eerily absent. After all, this was Deadtown—and whatever hell raged on its streets went unseen and unattended. The buildings would burn until they collapsed into their basements, the blaze spreading to the surrounding structures, without a single hand lifted to halt the fiery holocaust. Those injured had the choice of either dying on the streets or dragging themselves off to some safe place to lick their wounds.

As she leaned against an alley wall, struggling to catch her breath, she glimpsed a couple of Five Points gang members stumbling down the sidewalk. They had the look of young wildebeests that somehow had managed to elude a pride of lions, their eyes bugging from their heads as they moved as fast as their damaged limbs could carry them. So this was the Other's handiwork. It had awakened the predator inside the prey. For once she didn't feel guilty for her demonic counterpart's actions.

Taking a final gulp of air to steady herself, she rounded the corner and promptly stumbled over a body, landing hard on her wounded side. The pain was so overwhelming there was nothing for her to do but to lie there and ride it out. As she waited for the wave of agony to recede, she found herself staring at the corpse that had tripped her. It had recently been a man in his late forties, with the haggard features of a street crazy. He was dressed in a Marine Corps dress uniform, complete with decorations and white gloves. The brass nameplate on his breast read KOPECK. Someone had dropped a cinderblock on his head from one of the nearby buildings, crushing his skull. He still clutched an M16 rifle in one hand, but the action was jammed, rendering it useless. However, there was the bandolier of grenades to take into consideration. Biting her lower lip to banish the pain, the stranger hurriedly removed the weapon's harness from the body and looped it over her shoulders. Weighing a pound apiece, the grenades pressed against her leather jacket like deadly fruit, rattling against one another as she staggered to her feet.

She could hear the wordless howling of Esher's hounds closing in on her. She resumed her jog, although her right knee no longer seemed to want to bend the way it was supposed to. She ducked into a nearby doorway and yanked one of the spherical grenades free, holding the safety lever tightly with her left hand. She leaned forward and peeped around the doorway in time to see Esher's recruits emerge from the alley onto the street. The vampire in the lead had its head tossed back, scenting the air, while the rest pushed and shoved and snapped at one another, looking like a mix between a pack of hunting dogs and the Keystone Kops. If it wasn't her head they were after, she would have been tempted to chuckle.

The lead tracker pointed in the direction she'd taken and the group surged forward eagerly. The stranger darted from her hiding place and lobbed the grenade, praying its previous owner hadn't been carting around a bandoleer full of duds. The grenade sailed through the air and landed in the midst of the mob, exploding on contact. Two vampires were thrown into the gutter, their legs below the knees reduced to jelly, while a third discovered his intestines and stomach dangling about his calves. While the wounded shrieked in agony, their brethren darted for cover. Kindred could not die from such wounds, but none of them particularly relished being blown apart, and the weaker could even be sent into torpor.

The stranger grimaced as something inside her—her spleen?—ruptured, and blood frothed her lips when she coughed. She was trying to run while keeping an eye on the pack following her. The tracker was in the lead, waving his more timid brethren onward.

"Hurry, you curs! She's getting away! In the name of Lord Esher—get her!"

The stranger lobbed a second grenade, this time aiming directly at the leader of the pack. *"Heads up, asshole!"*

The tracker instinctively raised a hand to shield his eyes and shifted into overdrive, his silhouette blurring like a chalk painting caught in the rain, just as the grenade exploded. Seconds later the tracker reappeared several yards from where he first stood, only now he was missing his head. So much for the "faster-than-a-speeding-bullet" crap.

The stranger staggered out into the middle of the street, holding aloft another grenade.

"You want me so bad, you bloodless motherfuckers? Okay, come and get me! I'll take you all to Hell!

The remaining vampires exchanged glances, then turned and ran back the way they came. The stranger lobbed the third grenade after them, although her dimming sight and weakened arm sent it flying wild, exploding relatively harmlessly.

"Buncha wusses," she muttered under her breath as she watched them flee. She took an unsteady step backward, nearly collapsing as her right knee disintegrated. The vision in her left eye was fuzzy and her right flickered like an aging cathode tube. Every breath she took sent bloody froth out her nostrils and mouth. She winced and frowned at the rib poking through her shirt and rubbing against the inside of her jacket. Damn it, she'd just had that lining replaced, too. She only hoped she could hold out until she got to where she was headed.

She managed to get halfway up the steps before she collapsed. She lay there on her back, staring up at the gray shadows that crowded what was left of her vision. She knew she had to keep moving—that she had to hide before Esher's minions regathered their courage and came back—but her body simply refused to respond. She couldn't feel her legs anymore, nor could she move her arms. She couldn't feel anything except the pain, which started at the roots of her hair and extended to her toenails.

One of the gray shadows moved forward, coming close enough so that she could see it was a man. A human. His face was wrinkled and careworn, his jaw unshaven, and he wore a priest's collar that was the same color as his graying hair. He stared down at her with a mixture of fear, fascination and repugnance, as if she were a rare but exceptionally repellent insect.

Focusing what little strength she had left, the stranger lifted her right hand in supplication. The priest flinched, but did not move away, as her fingers brushed against the silver rosary draped about his neck. She tried to speak, but all that came out was a pained gasp. The priest leaned forward and she clutched the front of his cassock, pulling him closer so he might hear.

"Sanctuary."

Chapter

11

When she opened her eyes again, the first thing she was aware of was not sight, but smell. The odor of damp earth overpowered her. Her vision was still blurred, but she could make out the rough-hewn stone walls surrounding her. She was back in Esher's dungeon! A spark of fear surged through her battered body, prompting her to sit up.

"Don't try to move. You're safe," Father Eamon whispered, pressing his hand firmly against her shoulder.

The stranger squinted, trying to bring the priest's face into focus. He looked to be in his early sixties, with longish gray hair that hung to just below his clerical collar. He wore a cassock, the sleeves of which were badly frayed. He had a strong nose and chin, with gin blossoms giving his cheeks a mottled rosiness underneath the grime. But what caught her attention were his eyes—they were so blue it was like looking into a clear sky, making him seem younger than his years. She lay back down, biting her lower lip as her body cried out.

"Where am I? And who are you?"

"I'm Father Eamon. And you're in the vault beneath St. Everhild."

"St. Everhild—? The church across from the Black Lodge?"

The priest nodded and placed a cool cloth on her head. "I'm afraid I'm unused to visitors. I've made you a bed out of old choir robes, but some of them are rather mildewed."

"I'll get over it."

Father Eamon glanced in the direction of a distant explosion, followed by hoarse screams. He stood and peered out a heavily barred basement window set level with the street. His hand dropped automatically to the rosary about his neck. When he spoke, his voice was strangely calm, almost dreamy.

"Tonight I saw the hand of God come down and smite Deadtown. It is time for the just to rise up and make the guilty pay for their sins. Tonight I cast aside my fear of the dark and unlocked the doors of the church for the first time in twelve years." He glanced back to where the stranger lay on her makeshift pallet. "When I saw you sprawled across the stairs, I thought you were Esher's harlot. The one with the rings."

The stranger smiled wryly. "Seems to be a common mistake around here. Not that it'll be happening that much anymore. She's dead. I killed her."

Father Eamon lifted an eyebrow but his features remained immobile. "Is that a confession to me?"

"Just stating a fact."

The priest moved away from the window, staring down at her with a troubled frown. "I see a lot from the belfry. One of the things I've seen is you. At first I thought you were one of them, because you slept away the daylight hours in the attic. Then I saw you enter the Black Lodge. But this morning, in the light of day, I saw you with the boy. It was then I realized I'd misjudged you—you are a child of God, not Satan."

"I wouldn't go so far as to say that, Father," she rasped. "You got me pegged a lot closer than you know. See what I mean?" she grinned, baring her fangs.

Father Eamon gasped and took a step backward, his hand closing on the rosary. "Impossible—! You touched my rosary! You asked for sanctuary—I have bathed your wounds in water from the baptismal font! I myself saw you walking in the full light of day!"

"There's more to the Kindred than you realize, Father. It is in their interest to keep humans confused as to their exact weaknesses and abilities. There is wisdom in keeping your enemies ignorant. It's true sunlight kills them, but most Kindred would fear your rosary, not because of its religious significance, but because of your faith in it."

"I can't believe that."

"Believe what you like. It does not alter what I am—or the fact that I am here."

Father Eamon struck himself across his right cheek with his open palm. The blow was hard enough to send him staggering. "I have sinned again! I have brought into this holy place a thing of the devil! Unclean fool!" He delivered another blow to his own face, then another.

The stranger struggled to sit upright. "Father! Stop that!" she snapped. "You have betrayed no one! It is not the Church itself that makes this place anathema to the undead—it is the faith of those who believe in it! What white magic exists in this place is here because of you."

Eamon stared at her for a long moment. When he finally spoke, his voice and mannerisms contained no trace of the violence and self-loathing of a moment before except for his redly glowing right cheek. "This is your handiwork, isn't it?" he said, pointing in the direction of the window. "I can feel it in my bones. This all ties in to you, somehow. That is why you were brought to St. Everhild! That is why I felt compelled to help you!"

The stranger eyed the priest cautiously. Was it possible that the old hermit had some sort of low-grade extrasensory perception? Then again, the humans most susceptible to the shadow world were drunkards, lunatics, and poets. And it seemed that Father Eamon might qualify for two out of the three.

Something flickered deep in Father Eamon's eyes as he began to pace, speaking aloud more to himself than to his guest. "Deep within the bowels of Hell there dwells a divine monster—a creature both devil and angel. It goes by many names, but it is best known as the Angel of Destruction. It is the harbinger of punishment, vengeance, wrath, death and ire. Although the Angel of Destruction is in the thrall of Satan, it serves God, and no doom is visited upon mankind in which the Destroying Angel is not in its midst. When it executes its punishment on the world, it wields the Sword of God. And tonight I saw the Sword of God strike and split the sky!"

The stranger laughed and weakly shook her head. "I'm certainly no angel, father!"

Father Eamon halted his pacing and frowned, stroking his chin. "Perhaps. But I know what I saw tonight was a sign from God. A sign that it is time for me to do something besides cower in the shadows and drink myself into a stupor every night."

A burst of submachine-gun fire drew his attention back to the window. He peered out onto the street, then stepped back, crossing himself.

"What is it?" she whispered.

"Pointers. Dozens of them. They're walking five abreast in the middle of the street, headed for the Black Lodge."

The stranger pushed herself into a sitting position, although her head felt as if it was swinging on the end of a tetherball cord. "Help me up. I want to see."

"You're in no condition to move—!"

"I have to see what's going on," she grunted through gritted teeth as she struggled to stand.

Father Eamon clucked his tongue reproachfully, but looped his left arm under her shoulders, helping her to her feet. She staggered slightly, closing her eyes to the black specks swimming before her vision like a connect-the-dots game. Father Eamon helped her to the window, where she clutched the sill with trembling fingers.

The street in front of St. Everhild was indeed full of Pointers, mixed with members of Esher's enclave. Gang members and vampires alike carried assault weapons and military-issue machine guns. As she watched, a group of Black Spoons opened fire on the advancing invaders from a nearby alley. A couple of Pointers dropped as their fellows returned the fire. The exchange of fire ended with screams and splashes of blood. The Black Spoons' Glocks and Lugers were no match against Street Sweepers and M24s.

The overamplified thump of industrial-strength rap, laying down a bass-line as thick as boilerplate, signaled the Batmobile's approach, flanked by armed Pointers who trotted alongside the car like Secret Service agents in a presidential motorcade. The stranger grimaced as her molars vibrated in time with the beat.

"Looks like Esher's bringing the fight to Sinjon's door," she muttered. "I guess 'say it with flowers' really works."

The Batmobile halted directly across the street from the Black Lodge. One of the attendant bodyguards opened the rear passenger door and Esher stepped out. The vampire lord placed his hands on his hips and scanned the scene. A jumbled barricade of old furniture, broken masonry and timber had been erected in front of the Black Lodge, the top festooned with a bale of razorwire that glinted like tinsel in the flickering light of the fires from the burning tenements. Behind the barrier stood the Black Spoons and Sinjon's progeny, their faces smeared with blood and soot.

Esher motioned to one of his underlings, who reached into the front seat of the Batmobile and retrieved a bullhorn. Esher lifted the amplifier to his mouth and bellowed: *"Sinjon! I've come for what's mine! Do you hear me, Freemason?"*

Sinjon stepped out onto the third-story balcony overlooking the street and glowered at the assembled army at his doorstep. "What is the meaning of this, Esher?!? Have you gone mad like the rest of the rabble in this wretched place? It's less than an hour before dawn! First I have crazed derelicts attacking my men with torches and firebombs, now you!"

"Don't play coy with me, you bastard! You know very well why I am here! After all, it is you who cast the first stone!"

"You *are* mad!"

"I want my woman! I want the cocaine you took from me! But most of all—I demand that you hand over the traitor to me!"

"I have no idea what you're raving about, Esher! Return to your territory while you still can!"

"You give me no other choice, then!" Esher lowered the bullhorn and made a quick, chopping gesture with his hand.

The Pointers opened fire on the Black Lodge, the bullets gouging marble-sized holes in the building face. Sinjon flinched as a phosphorus bullet whistled by his ear and ricocheted off the brickface behind him. He quickly withdrew from the exposed balcony, shouting at his minions to return the fire.

"Daddy—what's going on?"

Vere, naked except for a black vinyl jockstrap, shivered on the canopied bed, clutching the purple satin sheets to his chest. His eyes were white with fear, and for the first time in months he looked like the frightened young boy Sinjon had picked up in front of the downtown bus terminal.

"The wizard's lost his mind! He's jabbering on about giving him back the girl and the drugs! And he seems convinced we're harboring Morgan's get!"

"Did you tell him she's not here?"

"Of course I told him, you ninny!" Sinjon shrieked.

There was the sound of breaking glass and a grenade landed with a thud on the carpet between Sinjon and the boy. The vampire lord stared at it, more stunned than frightened.

"The son-of-a-bitch has grenade launchers!"

The explosion sent glass and debris flying out the third-story window, where it pelted the Black Spoons like a lethal rain. Sinjon's progeny lifted their pale faces as one, their scarlet eyes glittering with panic, and raised their hands in supplication. *"Father!"* they wailed. *"Father, help us!"*

The situation behind the barricade was grim. Dead and dying Black Spoons lay sprawled three-deep. There were Kindred causalities as well— most brought down by phosphorus ammunition or grenades. The vampire called Tristan—his body blown away from the waist down—dragged himself along his elbows and belly, battening onto the wounded Black Spoons in hope of draining enough blood to hurry his reconstruction. The dying humans struggled feebly to escape his grasp, but were powerless to stop what was happening. Their cries for help went ignored by their former comrades-in-arms as they returned the Pointers' relentless fire.

The street in front of the Black Lodge ran red with blood, its sidewalks littered with bodies. Esher's minions fell back, taking cover behind garbage cans and repositioning themselves from the windows of the few nearby buildings that had yet to succumb to arson. Esher himself sat in the back of his bulletproof Caddy, watching the slaughter with a preternatural calm. During a brief break in the firefight, he glanced at the Rolex on his wrist and pulled a walkie-talkie out from under the seat.

"King Hell to Firebird. Begin the suite, over."

"Roger, King Hell. Firebird over."

Esher tucked the walkie-talkie back under the seat, leaned back, folded his arms across his chest, and waited for the show to start.

A pair of Pointers armed with grenade launchers zigzagged across the street, protected by covering fire from their fellow gang members, and set up their position on the steps of the church opposite the Black Lodge. One of the Pointers caught a bullet and dropped, rolling down the marble stairs, but his teammate kept working. When the first launcher fired, the Black Spoons watched what they thought was another grenade arc its way toward them. It wasn't until it hit that they realized it was napalm.

The jellied gasoline ignited instantly upon impact, splashing the troops huddled behind the barricade. Vampires and humans alike shrieked in terrified agony as the flames ate through their clothes and skin. The vampire youth Ethan leaped over the barricade, screaming and waving his arms in a futile attempt to escape the fire, only to be mowed down by Esher's men.

The second launcher fired, this time sending its fiery cargo directly through a second-story window. A chorus of shrill screams could be heard coming from the Black Lodge as thick smoke began to pour from the windows. A third volley crashed through the third-floor balcony Sinjon had been standing on minutes before.

Figures began to emerge from the Black Lodge, both human and Kindred. Some were on fire, others had their hands over their heads. The Kindred hesitated on the threshold, eyeing the lightening sky with apprehension, but were forced out by the flames. Not that it mattered—they were all mowed down the moment they cleared the barricades.

Esher smiled as he watched those trying to escape fall, the bodies piled four or five deep in places, and picked up the walkie-talkie again. "King Hell to Enclave Subcommand. Over."

"Enclave Subcommand here, milord. Over."

"Give the signal for the enclave to go to ground. Over."

"Understood, milord. But what about yourself? Over."

"Don't worry about me. I wouldn't miss this for anything. Over."

The Kindred recruits from Esher's enclave began to pull back. The sun was coming up and he had no desire to risk any more of his thralls unless necessary. He alone would remain behind, within the sunproofed Batmobile, and watch the fall of his enemy.

Tongues of flame leapt from every window of the second and third stories of the Black Lodge. Thick black smoke boiled forth like a biblical swarm of locusts. Vere came running out of the inferno, naked except for his black vinyl jockstrap, which the intense heat had melted to his skin. The youth's hair was on fire and his blistered flesh hung in large, flapping patches from his face, thighs and back. Blood trickled from his ears and nose from the damage done by the concussion grenade that had detonated in the boudoir. Vere waved his arms frantically in an attempt to escape his pain, his screams as high and piercing as those of a child.

"Help me! Somebody please help me! I don't want to die!" he wailed. *"Save me, Daddy! Save meee!"*

The crossfire tore the boy to shreds in a matter of seconds, spinning him around like a top. Vere staggered a few steps, a look of confusion on his ruined face, then collapsed onto the gore-strewn pavement.

"Merciful God!" Father Eamon whispered, crossing himself. He lowered his head and began to recite the Latin prayer for the dead.

The stranger wanted to tell the priest that the boy was better off, but held her tongue. As it was, she had to struggle to hide her delight in the carnage outside the window. Things were working out better than she'd hoped. As she returned her gaze to the burning ruin across the street, Sinjon appeared in the crumbling threshold of the Black Lodge. The vampire lord's finery was scorched and his powdered wig was gone, revealing a scabrous scalp through which his skull gleamed wetly.

The Pointer wing-commander consulted his walkie-talkie, then turned to bellow at the others: *"Hold your fire! Lord Esher says hold your fire!"*

"Lord of Hell—no! Vere!" Sinjon clambered over the barricade and made his way to where his favorite's body lay. He dropped to his knees with a pained moan. "Oh, my precious boy—look what they did to you—look what they did!" He pulled Vere's ruined corpse into his arms, cradling it as he would a child, and rocked back and forth.

All his boys were dead. Well and truly dead. Vere. Tristan. Ethan. All of them. His bloodline was no more. The loss struck him like a knife twisted in a wound. The kingdom he had built and shaped for over two centuries was dying all around him, consumed by flames and madness. Deadtown had been usurped.

Then he raised his eyes heavenward and saw, to his horror, the first fingers of dawn stretch across the sky.

"Esher!" Sinjon painfully got to his feet, swaying like a drunken man. He staggered across the debris of the battlefield to where the Batmobile sat, still throbbing out bass-heavy rap, like a bull alligator during mating season. "You win, Esher! Deadtown is yours! I surrender! I bend my knee to you and recognize you as my liege and lord!" He pawed with trembling fingers at the rear passenger window's heavily tinted glass as he glanced over his shoulder at the rising sun. His voice grew more and more panicked, until he was all but sobbing.

"I will swear fealty to you and gladly take your blood as my own! I will make myself your footstool and never once raise my hand against you, for as long as the oceans are wet! I promise you all that I am, Esher—*just don't let me burn!* "

Sinjon's skin prickled and itched as if he were covered in ants. Then it began to burn. He hissed in anger and pain and tried to shield his eyes with his lifted forearm. It was no good. He pounded his fist against the impassive black glass of the Cadillac, but it refused to shatter. He staggered away from the car, back toward Vere's body, but collapsed before he could take a half-dozen steps.

He had never known such agony in all the centuries of his undeath. He lay panting on the ground, his eyes filling with tears and blood as the fluids inside him began to boil. His instincts told him to find shelter, to go to ground somewhere dark and cool and safe from the burning rays of the sun, but it was too late. There was nowhere to escape. He clawed at the street beneath his belly for a few frantic seconds, in hopes of burrowing into the earth, but his wildly scrabbling fingernails met only unyielding cobblestones.

His flesh blistered like bacon in the pan. He could smell himself cooking. The skin on his face bubbled and sloughed away like wax. His eyes turned dull white as they were boiled in their own ocular fluid. Despite the magnitude of his wounds and the pain he was in, Sinjon continued to crawl forward, groping blindly with his fleshless hands. Although he no longer possessed a sense of touch, he knew he must be close. He wanted to tell Vere he was sorry it had come to this, but his tongue was a piece of blackened leather. He wanted to kiss him one last time, but he had no lips.

There was so much he wanted to do. Wished he could do. Needed to do. And now, after nearly five centuries, the unimaginable had finally come to pass.

There was no.

More.

Time.

Esher watched as Sinjon dissolved under the touch of the sun's rays, a smile pulling on his lips. As an early morning breeze scattered the Freemason's ashes, he could no longer contain himself and began to laugh. He was still laughing as he motioned for the driver to leave.

"It's time to return home," he managed to choke out between guffaws. "There is nothing more to see here."

The stranger watched the Batmobile bounce over the broken, bleeding bodies littering the street—its front wheels crushing Sinjon's fleshless skull to powder. The Pointers shambled behind their master's car, looking as dead as their enemies. They were too tired to be boisterous concerning their victory, and many of them limped and seemed to be nursing wounds of some kind. By the stranger's estimates, Esher had probably lost well over half his human servitors to the riots and battle with Sinjon.

Which reminded her that she didn't feel that great herself. The adrenaline rush that came from witnessing the *jyhad* waged between the vampire lords flagged, and she was suddenly aware of how drained she was. She let got of the window ledge and sank to her knees, pressing her forehead against the cool stone.

"You need to lie down," Father Eamon murmured as he bent to help her.

"That leaves only the one, now," she grunted as the priest helped her back to her makeshift bed.

"Sinjon was bad enough, but Esher—he is the devil made flesh!" Father Eamon spat. "Now the gutters of Deadtown will run with the blood of innocents!"

"D-don't be too sure of that. I'm not out of the game yet—do you have a pencil and paper, Father?"

"Pencil and paper?"

"I need you to take a message to a friend of mine."

Father Eamon shrugged and left the room. A couple of minutes later he returned with a tiny pencil stub without an eraser and a crumpled brown paper bag that had been flattened out. "This is all I could find."

She hastily scrawled an address and phone number onto the back of the bag. "I need you to take this to Cloudy. He's an older man who lives in a basement squat a block or two over from here...."

"You mean the hippie?"

"You're the only one in Deadtown who doesn't call him 'the old hippie',"
she said with a dry laugh, which abruptly turned into a violent coughing spasm, bringing up clotted blood.

"I can't leave you while you're in this condition!" Father Eamon protested.

"Do what I ask you!" she gasped, shoving the paper into his hand. "Do it or I'll die anyway! I can *feel* everything that's wrong inside me. Father, there's a piece of rib stuck in my *heart* and my right lung is completely collapsed! If I were human, I would have been dead hours ago! There's only one thing that can help me recover—and that's blood. The address on this piece of paper is that of a man who specializes in providing black-market plasma to those such as myself. I need Cloudy to contact him and arrange a buy. I need blood—and I need it bad."

Father Eamon frowned at the piece of rumpled brown paper. "If I do this thing for you—will I be acting as a tool of Satan or as a servant of the Lord?"

"I really couldn't tell you, Father."

"Yeah—what do you want?" Cloudy growled, peering suspiciously at the grubby older man on the other side of the door. He assumed he was a derelict of some sort, judging from his unwashed appearance and grizzled chin. Then he noticed the priest's collar.

"I—I was told to come here and give you this," Father Eamon said, holding up the scrap of paper by way of explanation. "She said you'd know who she was."

Cloudy's eyes lost some of their suspicion, but not their anxiety. "She sent you? She's alive?" He slipped the chain off the door and yanked it open, ushering the priest inside. "Sorry I didn't recognize you, Father! I'm just not used to receiving company. Especially after a night like last night! I spent most of it trying to keep those fuckin' loonies from torching the place (pardon my French). It was real Helter Skelter."

Father Eamon stood in the middle of the front room, staring at the piles of books surrounding him. "I see you are a man of letters," he said, not without some surprise. "I never dreamed there were so many books to be found in Deadtown."

"I've found they help pass the time at night," Cloudy replied with a shrug. "Now, what about her? Is she okay? Is she hurt? The last I saw her, that crazy bitch Decima was carrying her over her shoulder like a sack of flour. Then all Hell broke loose, and I had my hands busy the rest of the night."

"She is alive, but badly hurt. I found her, all but dead, on the steps of St. Everhild. She asked for sanctuary and I brought her inside. I tended to her wounds and tried to make her as comfortable as possible. She claims she escaped from Esher's stronghold by killing the woman called Decima."

Cloudy shook his head in amazement. "And you say she needs my help?"

"She—she says she needs blood." It was all Father Eamon could do to speak the words out loud. "She says she will die without it. She gave me this address and phone number to pass on to you. She says it's a black-market contact of hers."

Cloudy took the piece of paper and frowned at the scrawled information. "Tell her to rest easy, padre. I'll take care of it."

"May—may I ask you something?"

"Go ahead. And the name's Cloudy."

"Is this woman a thing of the devil?"

Cloudy blinked, surprised by the confusion and pain in the priest's voice. "I honestly don't know *what* she is, to tell you the truth. I kind of thought guys like you knew those things for sure."

"Satan is a devious foe. His devils wear different skins. Sometimes even those of priests."

"I couldn't answer about that, Father. But I can tell you what I know personally. I'll admit that what she is scares the bejesus outta me. She's saved my life twice—and both times she didn't have to. She helped that kid, Ryan, get back with his mom and saw that they got away safe. She didn't have to do any of that. But she did. I don't know who she is, or what brought her to Deadtown, but it's obvious she's not like Sinjon or Esher—or anything else I've ever seen in this screwy neighborhood. She ain't human—but I don't know if that's such a bad thing, really. As to her being a thing of the devil—well, aren't we all?"

Father Eamon picked his way through the streets of Deadtown, surveying the wreckage left by the riots. It was like a nightmare made flesh. Corpses littered the sidewalks and the stink of blood and smoke filled the morning air. Most of the dead bodies were human, and a surprising number were those of Pointers and Black Spoons. Judging from what was left of them, the gangbangers had been torn limb from limb. Dead men hung from street lamps, and at one intersection he spotted a pair of Nikes dangling from a telephone pole, the previous owner's feet still inside. Every now and again he would spot a fleshless skeleton with oversized canines among the carnage, proving that death had visited the devil's own as well as the sons of Adam.

Fires, whether accidental or the product of arson, had wiped out many of the ancient tenements, and several continued to smolder within the burned-out husks. He was reminded of the newsreels of the Battle of Britain and the Fall of Berlin he'd seen as a boy. The Street With No Name was as potent a symbol of the catastrophe as could be found. While the Dance Macabre looked to be relatively untouched, Stick's Pool Hall was little more than a charred and gutted shell. He noticed with a twinge of panic that the liquor store had been looted and torched, along with the handful of crack *bodegas* that served as the neighborhood's business community.

Everywhere he looked, he saw nothing but ruin. He knew it was his duty as a priest to go among the dead and administer last rites, but the task was a daunting one. Every now and again, he would glimpse something moving amid the debris, but for the most part there was nothing but death. Father Eamon found a grim irony in the fact that for the first time since its dark conception, Deadtown truly resembled its name.

As he continued to survey the damage, his mind kept turning back to the creature in the basement of St. Everhild. She was somehow responsible for the destruction of Deadtown. And although the devastation that surrounded him was indeed horrible—was it the product of evil? He wished he knew. He wished he could be *certain*. Was the woman a servant of Satan, or was she a Destroying Angel? She did not seem to know, nor was she willing to tell him if she did. What Cloudy had told him of her motives and actions confused him even further. Could a monster have a soul, or an angel bring suffering to the innocent? And what did it mean that he, the most wretched of sinners, was the one to whose doorstep she came crawling?

When he returned to St. Everhild, he found her where he'd left her, curled up in a fetal position. Her skin was cool and dry to the touch, like that of a snake, and she did not seem to be breathing. At first he was afraid she was dead, but when he prodded her she moved slightly and one of her eyelids flickered, exposing a blood-filled white. Satisfied there was nothing he could do to make her any more comfortable, Father Eamon headed back upstairs.

As he knelt at the altar-rail, he noticed his hands were shaking. He closed his eyes and bowed his head even lower, praying for forgiveness and strength. This was the first day in years he'd gone without a drink. Even if he'd wanted a bottle, there wouldn't have been a way to get one. The liquor store was no more—its meager stock of generic beer, wine and spirits looted and put to the torch. He cursed himself for being weak and afraid all those years and using the alcohol to hide from himself, if not his God. His body trembled and his tongue seemed dry as sandpaper in his mouth. The saints looked down at him from their reliquaries, their plaster faces staring at him in silent reproach.

"What am I to do?" he asked the Virgin Mary. "What is it that God wants of me? I have witnessed His judgment—but I am confused. Am I to help the creature or destroy her? How am I to know His will? Holy Mary, Mother of God, Bride of Heaven—give me a sign! Weep tears, sweat blood—do *something!* Anything!"

The plaster icon smiled placidly down at him, as she had every day for the last twelve years, and said nothing, as she had every day for the last twelve years.

♋

"Father Eamon—?"

He started at the sound of the stranger's voice, his cramped muscles shrieking from the sudden motion. Disoriented, he glanced up at the stained-glass windows—it was already dusk. He must have fallen asleep while praying. He turned his head toward his guest, trying not to grimace in pain. The muscles in his neck and shoulders were so stiff he could literally hear them groan and crack.

The stranger was standing at the end of the nearest upright pew, leaning against it uncertainly. Although she was pale to begin with, something told him she looked unhealthy even for the undead.

"Are you okay, father?"

"I'm—fine. Forgive me. I was lost in prayer. But you shouldn't be walking about like that!"

"I couldn't agree with you more," she grunted, easing herself into the pew. "But I hate being cooped up. Makes me feel—helpless."

Father Eamon got to his feet, wincing as the blood rushed back to his legs. It felt as if his extremities were being stabbed by hundreds of imps armed with pins. "I saw your friend. He said not to worry. He'll take care of it."

"Cloudy's an okay guy. I just hope he doesn't get nabbed by Esher's goons. The bastard knows I wasn't in the Black Lodge by now. If I had been, Sinjon would have tossed me out after the first grenade went off. Esher's not the kind to forgive and forget. I killed his childe and stole his bride. He wants me worse than he did Sinjon."

"How can you know all this?"

"Let's say I have a gut feeling," she said with a dry laugh, thumping her chest with her fist. "I can feel his blood calling to me—it's taking what little strength I have left not to get up and walk back to his stronghold."

"You must go lie back down—you look like Death warmed over."

She laughed and pushed the bridge of her sunglasses back into place with her forefinger. It was a surprisingly human gesture. "You really know how to flatter a girl, Father. No, I think I'll stay here for awhile, if it's all right with you." She glanced around, taking in the cracked stained glass, the toppled pews and the layers of dust. "Nice place you got. How long you been here?"

"Twelve years."

She nodded to herself, as if this answered something. "Uh, don't take this wrong, Father—but are you a *real* priest?"

Eamon surprised himself by chuckling. "I'm not offended—I can certainly understand why you'd ask that. But, yes, I am a *real* priest. I graduated from the seminary in 1959." He glanced up at the cross, then back down at her. "I hope you don't mind me asking you something personal—but were you religious before you, um, before you were—"

"Before I became what I am?" She looked thoughtful for a long moment, then shook her head. "I guess not. I mean, her family was as religious as your average Americans—which is to say, not very."

"'Her'? They weren't your family?"

"It's a complicated story, father. You see, back in 1969, a seventeen-year-old girl was seduced and raped by a vampire named Morgan. When he was finished with her, he threw her from a moving car into a London street. She was found and taken to a hospital, where instead of dying—she lapsed into a coma. When she awoke nine months later, it was to find herself—changed. She was no longer human, but because she had never really died, neither was she one of the undead. She discovered she was a thing unto herself: she could walk in the daylight; she could feed off of and control the negative emotions of the humans around her. But none of these wondrous powers made her happy. You see, she didn't like being a monster. She fought hard to keep from succumbing to the cruelty and bloodlust inside her. She even tried to create for herself a family, of sorts. But time and again she failed. So she dedicated her existence to hunting down the vampire who had stolen her humanity and making him pay for what he'd done to her."

"And—and did she find this man?"

"Oh, she found him all right." Her laugh was dry as dead leaves. "And she discovered her favorite food—was the blood of vampires."

"How does the story end?"

The stranger shrugged and smiled crookedly. "I don't think it does. Well, enough about me—so who's this Saint Everhild?"

"I doubt he exists anymore. He was removed from the Book of Saints sometime during the Second World War. He was an early English martyr who was chopped to bits and fed to a pack of wild boars by the Vikings. Supposedly the boars then tossed themselves *en masse* off a cliff into the North Sea. He was the patron saint of swineherds, I believe. Perhaps they chose St. Everhild because of the similarity between his martyrdom and Jesus exorcising the demon called Legion. "

"What's the history behind this place? Why did the Church build in Kindred territory?"

"I don't know. The history behind the parish is shrouded in mystery. There's no documentation concerning the construction and consecration of St. Everhild anywhere, yet rumors and myths concerning its existence have been floating around for over a hundred years. Some said it was raised as a challenge to the dark powers. It had a reputation for being a parish where the priests and nuns assigned to it routinely disappeared. Some said the Holy See sent its more troublesome, heretical clerics here deliberately. All I know is that it was abandoned sometime during the Depression."

"So what are *you* doing here?"

Father Eamon blinked and rubbed his mouth nervously. He really wanted a drink right then. He glanced over to the statue of the Virgin, then back at the stranger. With a deep groan, he lowered himself in the pew beside her.

"It's a long story."

"I've got time."

He stared into the stranger's mirrored gaze and saw the twinned reflection of what he'd become looking back out at him. Perhaps it was time, after all these years, to finally tell the tale.

"I never really knew my parents. My mother was very young when she succumbed to rheumatic fever. I was three months old when she died. My father was killed in a traffic accident when I was four years old. I was sent to live with family. My aunt and uncle were good enough people, I suppose—but they were elderly and childless. They did not know what to make of me, or what to do with me, except put me to work on their farm.

"They did not beat me or abuse me—at least no more than was considered normal for those days. But they were not emotional people—either with me or one another. As I said, they treated me well, but I was never anything but a distant relative. As I grew older, I proved to be a good student. I was bright and studied hard. But it was difficult for me to make friends. My aunt and uncle did not dance. They did not listen to music. They did not entertain. But they did go to Mass. It was there I met Father Raymond.

"Father Raymond looked at me and saw a lonely, fatherless boy. So he decided to take me under his wing. That is, after all, a parish priest's role— to be father to all children. It was Father Raymond who encouraged my scholastic ability—Father Raymond who arranged a scholarship for me to Loyola University. It was Father Raymond who saw to it that I got into the seminary. He showed me nothing but kindness and support, and I decided he was the kind of priest I wanted to become.

"As I mentioned, I graduated from the seminary in 1959. I was twenty-four and full of idealism and naive energy. Within a year America elected its first Catholic president and I was certain great things were in the offing. I wanted to help orphaned children find themselves, much as Father Raymond had helped me. My first few years in the priesthood were spent teaching in various parochial schools for the underprivileged. Then, in 1969, I was sent to the St. Ivo Orphanage for Boys.

"St. Ivo's was not a particularly well-funded institution, and the headmaster's duties were largely taken up with fundraising, so the priests and brothers who oversaw the welfare of the children weren't overly supervised. At first I did not think much of it—then I came to notice one of the other priests, a Brother Marten. It was little things, at first—how his hands seemed to linger when he touched some of the younger boys, for instance. There was something decidedly unwholesome about his interest in making sure none of the boys' underwear bore signs of "self-pollution." I had my suspicions, but I was unsure. I dared not mention them to the headmaster, for fear of causing a scandal that would damage St. Ivo's precarious economic security.

"Then one of Brother Marten's favorites, a frail little six-year-old with the face of an angel, was claimed by a long-lost relative. Apparently the boy said something to his family that aroused their suspicions, and they notified the police. The headmaster went to the bishop, who managed to smooth things over with both the boy's guardians and the police. Brother Marten was removed from St. Ivo's and, so I believed, the priesthood. That was 1971.

"I remained at St. Ivo's four more years, then I was transferred to St. Levan's Orphanage. You can imagine my shock and dismay when I arrived and found Brother Marten there. I was incensed! I went to the headmaster and told him what I knew of Brother Marten's proclivities, but he refused to take me seriously and accused me of being a troublemaker. I was forced to work alongside Brother Marten for over a year. I tried my best to keep an eye on the children and see that no harm came to them—but in the end I failed. There was a boy. He was no more then four. His name was Christopher."

Father Eamon stopped and took a deep, shuddering breath and turned his face to the rafters. His eyes blinked rapidly for a few seconds as he struggled to regain his voice.

"Christopher was a beautiful child. Absolutely beautiful. He had the biggest, softest eyes—like those of a fawn. It broke your heart just to look at him. He was the kind of child I had dedicated my life to stewarding. I—"

Father Eamon's voice wavered and began to crack. The memories were too much. Even after all these years, the pain was still sharp, the wound still fresh. He closed his eyes, but the image was still there, only now there was no whiskey to dull the edge and make it go away. He wiped the tears from his face with a shaky hand.

"I found him in the coat closet. His underpants were shoved so far down his throat he'd choked on them. I *knew* who did it. And knowing drove me mad with rage. I went looking for Marten. I found him in the basement, getting ready to burn his own undergarments in the furnace. There were blood and other things on them. I accused him of raping and murdering poor, sweet Christopher. The bastard attacked me with a coal shovel. He might have been a terror to small boys, but he was no match for a grown man. I ended up wresting the shovel from him—" Father Eamon's eyes narrowed and his face became rigid, like a man reliving the pain of unanesthetized surgery. "And for a brief moment I simply stood there, knowing that this would get swept under the carpet, just like it had at St. Ivo's. I knew Brother Marten would never see the inside of a prison. At best he would be defrocked. At worst they would simply ship him to a new parish, to start afresh. Either way children were in danger. Children like Christopher. Poor, innocent Christopher.

"I beat Brother Marten's brains in with the shovel.

"The police called it self-defense. The archdiocese absolved me of any crime as well. If anything, they needed a 'heroic priest' to counterbalance the murderous pedophile. I told myself that what I did was just—that I was acting as an instrument of the Lord's wrath. But it was a lie. As I stood there over Marten, listening to him bleat and beg for mercy, I felt nothing but *hate!* A priest is supposed to hate the sin but love the sinner, but I hated *him!* I hated him for what he'd done to that poor child! I hated myself for failing to be there when Christopher needed me! There was nothing of God in me when I brought that shovel down on his head, and I knew it. I began drinking shortly after that. I suffered a nervous breakdown in 1982. The archdiocese sent me to a sanitarium. After six weeks I went AWOL. I claimed the small inheritance left after my aunt and uncle passed away, and I've been living on that ever since.

"I'd heard the stories about 'the parish of the damned' while I was a student at the seminary. It took me a year of wandering to find it—but I finally located Deadtown. People have a funny way of finding this place after all other avenues of life have been closed to them. I have dwelt here for a dozen years, drinking myself into oblivion every night and praying for a sign from God that I have been forgiven. But I pray in vain—because I am not truly sorry for my trespasses. I cannot feel true regret for what I did. My soul is stained with the blood of another. But it is not Brother Marten's. "

"You can't forgive yourself because of the boy."

"I failed him. I promised that no harm would come to him—and I lied. There is not a night that has gone by in the last twenty years that I haven't closed my eyes and seen him lying there, cold and dead. Sometimes I wake up, choking as he must have choked in those last horrid moments."

"Father—it wasn't your fault. You're torturing yourself for nothing."

"That's what the doctors said at the sanitarium. But they were wrong. You're wrong. Everything that made me a priest died that day. I'm one of the damned, now. That's why I sought Deadtown out. I *belong* here." He pushed himself out of the pew, trying his best to control his tremors. "I—I have to get some air. Please excuse me. I'll be in the bell tower if you need me."

Cloudy scanned the alley, switching the cooler from his right to his left hand. The streets were unusually empty, even by Deadtown's standards. Still, taking a stroll wasn't the safest thing to be doing this time of night—but he had no choice. Tracking down the black-market blood dealer ended up taking up most of the day. By the time he finally made the buy and was on his way back to Deadtown, the sun was already setting. He'd promised to get the shipment to her, and he meant to stick to his word. And judging from what the priest had said, something told him she wasn't going to last the night without an infusion. Now all he had to do was make it to St. Everhild's without getting nabbed by Esher's goons....

As he stepped out of the alley, a burly Pointer materialized from the shadows, blocking his way.

"Yo! Look what we got here, cuz!"

A second, equally large Pointer emerged from the darkness behind Cloudy. "Looks like we got ourselves a curfew violator. Hey, old man! Don't you know you're under martial law?"

Cloudy shifted uneasily, trying to keep his eyes on both men as they moved to circle him. "Martial law? Under whose order?"

"Who else do you think, sucka? King Hell hisself—Lord Esher, the fuckin' king of Deadtown!" grinned the first Pointer. He jabbed a thick finger at the cooler Cloudy was carrying. "Whatchoo got there, motherfucker? We're to search and interrogate anyone we find on the street after sundown."

"Nothing you'd be interested in—just let me go, okay?"

The second Pointer loomed closer, scowling menacingly. "He asked you what's in the fuckin' cooler, old man. Mebbe we just take us a look-see. "

Cloudy sliced at the first Pointer's hand with his Buck knife, nearly severing the bigger man's thumb. The gangbanger grabbed his hand as blood spurted forth, looking more surprised than hurt.

"Mother*fucker*!"

Cloudy shot past the Pointer blocking his way, but the one behind him was too close. He felt the air leave him in a solid rush as the second man tackled him, driving him to the ground with bone-jarring force. He cried out as his shoulderblade snapped.

The first Pointer, the one holding his thumb, kicked Cloudy hard enough to lift him off the ground. "Motherfucker *cut* me!" he shrilled. "I'll fuckin' *kill* his ass!"

A third Pointer came trotting up out of the darkness, drawn to the yells and sounds of struggle. "What's goin' on here?"

"This asshole fuckin' cut me! *That's* what's goin' on!" the wounded Pointer snarled, delivering another vicious kick to Cloudy's midsection.

"What's in the cooler?"

"Dunno," the second Pointer said with a shrug. "Old fucker didn't want us to look. Probably his hooch. Ain't nothin' left now but the hardcore alkies and junkies."

"So why don't we take a peek at what Gramps here didn't want us t'see?" The third Pointer grinned down at where Cloudy lay half-conscious, blood staining his beard. "Is that what you got stashed in here, old-timer? A six-pack of Olde Sterno?" His grin faltered as he reached inside and withdrew a plastic bag full of human plasma. "Take him to Lord Esher. *Now*."

♋

Esher sat on his throne atop his dais, chin resting on his doubled fist, and stared into nowhere. It was supposed to be better than this. After long years of scheming, he was finally the unchallenged prince of Deadtown. The entire Eastern Seaboard's illegal drug and gun trades were now his, and his alone. After decades of waiting, he was finally one of—if not *the*—most powerful princes in America. But instead of experiencing the joy and satisfaction that come from grinding an enemy into dust, he felt only emptiness.

What good did his triumph over Sinjon do him without Nikola and Decima to share in his success? The stranger eluding capture made his situation all the more galling. He did not relish being played for a fool. The mirror-eyed bitch was going to pay dearly for what she cost him—dearly indeed.

"Lord Esher!"

He glanced up from his reverie to frown at the Pointer holding a plastic cooler. "What is it? Can't you see I'm busy?"

"We captured a prisoner, milord—one we thought you should see for yourself." The Pointer holding the cooler motioned to his companions, who dragged the bleeding and bruised Cloudy into the audience chamber. "We found this piece of shit breaking curfew. He attacked us when we asked to look inside the cooler he was carrying."

"Let me see that," Esher snapped. He took out the chilled bags of plasma, studying the labels like a wine connoisseur before dropping them back into the container. "Bring him closer."

The Pointers dragged the groggy hippie forward, forcing him to kneel before the vampire lord.

"I recognize you," Esher said. "You were the one who tried to rescue the boy. The one I told her to destroy. Tell me where she is, old one, and I'll let you live."

"Get bent, you rat bastard!" Cloudy spat. "You're not getting a thing outta me!"

Esher's smile was as thin and sharp as a razor. "I wouldn't be so certain, if I were you."

The stranger sat propped in the church pew, staring at the shadows cast by the flickering light of the votive candles. She hoped Cloudy showed up soon. Every beat of her heart was growing perceptibly fainter. It was strange, feeling yourself die one cell at a time. She wondered how long it would continue before her consciousness would finally be obliterated. Maybe it wouldn't. Perhaps that was the curse of the undead—to die and remain sentient the whole while, experiencing your own rot yet helpless to stop it. That was a cheery thought.

There was a loud bang as the door to the bell tower slammed open and Father Eamon hurried into the church. He was gasping noisily and his face was beet red.

"They've got him!" he gasped.

"They got who?" She struggled to sit up straight, but the exertion was too much for her.

"Cloudy! I saw it from the bell tower! They captured him!"

The stranger slumped even further in the pew. "That's it, then."

"You don't think he'll tell Esher where you are, do you?"

"That's beside the point. Without that blood, I'm as good as dead. " She pulled herself up onto wobbly legs, grimacing from the exertion. "I guess there's no point in delaying the inevitable...."

Father Eamon moved to block her path. "Where are you going?"

"I've got to help Cloudy."

"But you said you don't stand a chance without the blood!"

"Father, I can't sit here and let him die! He risked his life trying to help me—I've got to get him out of that hellhole! Now, please—get out of my way. Let me do what I've got to do." She pushed past Father Eamon and staggered into the aisle. Squaring her shoulders against the pain, she took a step forward—and collapsed.

Father Eamon knelt beside her, rolling her limp body over so she lay cradled in his arms. He gingerly removed the mirrored sunglasses, flinching at the sight of her blood-filled eyes with their elongated, reptilian-slit pupils.

"You're dying."

"So I noticed," she whispered.

"You need blood." He glanced up at the Virgin Mary, then at the crucifix suspended over the demolished altar. There were no miraculous tears or dripping stigmata to be seen, but he no longer needed such crude signposts to show him the way. He calmly reached up and removed the clerical collar from his neck. "Take mine."

The stranger's eyes widened, revealing even more blood-filled whites. "Father, you don't know what you're saying—"

"Yes, I do. For the first time in years, I know *exactly* what I'm saying. I don't know if you are a thing of Heaven or Hell, but I have no doubt as to Esher's origins. There is much I don't know or understand, but I know one thing for certain: all that has gone before in my life was to bring me to this place, so that I would be the one kneeling beside you at this moment. No one else could make this sacrifice but me."

He pulled her closer, lifting her head so that it rested on his shoulder like a sleeping child's. She closed her eyes, trying to blot out the sight of his veins pulsing in his neck. She could smell his blood, lurking just beneath his skin. She could hear his blood rushing through his arteries with every pulse of his heart. Her fangs ached to plunge into his bared throat.

"Father—no—don't do this to me. Don't make me kill you," she whispered as she tried to pull free of his embrace.

"You needn't worry about that. I've been dead for years. I died with Christopher."

She licked her lips, her tongue flickering across the skin of his throat. He tasted of sweat and dirt and human. She trembled as she felt her resolve give way to the voracious need within her. She opened her mouth wider, and her fangs unsheathed themselves.

Do it, the Other's voice hissed inside her ear. *If he is so desperate to martyr himself—let him! We'll die if you don't—and then where will we be? Heaven? Hell? Or back where we started, all those years ago?*

Father Eamon jerked when her fangs first penetrated him, then relaxed as the natural anesthetic in her saliva began to kick in. He could feel his blood being drained, but it was all very painless—even pleasant. It felt better than the buzz from a bottle of whiskey. There was no fear, no anger, no hate—only the dreamy detachment that comes the split-second you realize you are falling asleep.

He turned his gaze to the plaster Virgin and saw tears of milk and blood streaming down her cracked and peeling cheeks. Something fluttered in his chest like a piece of paper caught on barbed wire, and he heard something that sounded like the beating of muffled wings. Father Eamon looked up toward the roof-beams and saw Christopher sitting on one of the rafters, surrounded by a host of white doves, kicking his tiny legs back and forth. He smiled down at Father Eamon and waved.

The stranger licked the blood from her mouth as Father Eamon's head rolled lifelessly on its neck. She could not remember the last time a kill had died so easily. His pale features seemed peaceful, almost beatific, in the flickering light from the votive candles.

She could feel her body regenerating itself, her strength returning. She still wasn't in peak condition, but there was no helping that. She was sound enough to give Esher her best shot. She got to her feet, lifting Father Eamon's body effortlessly in her arms.

She placed the priest's body atop the altar, folding his hands across his chest. She looped his rosary about his neck and arranged the votive candles so that they formed the stations of the cross. She took her switchblade and carved into the wood of the altar this epitaph:

"Here Lies Saint Eamon—Protector of the Damned."

Chapter

12

The House of Esher stood stark and alone amid the rubble of Deadtown, its bulk silhouetted ominously against the rising moon. The graveyard quiet of its surroundings made it seem even more like a mammoth tomb—a place where the dead held sway and which the living shunned. The checkpoints were no more, and a handful of guards loitered on the curb outside the House, smoking cigarettes and talking among themselves in hushed voices.

The stranger watched them from the shadows for a long moment, pondering her options. Was it worth going into overdrive to handle these goons? Ghostwalking ate up a lot of energy reserves, and she didn't have much to spare. And the moment she set foot across the threshold, Esher would know she was there. The element of surprise would be over before it could begin. No—she needed a different entrance.

She crawled down into one of the open cellars that dotted the block like bomb craters. Halfway down, she realized there were dead bodies littering the bottom. The Pointers who had survived the riot and the assault on Sinjon's stronghold were using it as a mass grave, tossing their fallen comrades into the open cellar in lieu of actual burial. Although the stench was bad, it was nowhere near what it would be after another day or two.

She shifted through the corpses until she found the tunnel entrance, which was about the size of a manhole cover. Such a small tunnel probably meant it wasn't used very often, which suited her just fine. The walls of the tunnel were not shored up with planking of any kind, as if it had been clawed out of the earth by a huge burrowing creature, and she had to lie on her belly and worm her way forward on her elbows through the darkness. As she crept along, she hoped she wouldn't come face-to-face with one of Esher's enclave worming his way in the opposite direction. Things were complicated enough already.

After several long, claustrophobic minutes, she finally saw something resembling light. Carefully edging herself forward, she found herself peering out into the far end of the subterranean vault that served as the barracks for Esher's recruits. The huge room appeared to be empty of Kindred. She quietly slipped out of the tunnel, brushing the dirt from her hair and clothes with a couple of brisk swipes of her hand.

Now that she was inside, she had to find out where they were holding Cloudy prisoner—and in this crazed funhouse, there was no telling where he could be. Her best bet was to find the dungeon where she had been taken for interrogation, which had been in one of the corridors off the main catacomb. As she retraced her steps from the night before, she felt Esher's blood pulsing inside her like a second heart. While she was weak, the summoning had been easier to ignore, but now it was almost as insistent as the Other's malign influence.

In a perverse way, the Other had prepared her for dealing with the likes of Esher. She'd spent so many years learning to subvert her vampiric personality, she recognized the blood-wizard's attempts at controlling her for what they truly were. A weaker vampire would have mistaken Esher's desires for his own and acted without a second thought.

The door to the interrogation room was unlocked. She stepped inside. It was very much as she had left it the night before—except that Decima's body had been removed and someone had scrawled on the wall in human blood: *He's with me.*

"Ah! Look who's in the House!"

Esher sat beneath the stained-glass window suspended over his chair of office, one boot resting on Cloudy's body. The old hippie's beard was bright red and his left eye and cheek were so swollen it looked as if someone had surgically inserted a grapefruit under his skin, but he seemed to be breathing. Kindred and Pointers alike lined the walls of the audience chamber, their eyes glittering like those of rats in a sewer.

"Let him go, Esher," the stranger said. "You've got me here—he's nothing to you now."

"On the contrary, my beauty," Esher grinned, nudging Cloudy with the toe of his boot. "He means everything to me. After all, he was the brat's protector. That must mean he knows where Nikola is."

"Nikola's dead. She died in the Black Lodge."

"Don't piss on my head and tell me it's raining, bitch!" Esher snarled. "If Sinjon had her, he would have tossed her out the nearest window after the first three minutes! No, I realize now that my beloved's abduction was your doing, not his. I don't know why you wished to maneuver Sinjon and myself into a *jyhad*—did you think we would destroy one another, leaving Deadtown for you to take over? Is that it? Are you a mammal conspiring beneath the feet of dinosaurs?"

"You wouldn't understand my motivations if I told you. But you're right about one thing—I came here with the express purposes of getting rid of both you and Sinjon."

Esher stood up and stepped away from Cloudy, glowering balefully. "Who are you, woman? Did the Camarilla send you? Are you one of their Archons?"

"The Camarilla!" She turned her head and spat. "I have as much love for the Camarilla as I do for you, Esher!"

"Answer me, damn you! Who are you! Tell me your name!"

"You want to know who I am? I am the shadow that monsters fear! I am the nightmare that haunts the dreams of the dead! Look into the darkest corner of your black heart, and you will find me there! I am the slayer of the dead, the destroyer of the Damned! I am that which you fear above all things—I am your death, Esher!"

The assembled audience whispered among themselves, shifting about uneasily. Esher gestured for silence with a sharp cut of his hand. "Big talk for a little traitor!" he sneered. "Do you think your brag impresses me, anarch? Who are you to challenge me? Me—! A wizard of the Tremere! I am prince of this city—and your knee will bow to me!" He stepped to the edge of the dais and stabbed downward with his index finger. "You heard me, bitch—I command you to bow down before me!"

She could feel his will inside her, hammering away at her self-control. It felt as if an invisible hand had grasped the back of her neck and was trying to force her head down, but still she refused to budge.

Esher's eyes flashed angrily at her defiance, and he redoubled his efforts. "I said—*bow!*"

The audience echoed their master's cry, their voices merged as one: *"Bow! Bow! Bow!"*

The stranger set her jaw and grimaced as her muscles fought among themselves. It felt as if she were playing tug-of-war with piano wire. Esher's will burned inside her like a red-hot coal, worrying her mind with the savagery of a pit bull. She staggered under the psychic onslaught, but stood her ground, grimacing from the exertion.

"Defy me all you like, traitor!" Esher snarled. "It will do you no good! Kneel before me, and at least I will grant you an easy death!"

One of Esher's thralls darted forward and grabbed the stranger by the hair. "You heard Lord Esher! Kneel, bitch! Kneel before your master!"

The stranger drove her elbow into the vampire's ribcage, forcing him to let go of her hair. She then grabbed him in a headlock and turned it a full 360 degrees. The vampire's neck made a noise like fresh celery being snapped as his head popped off in her hands. She drop-kicked the grisly trophy at Esher, who instinctively caught it.

"You meddlesome fool!" he growled at the severed head. "I didn't need your help to bend her to my will!"

The severed head opened its mouth to apologize, but there were no lungs to fuel the larynx. Its eyes darted about for a second, as if realizing for the first time its situation, then glazed over. Esher snorted in disgust and tossed the dead thing over his shoulder.

The stranger stood surrounded by Esher's minions, who pressed forward with a hungry gleam in their dark-adapted eyes. They strained toward her, licking their lips and tittering among themselves like bats.

"Get away from her!" Esher bellowed as he waded through the crowd, booting Kindred and Pointer aside. "She's *mine!*" The others scuttled out of his way, lowering their heads in deference.

Now Esher and the stranger stood on equal ground, separated by less than ten feet. She and the vampire lord began to move, each cautiously circling the other in a counterclockwise position, like wary panthers locked in a cage. Esher growled deep in his throat, his eyes burning like twin hellfires.

The stranger pulled her right hand from her pocket and the silver blade leapt from her fist. Esher's eyes widened in surprise and alarm, but he stood his ground. The stranger darted forward, slicing at Esher's chest, only to find he had sidestepped her, turning on his heel with the grace of a matador caping a bull.

"You're fast, traitor—but are you fast enough?" he jeered, lifting a hand that glowed with crimson fire. He feinted, grabbing at her with burning fingers. She pirouetted like a jewel-box ballerina on a mirror lake, narrowly avoiding contact with the blood-wizard. She came out of the spin, slashing at Esher, but he whirled out of reach.

Esher's followers watched from the sidelines, hooting and chanting as the two vampires danced their deadly challenge. This was far more arousing than anything that had ever graced the runways of the Dance Macabre.

The stranger darted forward and Esher moved to meet her, catching her right wrist in an iron-hard grip. The stranger bit back a cry of pain as liquid fire shot up her arm. The pain was excruciating—it felt as if an acetylene torch was being held to her arm. She tried to wrench herself free, but it was no good. Esher would not let go, no matter how she struggled. Her fingers spasmed open and the switchblade fell to the floor. Esher grinned and quickly kicked it out of reach. The members of the enclave gasped and quickly moved out of the way, for fear of being nicked by the deadly silver blade.

"You are indeed strong and clever, traitor," Esher leered as he tightened his grip. "But you never stood a chance against me—just like that mincing old museum piece, Sinjon! You are nothing compared to me! Nothing!"

She could feel her blood burning her veins and scalding her arteries. It was as if acid were sluicing through her—or magma. Tears of blood began oozing from her eyes, leaving crimson streaks as they rolled down her cheeks. Steam leaked from her ears and nostrils. The Tremere's blood-magic would boil her brain until it had the consistency of a pudding; her organs would cook and rupture like sausages in a microwave. It was a horrible way to die, even for the dead.

She swooned, dropping to her knees. Esher let her wrist drop and grabbed her throat, holding her head so that her blood-filled eyes could not look away from his face.

"See? I told you you would kneel before me, my beauty! But what to do with you—? Shall I use your skull as my winecup? Or shall I dissect you, piece by piece—a kidney here, a uterus there—but do it slowly, letting you regenerate just enough so that you never die? Yes, that has a certain appeal, don't you think? You have cost me much that was dear to me, traitor. It will take me years to find and train another Decima—" A slow smile spread across his face. "Yes, *that's* it! I will use you to replace Decima! I will make you my thrall, and force you to serve me as your liege-lord. You bear a close enough resemblance; there will only have to be a few cosmetic changes. Then I will change your name, whatever it is, to Decima, and you will *be* Decima! It will be as if she never died—and *you* never existed!"

"No! Not that! *Anything* but that!" the stranger gasped. "I *beg* of you!"

"Your cries for mercy will do you no good, traitor!" The pulsing energy shrouding Esher's hands flickered and died, but he maintained his grip on the stranger's throat. He motioned with his free hand to one of his nearby thralls. "Bring me the claive!"

The lackey scurried to the dais and quickly returned with the ritual knife.

Esher held his left wrist out and the thrall sliced into the exposed flesh, gasping at the sight of his master's blood slowly welling from the gaping lips of the fresh wound.

Esher pushed his bleeding wrist against the stranger's lips. She shook her head and tried to pull away, but was held fast. "No—*please!* Don't do this to me!" she begged.

"Take this, my blood! Drink and be bound to me, now and forever! Drink and be one with my flesh, one with my will! Drink—and be damned!"

"Drink it! Drink it! Drink it!" the others chanted.

The stranger's eyes closed as she took Esher's blood into her mouth. She moaned in abandon and reached up of her own volition to grasp his wrist and arm. Esher's grin grew even wider than before. Now she was under thrall to him, subject to his every whim and command. This was better than killing her. Much better. Death was far too easy and swift a punishment to mete out to the likes of her. The complete and utter destruction of her mind and soul, however, was another thing entirely. To erase her identity and turn her into a continuation of his beloved Decima was inspired by his centuries-dead father's fondness for replacing his gun-dogs and wives with look-alikes, in order to create the illusion of them being the same creatures.

Esher moved to pull his wrist away from her feeding mouth, but the stranger refused to let go. Her grip tightened and she began draining the wound in earnest. A look of alarm flickered across Esher's face as he attempted to pull away a second time.

"That's enough!" he whispered hoarsely. *"Let go!"*

The stranger opened her eyes, peering up at him over the rims of her sunglasses, but continued drinking. A mantle of purple-black light crackled about her head and shoulders, like the halo of a fallen angel.

"Let go!" Esher yelled, grabbing her hair with his free hand. The dark energy flared and spat like a bug-light, causing him to jerk his hand away. His fingers and palm looked as if he'd just stuck them in a deep-fryer.

The orgasmic rush that came with the sharing of blood had disappeared, to be replaced by a feeling of genuine panic. "Don't just stand there!" he shrieked at his gathered minions. "Get her *off* me!"

The vampire who handed Esher the claive came forward, grabbing the stranger's jacket collar. Then he spontaneously combusted. His fellow Kindred drew away, hissing as they shielded their faces against the blaze. After a minute of shrieking and gesticulating, he fell over and stopped making noise. Meanwhile, the stranger was still feeding and Esher's hair was starting to turn gray.

"Fuck *this* shit!" one of the Pointers said.

"I hear you, man," replied another.

"Get her off me! I *command* you!" Esher wailed.

Two more thralls came forward, and two more burst into flames. Only these were a lot more athletic than the first—they dove directly into the crowd, igniting several of their fellow Kindred with their death-throes. Within seconds the audience chamber was full of rapidly burning vampires, running around in frantic circles as the flames consumed their immortality.

Esher gave out a sob of pain and dropped to his knees, too weak to stand. The stranger broke off her feeding, wiping her lips with the back of her hand, and got to her feet.

"Oh, please don't throw me in that brier patch, Br'er Fox!" she laughed. "*Anything* but the brier patch!"

Esher tried to drag himself away, but he was far too frail. In place of the powerfully built, virile vampire lord was a rail-thin old man with jaundiced, liver-spotted skin and thinning white hair. His fingernails were long and hooked, like those of a bird of prey, and his face was that of a cadaver.

"*What are you?*" he rasped, his voice as dry as parchment.

"I am the vampire who feeds on vampires," she replied. "And I have tasted your blood—and found it good."

Esher lifted a bony hand to his face, whether in self-defense or to blot out the sight of his doom was uncertain, as she pulled him into a brutal parody of a lover's embrace, her face pressed close to his. He flinched at the sight of her exposed fangs.

"You should feel honored, Esher," she smiled. "You're only the second vampire I have consumed. My first was my own sire. And, I may add, you are *much* better than he was."

"Please—let me go—I'll give you anything—everything!"

"If I set you free, would you let Cloudy and myself leave Deadtown unharmed?"

"Yes! Of course!"

"Would you leave Nikola and Ryan alone?"

"I swear by my blood I will never seek her out ever again!"

The stranger loosened her grip on Esher without letting him go, studying the vampire lord's aged features. "I'll tell you what...." she said, after a pause. "You're one lying son-of-a-bitch."

Her fangs drove into Esher's jugular like a tap into a keg. The blood that flowed from him was thick and dark and had the consistency of motor oil. And it tasted sweeter than any she'd ever known. She'd told him the truth— he *was* good.

The deeper she drank, the faster the vampire lord aged. His lips turned black and withered, pulling away from his gums in a hideous rictus. His skin flaked away in large sheets, while his hair, nails and teeth loosened from their moorings and fell like autumn leaves.

Esher hammered his arms and legs against her in a futile attempt to break free. The stranger's response to his attack was to tighten her embrace, snapping his spine like a dry branch. Esher's shrieks climbed into the ultrasonic register, until they sounded like the pips and squeals of a bat. His eyes retreated into the back of their sockets as his remaining flesh lost its resiliency, locking his features into a grimace of raw terror.

The House of Esher shrugged.

The stranger halted her feeding to blink and look around at her surroundings. The interior of the audience chamber was ablaze, the tapestries inadvertently ignited by the burning vampires running around. But the fire did not account for what she'd felt—

The House of Esher shrugged again. Only this time it was more like a shudder.

"What's going on—?"

"My magics—" Esher whispered, his voice that of a very, very old man. "My magics are tied to my blood...my life force...without me to sustain them, they can no longer keep the House stable.... It is a house of cards...and you...have removed...the king...."

The house shuddered again, and a two-foot-wide crack appeared in the floor of the audience chamber. The stranger let Esher drop and moved to retrieve Cloudy, who still lay unconscious at the foot of the vampire lord's throne. Esher lay sprawled on the dais, his useless legs twisted beneath him like gnarled sticks.

"Don't leave me here!" Esher wailed. "Deadtown is yours! I surrender all that I am and all that is mine to you—just take me *with* you!"

"You still don't get it, do you?" she sighed as she tossed Cloudy over her back in a fireman's carry. "You can keep your fuckin' Deadtown—in fact, I think you were *made* for this place! Now if you don't mind—I think I'll show myself out!"

There was a rumbling from deep within the building and the House jerked as if it were being pulled in three separate directions at the same time. The stranger nimbly sidestepped a fissure that opened up underneath her, pausing only long enough to snatch up her dropped switchblade.

"No! Don't go! Don't leave me here alone—!" Esher cried, his voice lost in the groaning of the House as it began tearing itself apart.

There was the sound of a metal cable snapping, and Esher looked up to see the stained-glass window suspended over the dais swinging dangerously overhead, like the pendulum from the poet's story. His last thought, before the ton of metal and colored leaded glass came crashing down, was of Bakil.

The stranger kicked open the doors to the audience chamber and staggered into the hallway. If the House of Esher had been hell to navigate when Esher was in control, it was even worse now. Eyes open or shut, the place was utter chaos. The walls were bleeding and the doors moved about on spindly, lobsterlike legs, their knobs extended on long antennae. The carpet underneath her feet was made from roasted marshmallows. She gritted her teeth and slogged onward, doing her best to ignore the things skittering about on the edge of her vision.

She rounded a corner and saw a clot of Pointers mired up to their waists in the hallway. They looked like roaches in a glue trap. She looked away as the floor convulsed, slamming them against the ceiling with the force of a hydraulic press. She looked down at her feet and saw the carpet runner flex and twist, trying to snare her ankles like a snake. She tightened her grip on Cloudy and stepped up her pace, swearing under her breath. There was another quake and the sound of timbers giving way. She narrowly dodged a rafter crashing its way to the basement. All about her were clouds of plaster dust, crumbling masonry, and splintered wood—it was as if the House of Esher was striving to disappear in its own navel.

She suddenly found herself outside without exiting through a door—the wall had simply disappeared. She staggered across the street, fearful of being buried under a toppling chimney or an avalanche of brick. While it might do little but inconvenience her, she doubted Cloudy would survive the trauma. Once she was satisfied she was safely away, she lowered her burden to the ground and turned to watch the fall of the House of Esher.

Her first impression was that the building was on hinges and was being folded inward by a pair of giant, unseen hands. She was reminded of a magic act she'd once seen where the magician had taken a box the size of a car and repeatedly folded it until it was big enough for a child to carry—except that the box hadn't made a quarter of the noise the House of Esher did. The sounds of masonry being ground to dust and glass shattering did little to drown the screams coming from within the convulsing interior. She glimpsed a few bloodied figures leaping from windows to the ground below, but it seemed that most of Esher's followers, both human and vampire, remained trapped inside.

There was a long, guttural groan—not unlike the song of a whale—and the House of Esher disappeared in a mushroom cloud of grit and plaster dust. In its place was an empty lot. The stranger noticed that wherever the House had gone, it had taken its catacombs with it, since the patch of ground where it had stood only moments before was perfectly flat.

"Well, thank goodness that's taken care of," she muttered as she knelt to pick up Cloudy again. The older man's breathing sounded funny—she needed to get him to a hospital. Then she noticed the Batmobile sitting at the curb.

She opened the driver's door and scanned the interior. The keys were still hanging in the ignition. No doubt the driver was dripping off the ceiling in whatever hell-dimension the House had returned to. She opened the back door and gingerly laid Cloudy across the seat. The old hippie's good eye flickered open and his body went rigid.

"It's okay, Cloudy," she whispered. "You're safe now."

"I—I didn't tell him," he mumbled through what was left of his teeth.

"I know."

Cloudy closed his eye and lapsed back into unconsciousness.

The nurse at the emergency-room receiving desk glanced up from her magazine at the sound of the automatic doors whooshing open. She was somewhat startled to find herself looking at a tall, thin Caucasian woman in her mid-twenties with unnaturally pale skin and short, choppy dark hair, dressed in a battered black leather jacket, jeans and mirrored sunglasses, holding a grown man in her arms.

"My friend's been hurt," the woman said by way of explanation.

A couple of ER attendants hurried forward with a gurney. The woman seemed hesitant at first to surrender her burden, but finally let them take him from her.

"Uh, ma'am?"

The woman in the sunglasses turned to stare impassively at the nurse behind the receiving desk, who was holding out a clipboard and ball-point pen in her direction.

"Ma'am—we need you to fill out some forms."

"His name is Cloudy," was all she said, and turned and headed back out the door.

"*Wait!*" The receiving nurse called after the woman's retreating form. "Wait! You can't just drop him off like that! How do we know if he's got insurance or not?!?"

Cloudy lay in his hospital bed, his left leg freshly slathered in plaster and hanging suspended from a sling. His right shoulderblade and arm were also newly mummified, supported by a metal strut that held his arm out at a jaunty angle. His beard and hair had been washed clean of blood and vomit and the swelling on the left side of his face had gone down enough so he could open his eye. He sat in the dark, sipping apple juice through a straw, watching the TV with the sound off. The privacy curtain that separated his side of the room from that of his roommate's was pulled shut, effectively screening him from the door.

"Cloudy."

He jumped, spilling his apple juice.

"Sorry—I didn't mean to startle you," the stranger said, stepping out of the shadows.

"Jesus!" he muttered. "At least I'm in the right place for a heart attack!"

"Are you all right? What did the doctors say?"

"That I'm fuckin' lucky. I've got a broken leg, a fractured arm, and a dislocated shoulder. I'm also going to have to be fitted for dentures. I've got a couple of busted ribs and a punctured lung, but there's no sign of brain damage and it looks like I'll get to keep my eye."

"What did you tell them?"

"That I was mugged. Which is kind of the truth, once you think about it." He tilted his head and fixed her with a quizzical look. "I wasn't expectin' to see you again, after last night. Why'd you come back?"

"To see how you were doing and to tell you goodbye. Oh—and I thought you might like something to read while you recovered." She stepped forward and placed the *Oxford English Dictionary* on the night table.

"Thanks. I appreciate the thought," Cloudy said with a crooked smile.

"You'll need it once you get out. Deadtown is no more, Cloudy—don't try to go back. In a year or more it'll be an urban shopping plaza or a new business development."

"Where do you suggest I go?"

The stranger shrugged. "I hear San Luis Obispo is nice."

Cloudy smiled, exposing his naked gums. "I gotcha. Thanks."

As the stranger turned to go, Cloudy called out to her one last time. "Lady—I know this sounds corny…but I don't think I caught your name?"

The stranger paused, her silhouette etched against the privacy curtain. It was too dark for him to make out whether she was smiling or not.

"It's Blue. Sonja Blue," she whispered. "Goodbye, Cloudy."

The patient on the other side of the curtain groaned and muttered something in his sleep. Cloudy glanced in his roomie's direction to make sure they weren't being overheard. When he looked back—she was gone.

Sonja Blue yawned, stretched, and cracked her knuckles, all the while steering with her knees while the Batmobile barreled down the highway. She glanced into the rear-view mirror, watching the lights of the city dwindle behind her. Where to next? She'd heard rumors about a vampire coven in Detroit, and there were some pretty weird stories coming out of Boston. Then again, there were some pretty nasty infestations Down South that needed tending to. An embarrassment of riches. What was a girl to do? Well, better decide her next destination in the usual way.

She fished her switchblade out of her breast pocket and flicked the trigger. Without taking her eyes from the road she tossed the knife at the atlas open on the seat beside her. She glanced down and grunted. Looked like she was headed north.

She punched the eject button on the Batmobile's cassette player and removed the rap tape, tossing it out the driver's-side window. She reached inside her breast pocket and produced another cassette and deftly inserted it into the empty slot. The distorted shriekback of Diamanda Galas' "Madwomen With Steak Knives" came flooding out of the Batmobile's suitcase-sized speakers.

"There," she said with a smile. "Now *that's* music I can relate to."

GLOSSARY

ANARCH: A young rebel Kindred with no respect for its elders. Something of a young turk or punk kid, by vampire standards.

BLOODLINE: A vampire's heritage, traced from a progeny via its sire.

BLOOD BOND: The most potent bond existing between vampires; the receiving of blood is an acknowledgment of mastery. If a vampire drinks another vampire's blood three times, he is eternally Blood Bound to that vampire.

BROOD: A group of progeny gathered about a sire.

CAITIFF: A vampire without clan or brood ties.

THE CAMARILLA: A global sect of vampires set up as a loose governing body over the Kindred as a whole.

CHILDE: A young, inexperienced vampire; the progeny of an older vampire (see Progeny).

CLAN: A group of vampires who share certain physical and mystical characteristics. Vampire clans include Brujah (rebels), Gangrel (shapeshifters), Malkavian (insane), Nosferatu (hideous), Toreador (artists), Tremere (wizards), and Ventrue (ruling class).

ELDER: A vampire who is at least 300 years old.

THE EMBRACE: The act of transforming a human into a vampire.
Enclave: A group of vampires unrelated by bloodline but sworn to a central leader.

FLEDGLING: See Childe.

JYHAD: Conflict or warfare between competing vampires.

KINDRED: A vampire.

LUSH: A vampire who feeds on winos or junkies in order to get high.

MINIONS: Vampires who follow or serve a more powerful vampire.

NEONATE: See childe.

OVERDRIVE: A state of hyperactivity vampires can access in order to move faster than the human eye and elude detection. It is physically draining and not all vampires can do it. Also known as "ghostwalking" and Celerity.

PRETENDERS: Creatures of myth and legend, shadow races that dwell among humankind by "pretending" to be human. Pretenders include vampires, werewolves, seraphim and ogres.

PRINCE: A vampire who has established a claim to rulership over a city.

PROGENY: A collective term for all the vampires created by a single sire.

SABBAT: A sect of vicious, inhuman vampires; rivals to the Camarilla.

SERVITOR: Human servants of a vampire, such as gypsies.

SIRE: The parent/creator of a vampire.

THRALL: A vampire who is held under a Blood Bond and is under the control and protection of another, more powerful vampire.

A tale of bloodlust, vampire chic, and the agony of living.

DHAMPIRE ™

Nicholas Gaunt has always felt different. He doesn't know the HALF of it.

by Nancy A. Collins and Ted Naifeh

Ongoing monthly on sale at your local comic book shop

VERTIGO
DC COMICS
suggested for mature readers

CALL TOLL-FREE 1-888-COMIC BOOK
TO FIND A COMICS SHOP NEAREST YOU.

MASQUERADE OF THE RED DEATH TRILOGY

WRITTEN BY ROBERT WEINBERG

For ten thousand years a race of immortal vampires has waged a secret war to control mankind. Beings of incredible supernatural power, they are driven by a thirst for human blood. They are the Kindred.

But now a new player has entered the game. Known only as the Red Death, he controls forces that make even the Kindred tremble. Who is this avatar of evil? And is his appearance the first sign that Gehenna, the dreaded apocalypse for both humans and vampires, is about to begin?

The only two people who can stop the Red Death are Dire McCann and Alicia Varney. Racing against time as the Red Death comes closer to achieving his goal, they desperately need to find the one historian who knows the vampire's identity.

BLOOD WAR
VOLUME 1
ISBN 1-56504-840-7
WW13000
$5.99 US/$7.99 CAN

UNHOLY ALLIES
VOLUME 2
ISBN 1-56504-841-5
WW12401
$5.99 US/$7.99 CAN

THE UNBEHOLDEN
VOLUME 3
ISBN 1-56504-842-3
WW 12402
Retail Price $5.99 US/$7.99 CAN